RESURRECTION OF THE HEART

A SOVEREIGN SONS NOVEL

A. ZAVARELLI

NATASHA KNIGHT

Copyright © 2021 by A. Zavarelli & Natasha Knight

All rights reserved.

No part of this book may be reproduced in any form or by any electronic or mechanical means, including information storage and retrieval systems, without written permission from the author, except for the use of brief quotations in a book review.

Cover by CoverLuv

Editing by Editing4Indies

ABOUT THIS BOOK

Santiago finally has what he wants. His baby is growing inside me.

I've rewritten her destiny, binding her to me for good.

Things are changing for us. I see beyond the monster he shows the world. See the scars he hides beneath the ink.

Love is a weakness men like me can't afford. I've decided to keep her, but I'll never forfeit my revenge.

His final betrayal proves his vengeance means more to him than our love.

I will have my pound of flesh, no matter the cost.

I made a mistake trusting him. I forgot how much he likes my tears.

When I am through, I'll have what I thought I always needed.

I'll run from him. I'll have to.

I'll bring her back when she runs. I'll always bring her back. She belongs with me.

But it's too late when I realize he's not the only monster in my world. And that mistake will cost us both dearly.

Resurrection of the Heart *is the third and final book of The Society Trilogy. You can find book 1,* **Requiem of the Soul here** *and book 2,* **Reparation of Sin here.**

1

SANTIAGO

The small gray house in Oakdale blends in amongst all the others. It is not the first time I have visited, but it will be the first time I have stood on the doorstep.

I know every detail of her schedule. When she leaves each day. Where she goes. What groceries she buys, how often she fuels her car. There isn't a single thing I don't know. And as I count the time passing on my watch, I know in fifteen seconds, she will open the door, rushing out to her car to take her son to school.

I stand and wait. Moments later, there is a commotion on the other side of the door. Something clatters to the floor, and she curses. She yells for her son, telling him they have to go. The knob turns, and when the door opens, she spills out in a rush, nearly colliding with me.

A small gasp flies from her lips, and horror washes over her face as she scrambles back inside, trying to shut the door to seal the monster out. My palm slams against it, and a dark smile bleeds across my face.

"Hello, Hazel. It's been a while."

"No!" She shoves against the door with all her might, trying to stop me from entering.

Panic seeps into every muscle in her body as she glances over her shoulder at her son and tells him to run.

"There's no need for such dramatics." I shove against the door, the force knocking her off balance. When she stumbles back, I enter the house and shut the door behind me.

Hazel is breathing hard, eyes wide, looking very much like her sister but not as beautiful. Nobody is as beautiful as my wife.

"Please." Her hands shake as she reaches for her son, who can't be older than five, securing him in her arms. "You don't have to do this."

"What exactly is it you think I'm here to do?" I cock my head to the side, studying her.

She glances briefly at her son, tightening her grip on him. He looks just as terrified, and I find that notion surprisingly distressing. I haven't ever given the feelings of children much thought, but considering my impending fatherhood, I think perhaps I should make an effort.

"Your name is Michael, right?" I kneel to meet his eyes, hoping I might be less frightening for him at his level, but he only curls his little fists tighter into his mother's shirt. "I'm Santiago."

He looks up at his mother, and she forces a smile that looks more like a grimace. "It's alright, sweetheart. Why don't you just go upstairs and play with your toys for a little bit? Mr. Santiago and I are going to have a talk."

"Okay," he whispers, and slowly, she releases him from her grip. He tiptoes up the stairs, pausing a few times to glance back at me.

He can sense the monster in his presence. But all children are like that, aren't they? My own will inevitably be the same. They will cling to their mother, too horrified to look at me.

I swallow, but it does not dislodge the painful knot in my throat. My wife is missing. She has taken my child with her. And the question I don't want to acknowledge lingers at the back of my mind. If it would be better to let her go—let them both go—so that I never have to witness that same revulsion from my own son's eyes.

Yet I can argue that this is exactly what I wanted. My wife pregnant with my children. A family. Heirs to the De La Rosa name. But it isn't just about heirs anymore. I'd be lying to myself if I said it were. I want her back. *I need her back.*

"What do you want?" Hazel hisses, putting some

distance between us as she takes a few steps back and straightens her clothing.

When I don't answer right away, she starts to pace, brushing loose strands of hair back over her ears. "I expect the cavalry is coming. That's why you're here, isn't it? You plan to haul me away for punishment? What will it be? How will I pay for my sins for leaving IVI? I can't leave my son alone in this world—"

"Do you really believe The Tribunal would end your life over such a minor slight?" I stare at her, incredulous. "You are panicking. Stop. Think. Breathe. What you're saying doesn't even make sense."

She shakes her head in denial, spewing more fragmented thoughts from her mouth.

"I expected this day would come... I knew it would. We should have left the state. But then it doesn't matter, I suppose. IVI is everywhere, aren't they?" She pauses to take a deep breath and continues, "Just leave my son out of it. That's all I ask. If you plan to take me, let me call someone to come look after him. He doesn't have anything to do with my decisions. I won't let him pay the consequences..."

"Hazel," I growl.

Her eyes snap up to mine.

"I'm not here to take your son away from you. And I have no intention of taking you from your son.

If and when you decided to come back to the Society, there would be punishment, but it wouldn't be nearly as severe as you are imagining. As it stands, I have no reason to turn you in as long as you help me."

"Help you?" She blinks. "How can I possibly help you?"

"Tell me where your brother would take Ivy to hide her."

Her face pales, and she shifts, averting her gaze. "Why would you want to know where Ivy is?"

"Because she's my wife."

"No." The protest falls from her lips with blatant disgust. "She wouldn't. She wouldn't—"

"She wouldn't marry the likes of me?" I sneer. "I assure you, she did. And now I need to find her. Time is of the essence, so tell me what I want to know."

She clenches her jaw, shaking her head. "Even if what you're telling me is true, I can't betray my sister. If she's gone into hiding, it must be for a good reason."

"Fine." I pivot toward the staircase. "Then I'll take your son and be on my way. And, in fact, I'd dare say you are correct. You should expect an army of Sovereign Sons to descend on your house before nightfall. You could run, I suppose, if you are willing to leave your son behind."

"You bastard!" She lunges at me, gripping my arm

and trying to drag me back. "You aren't taking my son anywhere."

"Then tell me what I want to know." I shake her off and glare down at her.

Her eyes move toward the staircase and then to the front door. I watch her face as slow acceptance sinks over her. There's nowhere to run. Nowhere to hide. She's trapped, and she knows it. But she's wasting my time, and it's time I can't afford to lose, so I throw another motivation at her.

"Not that you seem to care, given that you abandoned all of them, but perhaps it would interest you to know I have your youngest sister, Eva, at my house."

Her eyes narrow as she curls her hands into fists. "Is that a threat?"

"Take it as you will." I arch an eyebrow at her. "But understand this. If you don't help me find my wife, I will make life miserable for all of you. I have been kind enough not to divulge your location even though I've been aware of it for quite some time. However, that grace is quickly dissolving in the face of your resistance. So it seems you have a choice. Help me find my wife and bring her back home to me safely, or let your entire family pay the consequences of your actions."

Tears cling to the edges of her eyelids, and she turns away to wipe them, stewing over her current predicament with a stubbornness that must certainly be a Moreno trait. I recognize it well enough from Ivy.

"Fine," she whispers reluctantly. "I will help you, but I need to know that Ivy won't come to harm."

"She is safer with me than anywhere else."

"That must be why she ran from you in the first place," Hazel hisses.

"We're running out of time." I nod to the staircase again. "And I'm running out of patience."

Her eyes dart to the keys she dropped on the floor, and she moves woodenly to pick them up. "One more thing." She tilts her chin up defiantly. "How can I trust that you won't give up our location or hand me over if I go with you?"

I consider my words carefully. I am accustomed to taking what I want without regard for the feelings of others. I am a De La Rosa, after all. But some sliver of humanity in me wants her to trust me because she's my wife's sister, and I know Ivy loves her. It feels strange to acknowledge this truth, particularly because I still don't want to believe it myself, but the longer I am without my wife, the more obvious it becomes.

"You can trust that I won't betray you," I answer stiffly. "Because my wife would never forgive me if I did, and despite what you might think, I... I care about her. I want her home with me where she belongs. That's all I want. And I have no reason to turn you over unless you refuse to help me get her back."

Hazel's face softens just a fraction as she studies me, searching for lies. When she is satisfied I am telling the truth, she offers a small nod.

"Okay. Let me get my son. We'll need to drop him off at school first."

"What is this place?" I ask.

Hazel shifts the car into park and turns off the ignition, staring up at the yellow house that looks just like any other on the street.

I was beginning to think she was driving without any set purpose in mind, intent on fucking with me, before she finally took the exit for Lafayette. From there, she drove the route to this house as if from memory, and watching her now, there is a wistfulness in her features as she studies it. This place is obviously familiar to her.

"This is the house my father bought for his first wife before he had to leave her," she answers solemnly. "I came here before I left The Society. It's in Abel's mother's name, so IVI was never aware of it. Not until now, anyway."

"Do you have a key?" I ask her as we exit the car and step onto the driveway.

"No, but I know the code to the front door."

I nod and follow her toward the door, but something catches my attention on the driveway. Hazel pauses at the same time I do, peering down at the red fragments of plastic. "What is that?"

I bend down, picking up a piece to examine it as a cold chill settles in my spine. "It looks like a taillight."

"Look at that." Hazel croaks, pointing a shaky finger at a crushed black plastic case.

We both move closer to examine it, and Hazel recognizes it first.

"It's lipstick."

My eyes move over the red smear on the concrete as a sick feeling twists in my gut. For as long as I live, I will never forget that shade of red. It has to be the same. The question is why is it here, smashed in the driveway?

"Do you think something happened here?" Hazel whispers.

"Open the door."

It's the only thing I can say. I can't accept the thoughts swirling the drain of my mind. I can't give those ideas space. Not until we go inside and I see for myself that she isn't here.

Hazel punches in the code, and I grab her by the shoulder to halt her before she turns the knob.

"Let me go first."

She swallows and nods, stepping behind me as I enter the space. For a moment, I stand there, taking it all in. The silence. The musty odor. The messy contents of a house that hasn't really been lived in for some time.

There aren't any lights on. It's morning, and Ivy would be up by now. But I can't give up that last lingering hope as I stalk through the living area and down the hallway, checking every room. They are all empty. It doesn't stop me from checking under the beds, inside the closets, showers, and any other space she could hide. But every search turns up nothing. Not a single trace of her. Yet I can feel it in my gut that she was here.

"Something bad has happened, hasn't it?" Hazel echoes my own thoughts, her voice trembling. "Something has happened to my sister."

2

IVY

They've removed the bag from over my head, but my wrists are still zip-tied behind my back, and the ties are digging painfully into my flesh. I wonder if it's to keep me off balance to prevent me from running, but they don't have to worry about that. My door isn't locked, but I'm not going out there. I can still hear them, and if I look out of the window of the run-down single-story house they've brought me to, I can see their cars on the driveway. They took mine somewhere a few hours ago, I guess to get rid of it. I didn't even realize Abel had held on to it.

Abel. Did he intend for this to happen like it did? Or did things just go wrong?

My head hurts where the one punched me, and a bruise is forming at my temple. I guess I should be grateful it's not my eye. My stomach growls. I'm hungry even though I can't imagine eating right now.

One of the men raises his voice and curses at whoever he's talking to in the other room. It's startling. It all seems disorganized as though they didn't really have a plan, and I'm not sure if that isn't more dangerous.

I hear a car and get up to go to the window. The room I'm in is around the side, so if I stand at the very edge of the window, I can see a part of the driveway. A light goes on. It's not very bright, and it must be triggered by motion. I watch a car pull up. It's an old, unremarkable black car with a muddied license plate at the front. My guess is that's on purpose.

But when the door opens and I see Abel step out, my breath shudders, and I feel a physical sense of relief. He looks around as he slips the keys into his pocket before the light switches off as he moves to the front of the house.

"About fucking time," one of the men says loud enough for me to hear.

I go to the door to listen to my brother's quieter response. I can't make out his words, but the men speak urgently, voices lowered now.

A few minutes later there is a raised voice again. This one is Abel's. "Well, I guess it's going to take a little fucking longer. I don't pay you to think. I pay you to do as I say. Don't fucking forget it."

More muffled sounds, someone curses, and then

something falls over. For a moment, I'm worried about my brother, and when I hear footsteps headed toward the bedroom I'm in, I hurry away from the door and watch, heart pounding, as it opens, relieved once again when Abel enters.

"Abel!" My voice quakes.

He takes me in as he closes the door. He looks angry, unkempt, and tired. Coming closer, he grasps my chin in one hand and turns my head to look at the bruise.

"I told you not to give them a hard time," he says, letting me go.

I rub my chin against my shoulder still feeling his fingers on me, and I don't know how to answer him. Wild thoughts swim in my head as I remember the last few moments on the driveway. The lipstick I'd found. Abel's silence when I'd asked him about it.

"Abel?" I look at his back as he walks to the window and tries to open it. It doesn't budge. He's wearing a button-down shirt and jeans. I don't think he had a jacket on when he got out of the car and the shirt looks like he's slept in it. "What's going on?"

When he looks at me, he notices my arms are still behind me. He turns me a little to look at the bonds.

"Don't pull against them," he says. "You just tighten them when you do that."

"What?"

His gaze falls to my stomach as if he's searching

for signs of the pregnancy, and I find myself taking a step backward, suddenly wishing I hadn't told him about it. I want to wrap my arms around my middle and protect my baby.

"Abel?" My stomach tenses. "Cut the ties off." Because why hasn't he already? Why am I bound?

He shifts his gaze back to mine. "Not yet."

"I thought you were helping me."

"I am. Believe it or not, I am."

"Those men, your...friends...they did this to me." I turn my head to make him look at the bruise.

He presses his lips together at least like maybe he doesn't like it either. "And I warned you not to give them a hard time, Ivy."

"They carried me off, put a sack over my head. I thought...I thought you were sending men to *help* me."

"Like I already told you, I *am* helping you," he repeats, sounding irritated while he checks his phone again.

"Then why can't you untie me?"

He gestures to the men at the door. "I don't want trouble with them. Not for you, not for me. So you're just going to have to deal with the zip ties a little longer. Don't struggle. It'll be easier."

"A little longer? How much longer?"

"Few hours."

"Why?"

He shifts his attention to his phone, typing something in, not answering me.

"I want to go home, Abel," I find myself saying the words before I can stop myself. This is wrong. This is all so wrong.

He tucks his phone away and tilts his head questioningly when he looks at me. "Home? Where exactly is that?" he spits. "That bastard's house?"

It's me who doesn't speak this time. He is so angry, angrier than I've ever seen him. My throat works as I swallow, as I struggle to stand my ground and not back away.

"I have worked my ass off to get this done," he starts, stepping toward me, dark eyes full of malice. I remember what I'd thought at the hospital. That even though Abel hates me, he hates Santiago more. But is he capable of hurting me to hurt him?

"Do you have any fucking clue what it takes to organize something like this? Getting you out of that hospital. Giving you the location of the safe house. Making the arrangement for the fucking doctor. Do you have any—"

"What doctor?" I ask, the room feeling icy suddenly.

His glance shifts again to my stomach, and he seems calmer when he looks back at me again. "I'm doing what you want, Ivy. For you."

"What doctor, Abel?" I push, panic rising.

"I'm going to get *that monster's* baby out of you."

"What?" My voice trembles even as I hear my own words repeated with so much venom.

"Isn't that what you said? What you wanted?"

"No. God, not like—"

"It'll be another two hours before the doctor gets here."

"I don't want any doctor."

"You just stay put," he says, ignoring me, refusing to hear me. "Stay in this room, and do not go out there. It's safer for you. Do you hear me?"

"I don't want a doctor." I'm shaking my head, my entire body beginning to shudder. "I'm not..." My voice cracks as I try to speak the next words. "Abel... it's a baby." I square my shoulders. "And I'm not going to hurt my baby."

He's on me so quickly I just have time to let out a scream before his hand squeezes around my throat and he has my back pressed to the wall.

"You need to learn to be fucking grateful, Ivy." Spittle lands on my face when he says my name. "I could have one of those men beat it out of you, but I'm not doing that, am I?" He cracks his neck, eyes strange, the look inside them unhinged.

I try not to struggle, try to stay perfectly still and breathe.

"Fuck!" He squeezes hard once before he releases me, and I wonder about the rage inside him. The violence. I remain where I am as he walks to the door.

But I can't let this happen. I can't let him do what he's planning.

"It's my baby too. Not just his."

He spins back so fast, right arm raised, his hand a fist, and all I can do is drop to the floor. Turning away from him, I try to protect my baby before he does what he warned. Before he beats the child out of me.

"And you just spread your legs for that bastard like a whore! Fuck you, Ivy. This isn't how this was supposed to go, but you just keep fucking things up!"

I jump when he kicks the wall beside me, and I see the effort it takes him to stop. To force in an audible breath. He's angry, so angry, and out of control.

He mutters a curse as he walks to the door and opens it.

"Abel?" I call out once because I have to know.

He doesn't stop.

"Was it you? The poison?"

That makes him stop. And I know it's stupid to ask. I shouldn't ask it. Not now. But I can't help myself.

I shudder when he turns slowly, face expressionless, eyes dead. And I know the answer. I knew it at the safe house too. As soon as I found that lipstick, I knew.

A moment later, without a word, he's gone.

I don't get up when I hear the front door open

and close. I don't get up when the motion detector goes on outside of my window and I hear the engine start, the car whining as he reverses too fast off the driveway. I remain where I am, feeling sick for what is to come. For the mistake I've made. For the terrible cost.

3

SANTIAGO

Marco pulls his car up beside mine in the empty parking lot of a strip mall that's long since closed for the night. I stopped here to get my bearings and rack my brain for any other place I might check.

I've been back by the hospital and Eli's room twice. I've checked her old apartment building. Her school. The few people outside of the Society who she spoke to in passing. Her family's house is under watch. They are all under watch. And driving the streets without any particular destination is only serving to exacerbate this insanity looming in the darkest parts of my mind.

Abel hasn't shown his face anywhere, which can only mean he must be with her. And all I can think about are my sister's words. The conversation she overheard.

He said he would sooner rot than let you impregnate Ivy. And if you did, he would cut the baby out of her himself.

My eyes feel raw when I blink and try to shake away that thought. I can't go there. Thinking about it won't do me any good. Not until I find her and fix this once and for all.

"I've got the situation with Hazel handled," Marco informs me. "Two guys are watching her place for the night."

"Good." I nod at him, staring out at the street.

"We have men everywhere," he says. "If she's anywhere on any of these streets, I can promise you we'll find her."

He's trying to put me at ease, I think. But those assurances mean nothing. Abel would know I'd bring down the full power of IVI on him. I have an army at my disposal. He would have planned for that. And in my gut, I know Ivy won't be on these streets. She'll be hidden away somewhere he thinks I can't get to her.

He hasn't responded to any of my texts. Not even the one about his father being alive. It seems my threats to torture Eli can't even draw him out, proving he truly has no loyalty to anyone or anything.

"I think you should go home and get some rest," Marco says carefully. "There's nothing else you can do right now. You need to eat something and close your eyes for a few minutes."

"I can't," I growl. "I have to do something."

He watches me as I stew in my frustration. He doesn't know that every time I close my eyes, I see her face. I feel her body against me. And I smell her. The ghost of her scent haunts me, even when she isn't here.

Something has snapped inside me. I don't know what it is, but I feel... *broken*. I never truly knew what that word meant until now.

"We have to find her, Marco." I grab him by the shirt and shake him because I don't know what else to do. "I need her back."

"I know you do, boss." His hands come up to grip my arms, gently removing them from his shirt. His lips are set into a grim line, reflective of the way I feel. He knows as well as I do this won't end well.

"There's one other option," he says quietly. "It isn't a pretty one."

"What?" I demand. "What is it?"

"The little girl," he says. "She might know more than she's letting onto. And I don't like bringing children into this, but if this is a life-or-death situation..."

He's right. Evangeline is the key. She could give me answers. More places to search. Something on Abel. Anything.

I'm already moving for my door handle when I

freeze and turn back to Marco. "I don't know how to talk to children. I terrify them."

"That may be true." His lips tilt up at the corner. "But not this one. I've seen the way she looks at you. She's not scared."

"Scared, no," I admit. "She's defiant. Like her sister. But she's still young—"

"Talk to her like an adult," Marco suggests. "And maybe she will surprise you."

Evangeline is still awake when Antonia opens the door and leads me inside. She's curled up in a chair next to the window, staring outside in contemplation. She's only thirteen, but she looks like someone burdened with the responsibilities and worries of an adult, and I realize Marco was right. She hasn't ever had the chance to be a child, I suppose. Not with a mother like hers, who would abandon her to the wolves for the sake of her own self-preservation.

"What do you want?" She glares up at me as I move toward her.

Despite the somber mood, I can't help but smile a little at her response.

I pull the chair from the desk and come to sit across from her while Antonia lingers in the doorway.

"You can go, Antonia."

She hesitates for a moment before shutting the door softly and taking her leave. Eva watches and swallows before turning her gaze back to me. Her hands curl in her lap like she's preparing herself for a fight.

"You are so much like your sister," I tell her.

The softness in my tone seems to catch her off guard, and she jerks her chin in agreement. "I know. I don't need you to tell me that."

"I think I never really saw it until now," I confess. "She must have been just like you at this age. Hardened by the world around her. Parents who are oblivious to her needs. It couldn't have been easy for her, as I'm sure it's not easy for you."

Eva's lip trembles, despite how much she's trying not to let it show. "You don't know anything."

The tears clinging to her eyelids tell me otherwise.

"I know that you think I'm a monster, and I suppose in many ways it's true. But your sister has shown me that I am capable of more. I am capable of feeling things I never thought I could."

Eva shifts, her eyes darting to the floor as her hair falls around her face. "If you care about her, then you wouldn't make her cry. You wouldn't have made her end up in the hospital like she did. That's not love."

Love.

The word hits me like a bullet, fragmenting inside my soul.

"I'm not capable of love," I confess, throat raw. "But I have... *feelings*."

My voice sounds foreign to my own ears as I try to unpack these thoughts to a child. I feel like I'm fumbling through this, and I don't know that I'm making any progress. But when Eva looks up at me, the tears have fallen from her eyelids and streamed down her cheeks, and she does not try to hide them. She is showing me her own vulnerability.

"Everyone is capable of love," she whispers. "Even monsters. Because monsters are still men, and men have hearts. Even you, Santiago De La Rosa."

I can feel my grimace. My doubt. It must show on my face. But Eva leans forward, studying me with an intensity that no girl of her age should possess.

"I hate you for taking her away from me," she says. "You don't let me talk to her or see her. And you keep her locked up like a prisoner. If I'm being honest, I don't think you deserve her."

"Those might be... valid points," I answer uncomfortably.

"My point is you shouldn't go after her. Not if you don't love her."

I dip my head and rub my aching temples. I don't know how to answer that. But I know that not having her here is not an option.

"Eva, she's in danger," I tell her. "She's been taken,

and she's being held somewhere against her will. Abel is involved somehow, and you're the only person who can help me right now. If something happens to her, if I don't get her back..." My voice fractures, and I reach out to touch her arm but stop short. "I am begging you."

She frowns, worrying her lip between her teeth. "If that's true, how could I help?"

"I need to know where Abel might have taken her. It doesn't matter how small or insignificant you think it might be. It can be any place at all. We are running out of time, Evangeline. Your sister is pregnant, and he plans to take her baby. Our baby."

Her eyes widen in disbelief. "Abel would have told me if that were true."

"He didn't tell you because he doesn't want her to have the baby," I answer.

She sits there quietly, peeking up at me several times while she digests this news. I gather she's trying to determine what's true and what's not.

"I have no reason to lie to you," I say. "I'm not a man who needs to be deceptive. I might say something you won't like, but I won't lie to you."

Her brows pinch together in challenge. "Why was my sister in the hospital?"

"Because she overdosed on aspirin. And if you'd like to see her medical records, I have copies in my office. With proof of her pregnancy."

She flinches at the news I deliver without any

sugar-coating, considering it for a long moment. When she speaks again, her voice is softer. "Why would Abel want to get rid of her baby?"

"Because he hates me, and he can't stand the thought of her having my baby."

"I know he hates you," she admits.

I meet her gaze, so there can be no misunderstandings that what I'm telling her is the truth. "He tried to kill me, Eva. He hired someone to poison me, and I almost died. Your brother is a dangerous man, and I don't know what he might do to Ivy. But I know she isn't safe, and I need your help."

She sucks in a sharp breath and stands up, tucking her hair behind her ears. "Then why are we here? Let's go look for her."

A knock on the door interrupts us, and when it opens, I'm surprised to see Marco standing there. My eyes move over his face, searching for any sign of the news I've been dreading.

"Boss." He nods at me and then Eva. "Someone left a package at the front gate. There's an address inside."

"Ivy?" I breathe.

He jerks his chin. "I think that's the meaning of it. But it could be a trap."

I glance down at Eva, who's now tugging at my sleeve. "Take me with you," she pleads.

"I can't." I frown. "It's too dangerous."

She glares up at me and shoves me away. "Then

go get my sister and make sure she's safe. Don't waste any time."

I turn around and head for the door, but the next thing she utters follows me out, echoing all the way down the hallway.

"I guess that means you do love her."

4

IVY

Several hours pass as two of the men leave with one of the cars. I'm so tired and feel myself drifting off when I hear a car door open and close. By the time I get to the window, whoever it is is already inside.

I wonder if it's the doctor. Will he force me to have an abortion? I think about Dr. Chambers giving me that birth control shot, knowing I didn't know what it was. But a birth control shot and an abortion are two very different things.

I don't know if it's relief I feel when one of the men, the wiry one, walks into the bedroom carrying a bag of food from a fast-food place. My relief is short-lived when he gives me a gap-toothed grin and sets the bag on the nightstand. That and the single bed are the only pieces of furniture in the room.

"Doc's running late," he says and turns to go. "Dinner."

"Wait!"

Stopping, he turns to face me, and I feel myself shrinking back. "My wrists. Please undo the zip ties. They hurt."

"No can do." He takes another step out.

"Tie them in front then. I need to use the bathroom, and I can't like this."

The other man comes into view, this one so big he has to hunch down to fit through the doorway. "What's going on in here?" he asks.

"She wants her hands untied."

"No, just...you can tie them in front. Please. I'm not going anywhere. Please. I really need to use the bathroom."

"Check the window," the big one says to the wiry man as he reaches into his pocket to pull out what I realize is a switchblade.

"Painted shut," the other man confirms.

"Get me another zip tie," the one with the knife says as he walks toward me. "You, get up."

I stand and turn, assuming he's going to cut the ties. But he grips my arm above the elbow and holds the knife to my throat. With a slight shifting of his hand, I feel the slicing of skin, the warm trickle of blood.

Tears burn my eyes as I try to stand perfectly still.

"You try anything, any fucking thing, and I'll slit your throat ear to fucking ear, you got it?"

"Yes," I manage, terrified.

"Your asshole brother fucked up," he says, roughly taking one arm as he slices through the zip tie.

The other man walks in with another zip tie as I wipe my neck with the back of my hand. It comes away smeared with blood, but it's not bad. He barely cut me. A warning. I look down at my bloody wrists, the skin rubbed away.

"It hurts, please," I start, but the man with the knife wipes my blood off his knife on the bedsheet and signals to the wiry one to rebind my wrists in front of me. But at least they're in front.

I hear the click of the switchblade as the big one closes it, and they both walk out the door.

"When is the doctor coming?" I ask before they close it.

"Not soon enough." The door closes.

The first thing I do is try the window, which I know won't open. Both Abel and the other guy couldn't get it open, so I doubt I'll be able to. I could probably break the glass with the nightstand, but they'd be in here before I could climb out, not to mention I'd have to contend with the shards of glass.

I go into the bathroom and switch on the light. It blinks twice, then goes on with a buzz. It's fluorescent, and I think about the lighting at the manor.

How dim it is. How subdued and soft. I think about Santiago and wonder what he thinks has happened. If he's looking for me. He must be. I don't even know where I am. I think we drove for a good hour from the safe house, but I can't be sure. How will he find me? And if he does, will he be in time?

A feeling of loss overwhelms me suddenly. This need to be home. To be safe.

Home. Home in Santiago's house. In my bedroom even though it's felt more like a prison than anything else.

He must be so angry. I ran away from him. I took his baby from him. I tried to kill myself even if I did change my mind. I knew what could happen when I took all that aspirin. It wasn't a conscious choice, though. I was desperate. But desperate for what?

For his attention.

For him.

And now we're farther apart than ever.

My throat feels tight as I turn on the water and wash my hands and face. I run cool water over my burning wrists. It only makes it worse, though, so I dry my hands on my pants—the towel looks nasty—and return to the bedroom.

My stomach rumbles at the smell of the food. I haven't eaten in so long, so I open the bag and take out the cheeseburger. I unwrap it and take a bite, then another, and before I know it, I've finished it. I look inside the bag for more, but it's empty, and I get up and go back into the bathroom to drink water from the tap.

That's when I hear commotion outside. A car door slamming. Voices in the living room.

This is it. He must be here. The doctor.

I hurry back into the bedroom just as the door opens, and the big guy walks in, followed by a thirty-something man in a suit. He looks shabby in the worn-out suit, and the bag he's carrying is tired-looking. His dark hair is oiled back and curling behind his ears like he needs a cut, and overall, he gives me the creeps.

"You must be Ivy," he says, his smile making my skin crawl. "Your brother said you have a little problem you'd like to be rid of. Why don't you come lie down on the bed, and we'll take a look-see."

"No, my brother was wrong. I don't want to get rid of the baby. This is a mistake. I just want to go home," I plead, holding out my arms in appeal, almost forgetting my wrists are bound because for a moment I think I have a chance. A choice. He's a doctor. He won't force this. He can't.

He smiles as the big man closes the door and moves toward me.

"Your brother told me you were confused. Now let's get this done," the doctor says, setting his bag down on the nightstand and noticing the empty bag of food. He picks it up, looks inside, and turns on the man. "When did she eat?"

He shrugs. "Now?"

"You idiots. That changes things."

When he opens his bag, I make a run for it, but the big man grabs me.

I scream as he drags me toward the bed, lifting me off the floor when I struggle.

"Gentle now," the doctor says when I'm slammed anything but gently onto the bed.

My gaze flicks to his just in time to see him pushing the air out of a syringe. They'll knock me out and abort the baby. And I won't be able to do a thing about it.

"Just something to relax you. Can't give you what I would have since you've eaten," he says, eyes on the syringe. "You shouldn't feel a thing."

"Please!" I scream and kick as the giant keeps my shoulders pinned and traps my wrists under one knee. "Please! I don't want this. Help me. Help!" I scream and scream, flailing, kicking all to no avail as I smell the alcohol of the swab then feel the coolness of it as he cleans the area before plunging the needle into my arm, emptying the contents, my body beginning to go limp before he even pulls the needle out.

5

SANTIAGO

Marco hands over the yellow envelope with a strained expression on his face and watches me open it. Inside, there is a handwritten note.

Want your wife back? Come and get her.

Beneath that is the address. Whoever dropped this at the front gate either wants me to know where Ivy is, or they want to lure me out. I'm erring on the second option. An obvious power play. Marco seems to confirm those thoughts when he trails me as I head for the car.

"Boss, I have men on the way there now. They can get her out if she's really there—"

"I'm going, Marco."

"That might be exactly what they want," he mutters. "We still don't know who tried to kill you the first time. And then the poisoning. I just think—"

"Are you driving, or am I?"

I yank open the driver's side door, and he sighs.

"Get in. I'll drive."

I walk around the car and slip into the passenger seat as he fires up the engine. While Marco drives, I study the paper, looking for any clues. I don't recognize the handwriting, not that I would. That is perhaps the one thing about Abel I haven't examined closely.

"Abel could be trying to lure you straight into his trap," Marco says, eyes focused on the road.

"Possibly," I admit. But it doesn't feel like that. "Or it's someone else."

He glances at me briefly. "You're thinking one of his men?"

"I don't see Abel coming anywhere near The Manor. He knows he'd be caught. So either they delivered the message for him, or they have their own motives."

"He must be getting desperate to go to these lengths," Marco says. "These men wouldn't be working for him if there wasn't something in it for them."

"Power," I mutter. "It's always about power. The little dogs always want to destroy the big dogs. Clearly, Abel has failed to do this one simple thing. Perhaps his men are growing tired of waiting. Knowing him, I wouldn't be surprised if he's made them all sorts of outlandish promises. But you can only borrow so much loyalty with unfulfilled assurances."

"Could be." Marco nods, but he doesn't look any less concerned.

I google the address on the note and find that it's just an average house in a suburb about two hours away. The journey passes far too slowly for my liking. I'm on edge, my foot tapping against the floorboard as scenery flashes outside.

Every text that comes through on Marco's phone has me checking it like a fiend. He handed it over after the first three times I demanded to know exactly what the updates were.

His men aren't there yet. We are all traveling from different locations, and I don't know who will arrive first. But when we finally turn down the street, another text comes through. There is one team waiting outside for us.

I type a response and tell them to hang back, and within a minute, Marco is pulling up behind them. I'm out of the car and barking out orders before he can even shift it into park.

"You two go in the front," I tell them. "I'm going in the back."

"Here, boss." Marco hands me a pistol and a knife. Following me around the side of the house, he pushes a path through the overgrown shrubbery.

The backyard is small, and the old door is wood, which works in my favor. Marco uses his giant frame as a battering ram, blowing it wide open with one grunt.

Chaos ensues within seconds. A shot rings out, and then a series of curses as Marco's men push their way through the front and take on two men I don't recognize. One of Marco's guys takes a bullet in the shoulder, and he repays the favor by shooting the asshole between the eyes.

Another man in the living room fires off several more shots as he dives behind a coffee table, pulling it up against him for cover. The sound of glass shattering and gun blasts ringing out pierce my ears, but I can't focus on any of it.

I move toward the hall, Marco at my side as we begin to check the rooms. The first bedroom we stop at has a guy scrambling to try to crawl out the window. Marco raises his weapon and shoots him in the head. His body slumps to the floor, blood pooling beneath him as we clear the space. When we don't find anyone else, we move along to the next room.

A strange sound is coming from the other side of the closed door. It's a rustling and grunting as though someone is trying to move a piece of furniture, presumably to barricade themselves in.

I look at Marco, and he nods, slamming his body into the door. It breaks open, sending splintered wood everywhere as we spill into the room.

There's a moment when I stop to take everything in. From the corner of my eye, I can see a figure charging at Marco. But it's the mess of dark hair on the bed that has my attention. It's the first sign of life, and relief fills my chest, only to be drowned out by the man lurking above her. A doctor?

He discards the instrument in his hand and turns to face me at the same time Ivy stirs from a hazy state, trying to open her heavy eyes. *My wife. My beautiful fucking wife.*

She blinks, murmuring something unintelligible as her hand twitches. For a split second, our gazes lock, and then her eyes are shuddering closed again. She fights it but falls into stillness, her chest rising and falling slowly.

The man above her pivots toward me carefully, holding up his hands.

"What did you give her?" I growl.

He whips his head in the direction of the other man. The one Marco now has in a chokehold on his knees. Clearly, he expects that man to save him.

"Want me to break his neck, boss?" Marco nods to the guy in his grasp.

"Save him for me," I answer coldly.

My eyes never leave the doctor, and when I stalk toward him, he cowers back, slowly reaching into his pocket for something. He's still fumbling around for it, only to drop the pen as soon as he produces it because his hands are shaking so badly.

"I don't want any trouble," the doctor says. "I just came here to do a job. That's it. I swear."

"And what exactly was that job?" I cock my head to the side, studying him like a pest.

"It was... an abortion," he croaks. "The woman didn't want the baby. That's all I know."

All the pent-up rage that's been breeding inside me boils over as I grab him by the throat and lift him off his feet.

"That woman is my wife," I snarl. "And that is my baby inside her."

"I didn't know," he gasps, feet kicking as he fights for air. "Please."

"Tell the devil I said hello." I produce the knife and stab him in the gut three times, dropping him to the floor. "I'll see you again in hell."

He's choking on his own blood when I kneel on his chest and grab him by the hair, slashing the blade across his throat. Blood sprays across my face, and I wipe it from my eyes before turning my murderous gaze on the other man.

Marco's got him locked down so tight, he's half-dead already. It's more than he deserves to die so quickly, but I don't have the luxury of time to torture him.

Marco releases him, and he drags in a long breath as I grab him by the collar and haul him up onto his feet.

"Where is Abel?" I demand.

"I don't know," he answers, his voice almost too hoarse to understand. "He took off and said he had some business to handle."

"What business?" I dig the tip of my knife into his forehead.

"Fuck, I don't know," he wheezes. "He doesn't tell us anything."

I drag the knife down and to the right, carving an F into his flesh. Blood gushes from the wound, and he nearly collapses again. Sensing a need, Marco comes to hold him upright for me.

"I can do this all night." I stare at him.

It isn't exactly true. The sirens in the distance are getting closer. Someone undoubtedly heard the gunshots, and I need to get my wife out of here. But the last thing I want to do is drag this piece of shit back to the compound to finish him off.

"He's gone off the rails," the guy tells me. "I don't know where he's been. But he was supposed to handle this shit, and he left it for us."

I carve a U into his forehead next, and he starts talking faster, spewing whatever he thinks will save him as I move onto the C.

"He said you'd be looking for him, and he couldn't let you find him. He was getting too paranoid, so he wouldn't tell us anything. But we knew the gig was up. Abel was going completely insane. That's why one of my guys delivered the note to you. So you could come get her."

"Purely out of the kindness of your heart?" I muse, slashing the blade to complete the K.

"Look, we fucked up, okay? I know that!" he screeches. "We just wanted some respect. You can't blame us for that."

"Respect is earned," I remind him. "Now tell me what the doctor did to my wife."

"All he did was give her the sedative," he pants. "Come on, man. You're carving me up like a fucking pig."

"It's the least of what you deserve." I move onto the Y and O as blood pours down his face, blinding him.

"I'll help you find Abel. I swear it. Just give me a chance."

"Your chance was up the moment you decided to fuck with my wife." I finish off the U with a flourish, stepping back to admire my handiwork. "Which one of you left the bruise on her face?"

He swallows, and I know it was him before he even conjures up a half-ass denial.

"Boss." Marco glances at me from behind, signaling I need to hurry things along.

I nod and then look at the piece of shit in front of me one last time. "Did you touch her anywhere else?"

"What?" He shakes his head in disgust. "No way. Abel wouldn't let us do that."

"You're lucky I'm in a forgiving mood," I tell him.

"Really?" He perks up, blinking his bloody eyelids hopefully.

"Yes," I answer flatly as I drag the tip of the knife to the pulsing vein in his throat. "I forgive you for being so fucking ignorant. You didn't know not to touch what belongs to me."

I stab him in the throat. Once. Twice. Three times, until his blood flows in rivers down my arms and the gurgling noise in his mouth fades to nothingness. When I drop him to the floor, Marco kicks him in the face for good measure.

"Just checking." He shrugs when I look at him. "We gotta go."

I pivot toward my wife, pausing briefly to untangle the hair from her face. Blood smears over her cheek when I stroke it, and warmth fills my chest when I pick her up and cradle her limp body in my arms.

"Time to go home." I whisper the words against her ear, finishing them with a kiss. "Where you belong."

6
IVY

I feel heavy. Arms and legs like lead. But he lifts me without effort, and when my arm falls away, he carefully adjusts his hold, tucking that arm over my belly. I realize the zip ties are gone and try to open my eyes, but I can't. I only get glimpses as we hurry through the small house and what I see is a massacre. Blood. Death.

I groan, and he hugs me closer, and when I'm alert again, I feel the vibration of the moving car beneath me, and panic sets in. They're moving me again. I'm on the floor of that car again.

"Shh. You're safe. I'm here."

Santiago.

He pets my hair, fingers gentle, and I take in the scent of him. It's not those men. I'm not on the floor of the car. I'm lying on leather, and my head is on his lap, his hands gentle. He wasn't gentle a little while ago. Not with that doctor. Not with the man.

"Shh," he repeats, telling me over and over again that he's here, and that I'm safe.

I'm quiet again. Heavy. When I stop fighting it, I feel myself relax so completely it's tempting to give over to it.

I'm safe.

Santiago is here. I am safe.

The baby, though. Our baby. I try to concentrate, to mentally scan my body. I'd feel if they'd done it, wouldn't I? If they'd taken the baby. Does Santiago know what they did? Did he arrive in time to stop it?

An immense sadness tugs me back into a reality I can't quite join yet as the drug continues to leave me paralyzed.

"Shh," Santiago starts again, repeating those same reassuring words again and again and again. I want to ask him about the baby. I need to know. But my mind is as fuzzy as my limbs are heavy, and I drift off again to the soothing sound of his voice.

I hear lowered voices as I begin to wake. I turn my head and breathe in a familiar scent. The pillow I'm lying on is soft and warm. His. One of the voices I hear is Santiago's. He's talking to another man, but

I don't recognize the other voice, and I can't make out their words.

When I finally manage to open my eyes, I see the empty pillow beside me. The armchair across the room. And I know I'm home. In Santiago's room. In his bed.

He has his back to me. He's standing just outside the open door, whispering to another man.

I open my mouth to say something, but all that comes out is a croaking sound. My throat is so dry. But it's enough because Santiago turns, and our eyes meet. He hurries to me, and all I can do is reach for him, hold on to him. My fingers curl into his shoulders, the nails broken, the skin of my wrists bruised as he sits on the edge of the bed, takes my face into his hands, and just looks at me for a long, long time.

I think in the days we've been apart, he's aged.

Again, I try to speak, but I can't. He puts a glass to my lips. I sip the cool water but only manage a little.

"You're back," he says, attempting a smile, and without warning, it's as though a dam breaks. All the anxiety, the doubt, the fear comes pouring out of me in loud, ugly, choking sobs. He pulls my head into his chest, holding on to me. One big hand cups my head while the other rubs circles into my back.

I cling to him. I cling as if I would die without him.

"Did they..." I trail off.

He draws back, shakes his head. "No. We were in time."

I suck in a sob. "Thank goodness."

The door clicks as someone closes it. He kisses my forehead, my cheeks, my mouth, all the while whispering that it will be all right. That I'm safe. The baby is safe. That we're home.

Through the blur, I see his face, familiar and dark. I take it into my hands, feeling his warmth, the soft, scarred flesh, thumbs on lips, lips on lips, the salt of tears as we kiss. I push away his shirt, popping the buttons when I slide my hands underneath to touch him, needing his skin, needing to burrow closer, kissing him while my fingers brush over years-old scars. I want them to become familiar. I want to memorize them. To know the past the ink hides. To see the broken man hidden beneath.

He draws back, but I pull at him. I need to be close. To touch him. To feel him.

"I need you," I manage.

He hesitates, but a moment later, he slips the nightgown I'm wearing over my head. I'm naked and shivering until he takes me into his arms again, skin on skin, his shirt gone, ripped away, my hands on his face as I memorize his eyes, feel the stubble that grows on the un-inked side of his face. My gaze follows the path of my own hands over his neck, shoulders, chest as he lays me on my back and straddles me, keeping his weight on his forearms while my fingers trace over skin and scars and ink.

I see the bandages that circle my wrists before I close my eyes and feel him kiss me, kiss my face, my neck, my breasts. I wrap my legs around him, wanting him inside me. Needing him inside me.

He draws back just a little, eyes locked on mine, and I hear the buckle of his belt, the zipper of his pants, and then he's at my entrance. I draw in a rattling breath, and I watch him as he pushes inside me, watch how his eyes shift, darken, pupils dilated, skin flushed, mouth open just a little as he dips his head down to kiss me, gentle at first, then as the fucking grows more frantic, teeth scraping teeth as he says my name again and again like he needs this too, as much as I do.

One hand wraps around the top of my head, and the other closes over my shoulder. His eyes lock on mine with the final thrusts, and when we come, it's a deep, slow thing, not frantic, not hurried, neither of us taking but instead giving, and I feel tears again sliding down over my temples when he kisses me, the thudding organ inside my chest not twisting but something else, something different.

I draw a shuddering breath, look at the top of his dark head as he bows it into the crook of my neck, his breathing labored, cock still throbbing inside me. I bite my lip so hard when the words come that I taste the copper of blood to swallow them back and shove them down. And when he looks back up at me, something's inside his eyes I can't name, and I wonder what he's swallowed down. If it's lodged in his throat like the words are lodged in mine. And I think how sad we are. Even now.

Santiago rolls to lie beside me, our heads on one pillow, face-to-face. He brushes my hair back, wiping away stray tears, and here come those words again, that choking emotion. They want out, but I swallow hard.

Because I can't say them.

Because I can't love him.

"Did you come for the baby?" I ask instead. It's important we're clear. We're each where we belong and know where we stand, even if it hurts.

He looks confused, and it takes a moment for him to reply as if he's considering. "I came for you."

7

IVY

Santiago doesn't leave my side. After bathing me and helping me dress, he stands at the wall, arms folded across his chest, watching as the doctor asks me questions and explains what they'd injected me with. A muscle relaxer rather than an anesthetic, albeit a strong one.

Santiago snorts when this doctor uses the term doctor about that other man. "He was no more a doctor than I am. More like a piece of shit."

"It wasn't harmful to you or the baby. That's the most important thing," the doctor continues after clearing his throat. He turns my head to study the bruise at my temple. "You were lucky."

"Lucky?" Santiago interrupts again. "I'm not sure I'd call her lucky."

"I meant any damage will heal." He smiles, giving me a wink. He takes a card out of his pocket and sets it on the nightstand. "If you need anything or have questions, I'm available day and night to the members of The Society."

He's a Society doctor.

"We want our members to feel safe and well cared for, and you certainly are, Ivy. Especially during such an important time." I guess he means the pregnancy.

I glance at Santiago. His hair is still wet from the shower, but he's dressed in a fresh white button-down and dark slacks and looks more like himself. It makes me smile a little. He'll be a cantankerous old man, I think.

He shifts his gaze to me and momentarily appears puzzled by my expression, but then there's a knock on the door, which is open just a little, and to my surprise, Eva peers inside.

"Eva!"

She pushes the door wide open and gives me a big smile that shows all her teeth as she hurries to hug me even tighter than she had at the hospital. I hear her sniffle and rub her back.

"I'm so glad you're safe and home," she says, voice quiet so only I can hear her.

"Me too."

I look at Santiago over her shoulder and gesture to the door. I know he understands I'm asking him to give me a minute with my sister, but he just carries on talking to the doctor like he doesn't, so I clear my throat as Eva pulls away.

"Can you give us a minute?" I ask outright.

The doctor smiles. "Of course. I need to be going. If you need anything, just call."

"Thank you," I say and shift my gaze to Santiago, who just keeps on standing there. "Why don't you walk the doctor out? I promise I'll be right here when you get back."

He shifts his gaze to Evangeline, who I can see is smiling, then back to me. "Fine," he says, but he sounds far from fine. "I'll be right back." They head out a moment later, Santiago making a point to leave the door open.

"He's sweet, I guess. In his own weird way," Eva says.

I'm confused. "Santiago?"

She nods.

"Sweet?"

"You should have seen him when you were missing. He was really worried about you."

That makes me smile. I want to believe it's true.

"I came for you."

A thought niggles at the back of my mind. Did he just say that because I'm pregnant? Because he doesn't want to upset me for fear of something happening to the baby? I can't forget the days leading up to the hospital. I can't pretend they didn't happen.

"Hey, are you okay?" Evangeline asks, dragging my attention back to the present.

I try to smile and nod. "What are you doing here?"

"Your husband took me as collateral," she says hesitantly.

"He did what?"

"It's not as bad as it sounds. I mean, what's the alternative? Being at home with Mom? At least here, there are people to talk to like him or Antonia. She's nice. She was super worried too, Ivy."

"You talk to him?"

"Mm-hmm. He's crazy in love with you, you know."

My mouth falls open, and I'm about to ask what she's talking about when Santiago is back standing in the doorway. "Antonia has dinner for you in the kitchen, Evangeline. French fries and some other crap you should enjoy tonight because you won't be having it anymore. Not under my roof."

Eva looks at me, rolls her eyes, and gets to her feet. "Want me to bring you some?"

"Ivy will not be eating that. Thank you," Santiago answers for me.

"I got you covered," she mouths with a wink, then gets up and leaves the room.

Santiago watches her go, then closes the door. "She's something else."

"She is. Would you mind explaining how she came to be here?"

"Would you prefer she wasn't? I can send her home, but considering your brother is still out there, I didn't think you'd want that."

"Did you kidnap her?"

"Kidnap is a big word. I..." He considers. "Borrowed her."

"Hm."

"And I've treated her with kid gloves."

"She thinks you're sweet."

His eyebrows rise high on his forehead.

"Exactly. Where's my brother, Santiago?"

He comes to sit on the bed. "You don't have to worry about him. He won't hurt you again. He won't get near you ever again." His expression darkens.

"Did you do something to him?" I ask when I remember the scene I glimpsed as he carried me out of that house.

He sets his jaw and studies me. "I'm going to ask you something, and I want the truth."

I nod.

"Did you run because you wanted to get rid of the baby? Is that why your brother arranged for that idiot doctor?"

"What?"

"I know how you feel about me, and honestly, I don't blame you. Having my baby inside you—"

"Our baby. It's *our* baby. Stop calling our baby yours!"

"Fine. Our baby. It doesn't change the fact that it's not what you wanted."

I stop to consider this. He's right. I wouldn't have chosen a pregnancy, not right now. But I am pregnant. And things are different. Everything is different.

I reach out and touch his arm only to feel his muscles tense when I do. "I never wanted to get rid of our baby. Not for a minute. That was Abel. And I don't know. Maybe he thought he was helping me in his warped mind. Maybe I gave him the impression even—"

"Don't you dare take the blame for what your brother did and do not make excuses for him."

"I don't know. I mean, when I called him, I was scared. But Santiago, I already love this baby. It was never my intent to hurt him or her."

He remains silent, face unreadable.

"Did you hurt Abel?"

He shakes his head. "Not yet."

I'm relieved. Should I be? I mean, maybe Abel did get that doctor thinking I wanted it. But the zip ties? Those men? I can't think about that right now. "Did you mean what you said?" I ask Santiago before I can stop myself.

"What did I say?"

"That you came for me? Not just for the baby."

He studies me, a momentary flicker of emotion in his eyes, a single second of something I can't quite name there. "You would rather have died than stay with me."

I look down, unable to hold his gaze. Because I know what that emotion is. It's hurt.

It takes all I have to look back up at him. "I just wanted you to come for me. With the aspirin, I mean. I didn't think it through. I didn't...when Colette told me you have my father—"

"Ah. Colette."

"I just...I felt betrayed. After everything that happened, the progress we'd made, you were keeping that from me. And you never came back, Santiago. For days after you got that call, you didn't even call or talk to me. I got angrier the longer I waited, and I was going to confront you, but then I saw the sheet, the stupid bloody sheet, and I remembered what you said you'd do with it on our wedding night. That you'd show it to my father. I was burning it. Not the pictures of your father or brother. I went out to the chapel so no one would find me to stop me. And then you got so angry. What you did..." I feel my face heat, and I can't hold his gaze. "And then locking me in my room." I look up at him. "You can't do that anymore. I can't stand that. Punish me any other way but not that again. If—"

"I won't." He cuts me off.

"I'm just...if I'm going to stay, I won't be put back in that room."

"If?"

"I mean it. I can't do that again, Santiago. Send me away if you can't stand to see me, and when the baby comes, we can work something out—"

"Are you completely daft?"

"What?"

"Or just hard of hearing?" He takes my hands in his. "I came for you. *For you.*"

I swallow hard.

"You are my wife, Ivy."

"In name."

"No. Not in name. Not anymore. Not for either of us. And you know it." There is a long moment of silence between us before he continues. "What exactly did Colette tell you?"

Shoot. "I don't want to get her into trouble."

"What did she tell you?"

"Nothing. She just thought I knew that you'd taken over my father's care. Have you?"

"How did she know that?"

"This isn't about Colette, Santiago. Did you take over my father's care?"

He nods.

"How long ago?"

"Since my poisoning. Your father was poisoned too, Ivy. That's what caused him to go into cardiac arrest and eventually a coma. Someone tried to kill him, and I can guess who."

I feel the blood drain from my face. "You think it's Abel? You think he tried to kill our father?"

He doesn't answer. He doesn't have to.

"Why?"

"I don't know."

"It doesn't make sense."

"Doesn't it?"

I shift my gaze momentarily away, then back to him. "How is he? My dad?"

"Awake. Alert. But weak."

"Can I see him?"

"In time."

"What happened between you? Why do you hate him? Hate us?"

He winces at that last part. It's just a twitch, but I see it. "Chambers is dead," he says instead of answering me. He stands.

"Chambers?" It takes me a moment to place him. "When? How?"

"Found his body a few days ago. His maid too. And his family is missing. You and your sister will stay inside The Manor at all times. I'll arrange for her schooling until she can return to classes. Your brother—"

"You think Abel killed him?"

Santiago stops pacing, looks at me like he's waiting for me to catch up.

"No," I say, shaking my head. "As bad as Abel is, he's not a killer." But then I remember the lipstick. "Oh my god."

"The poison that was used to poison me came from the tube of lipstick I found on the driveway of the house Hazel took me to. Abel's safe house. I'm still trying to make sense of the things we found inside, all those files, names of my—"

"Wait, Hazel? What? When?"

Just as I ask, his phone rings. He checks the display, swipes, and puts the phone to his ear. "I'll call you back." He disconnects.

"Where's Hazel?"

"Hazel and her son live in Oakdale. They're safe. I have a man watching the house."

"Her son? She has a son, and they've been in Oakdale all this time?"

"You're getting worked up, and I need to return a call. We can continue this conversation after you've rested."

"I'm not tired."

"You need your strength. Not just for yourself but for the baby. I promise to tell you more, but I won't risk your health or that of my child." He stops as if he's just caught himself. "*Our* child," he modifies, and it somehow soothes me. He must see it because he sits back down and adjusts the pillows, easing me onto my back. "Rest. We'll have dinner together later."

I bite the inside of my lip. "Who do you have to call?"

"Society business." He leans down to kiss me on the forehead. "Sleep, sweet Ivy. And trust me to take care of you."

8

SANTIAGO

"Santiago?" Judge answers the other line on the second ring.

"Sorry, I've been getting my wife settled back in," I explain. "I'm back in my office now."

I take a seat at my desk and stare at the bottle of scotch that's been taunting me. It would be nice to have a drink after the past two days, but I don't want to risk it. Not when Ivy's safety is in question. I won't let my guard down for even a second.

"How is she doing?" Judge asks, polite but seemingly not too concerned. He doesn't foster attachments to useless emotions for people he barely knows. And I have to remind myself that I am much the same, and I shouldn't take offense.

"She's tired," I tell him. "She needs rest, but the doctor assures me she's going to be fine. The baby too."

"All well and good," he says. "I'm assuming the paperwork that was hand-delivered to my desk today is something you'd like to discuss."

"Yes." I glance at the clock on the wall, realizing he's still at work. Marco didn't waste any time.

"Where did these files come from?"

"Eli has a safe house. A place Abel has been using for his own purposes apparently. It's in his mother's name, so it wasn't ever connected to The Society. Ivy had been hiding..." I clear my throat and cringe at that word. "Staying there during her absence. I sent Marco to search the place for anything useful, and he produced these files."

"I see." There's a sound of a chair creaking, and I can just imagine Judge leaning back as he considers this news. "These are all IVI members. Myself included."

"Yes."

"Names, birth dates, family lineage," Judge murmurs.

"You may have noticed a connection."

"Indeed," he answers solemnly. "There seems to be a dossier for every member who was killed in the same explosion that took your father and brother. Do you know if it was Abel or Eli who compiled them?"

"They are one and the same as far as I'm concerned. I'll be having a conversation with Eli. But what concerns me are the files on Jackson and

Marcus Van der Smit. They are connected to The Tribunal. Marcus served before he died, and Jackson still serves."

"You don't think they have anything to do with this?" Judge asks.

"It's difficult to say. But his wife has been feeding my wife information. Befriending her. And it was Jackson who inserted himself into The Tribunal's investigation with Ivy. He made himself out to be a hero, but there's always a chance—"

"Not to mention what he did to Mercedes," Judge adds bitterly.

"Mercedes?" I repeat. "You mean because he didn't marry her?"

Judge is quiet for a pause before he answers. "He should never have courted her if he had no intentions to marry her."

His remark surprises me. I know he's protective of Mercedes because she will be his charge should anything ever happen to me. I detect a hint of something that sounds like resentment in his tone, yet I can only laugh as I consider the notion that his attachment runs any deeper. Judge will never marry. He is taking care of Mercedes, looking after her best interests, but I find it highly unlikely he could harbor any real feelings for her. Judge doesn't involve himself in romantic entanglements. I know because I've seen him at the IVI Cat House, picking out a woman as one might pick out a pair of shoes for the evening. He chooses what suits him, uses them for their purpose, and then returns them without any emotional investment.

"You shouldn't worry about Jackson hurting Mercedes again," I tell him. "Once she is scorned, she doesn't forgive. I am quite certain she only wants to make him sorry for it."

"I'm aware," he muses. "But is there a possibility that Jackson could have been courting her to serve some bigger purpose? If he never intended to marry her, and you suspect him of being dishonorable... it isn't much of a stretch of the imagination."

"I don't know," I admit. "I would find it difficult to believe he'd get into bed with Abel on any dealings, but Eli is another matter, perhaps. He was a respectable man, once. I believed so too. Perhaps they were scheming together."

"I think the only way to know for sure is to crack Eli while you still have the chance," Judge says. "You've been too lenient with him, and you don't know how much time you'll have. Someone already tried to clean up that loose end once. How long will it be until they do it again? It's time to put the screws to him. I can help if you require my assistance."

I don't want to tell him that he's still recovering, and it gives me pause to torture such a weak man. Or that he was right to assume Ivy's presence in my life has given me doubts about my own intentions. I can't think of torturing Eli without considering the consequences to my relationship with her, so I give him the only assurance I can.

"I'm going to speak with him tomorrow."

There's a slight pause, and then Judge answers. "Weakness will get you killed, Santiago. You can't afford it. There are already holes in your armor."

"I know." I lean my head back and close my eyes. "I won't deny it."

"Speak to Eli," he says. "And I'll keep looking through the files you sent. If anything else catches my attention, I will let you know."

I thank him and say my goodbyes, and when I open my eyes again, Evangeline is standing in the doorway to my office, staring at me.

"What are you doing?" I frown.

"Nothing." She shrugs a shoulder and ventures inside without being asked, her eyes moving over everything with interest. "I'm bored."

"Bored?" I repeat. "And what would you like me to do about it?"

"Want to play a game?" she asks.

I stare at her, incredulous. "I have to take care of your sister."

"She's sleeping," she says. "How about Tic Tac Toe or Hangman?"

When I don't respond, she sighs.

"Fine. MASH then."

"I don't even know what that is," I answer dryly.

She makes herself at home, settling into the seat

across from me, grabbing a pad of paper and a pen from my desk. "I'll show you. It's easy."

Somehow, she ropes me into answering a bunch of inane questions, which she follows up by marking lines into the paper until I tell her to stop. I watch her as she proceeds to count, scratching off items one by one until she's circled a word in each column.

"Okay, you're going to live in a mansion, and you're married to my sister, obviously. You drive an Aston Martin, and you're a math geek for your job. You'll have five kids and no pets."

"This is the dumbest game I've ever seen," I tell her. "What's the point of it?"

She laughs and rolls her eyes. "Um, duh. It's just for fun. Do you know how to have fun?"

"Clearly, I do not."

"Okay, now my turn." She slides the paper toward me, and I consider telling her this is ridiculous. But when I notice how at ease she seems to be around me now, it makes my chest feel strange.

"One game," I say firmly. "And don't expect me to know who Damon Bieber is."

"Those are two different guys." She laughs. "God, you are so out of touch. Okay, let's do this. Put down mansion in every column for me. Pink, purple, blue, and red."

"Isn't that cheating?" I arch a brow. "I had a shack and a normal house."

"Nah, not really. It's all pretend, so just go with it."

I suspect she's not being completely truthful, but I do as she asks. And somehow, over the next ten minutes, I end up describing her imaginary future life full of cats and dogs and some vampire named Salvatore for a husband in their pink heart-shaped mansion. I'm too uneasy to admit how strange this is, talking to a child as if I know anything about dealing with them. It isn't until Marco finds us there and he heaves out a strangled laugh at the spectacle before him that I realize it's not just me. I really am unequipped to deal with small humans, and it shows.

"Hey, boss." He wipes the smirk from his face as he steps inside. "Sorry to interrupt. I was just going to give you an update for the night like you asked."

Eva cranes her neck to look up at him, giving him a little wave, which he returns before he takes a seat beside her.

"Eva, I have some business to take care of." I nod at her.

"Yeah, yeah, I get it." She tugs the piece of paper from the pad and folds it up, placing it in her pocket. "I'll go wander the house and find something else to do."

"Go to the kitchen if you'd like," I suggest. "Ask Antonia for one of her famous sundaes. But just this once."

"Really?" She perks up.

"Yes. Really."

Marco is grinning at me like an idiot when I shake my head.

"I think this house needs a few kids running through the halls. Brings it to life," he remarks.

I nod stiffly, hoping he can't see the terror that's slowly beginning to sink in. It was always a given that I would do my duty and have heirs, and since Ivy has been here, that's been my goal. But now it's real. Now that I seem to be reminded of it at every turn by a child in my midst, I can't stop doubting my abilities as a father.

"What is it like?" I ask.

Marco blinks at me slowly, trying to comprehend the question. I'm about to tell him to forget it when it occurs to him.

"Being a father?"

I nod, wishing I never mentioned it.

He brushes a hand over his stubble and sighs. "Honestly? It's fucking terrifying." A laugh bursts from his lips as he shakes his head and then smiles. "But it's the best thing I've ever done. I'm always thinking about them. Wondering if I'm doing enough. If they are safe at home. What they are doing when I'm at work. They never leave my mind. You can't even imagine half the scenarios that will go through your head... all the questions you'll have about whether you are doing it right. You'll never stop thinking about it."

His answer isn't what I expected, and I can't wrap my head around it. Surely, that isn't the case for every man. He must be an anomaly. My own father never seemed to think of us except when we did not perform to his standards.

But I won't be that way, will I?

I feel a headache starting to form at the base of my skull. Right now, the only thing I know for certain is that Ivy will be here to help me muddle through the process. Between her and Antonia, I suppose they will not even need me around very much. Yet I think I would like to be around. But will I just get in the way?

"Boss?" Marco is staring at me, and I realize I haven't responded.

"Yes, you came to tell me about the progress on Abel." I force myself to focus on the present clusterfuck. One problem at a time.

"There still haven't been any sightings," he informs me. "But there is one courtesan who has been absent from the Cat House the last two days. I've been informed that she is another one of Abel's regular conquests. There could be a connection there."

"So, what's the issue?" I ask.

"Unfortunately, it appears we don't have her current address on file, so we are trying to track her down. My guys are shaking down the whole place as we speak. If any of the ladies know anything, they'll give her up."

"What about her family? There must be something on the paperwork we have for her."

"No family listed," he says. "Both her parents died. No siblings."

I sigh. Of course, Abel would choose someone like that to use for his own purposes.

"I hope he didn't do anything to her," Marco says quietly, echoing my own thoughts.

"If he has, he will pay. He will pay for every last sin."

He nods. "The guys are taking shifts. We have men out looking for him round the clock. And the Society posted ten more guards outside The Manor walls. So far, he hasn't been dumb enough to pass by, but you never know."

"Thank you for keeping me informed, Marco. It's difficult to sit here and wait him out, knowing he's still out there."

"We'll get him," he assures me. "This is the safest place for your family to be. Your wife needs you right now."

"Yes," I agree. "I think she does."

9
SANTIAGO

"Santiago?"

Ivy's soft murmur as she stirs from her slumber fills the cavity where my heart should be with something I can't identify. All I know is that I never want her to stop calling out for me like that.

"I'm here."

My fingers brush over her face, and she opens her heavy eyes, blinking up at me. She relaxes when she sees me perched on the edge of the bed, watching her. Even in her sleep, she manages to sense me somehow.

"I'm sorry," she croaks. "I've been so tired."

"It would be expected in your condition even under normal circumstances," I tell her. "But given what has happened, I think you can accept your body's requirement for rest."

She rubs her eyes and leans up on her elbow, studying me. "How do you know what's normal in pregnancy?"

I feel heat rise to the surface of my neck as I offer a half-hearted shrug. "I've done some reading."

A small smile curves her lips. "You've been reading about pregnancy?"

"When I have time," I answer dismissively.

Her face falls slightly at my short tone, and I regret it immediately. But when I lean down and press my lips against hers, she seems to forget about it entirely. Her fists curl into my shirt, trying to drag me closer.

I groan into her mouth and force myself to pull away, half breathless. "You need to eat something first."

She frowns. "I can eat after."

"No." I soften the blow by bringing her hand to my lips and kissing the back of it, which seems to surprise her. "I want to have dinner with my wife. That is, if you're feeling up to it."

"I think I am." She yawns and pushes the covers off her. "It would be nice to get something in my belly. And then we can come back here and take care of other needs."

"I would be flattered," I answer dryly. "If I didn't know that too was a side effect of the pregnancy."

A pretty flush spreads over her cheeks. "It is?"

"Yes." I help her up and keep my hand on her

elbow until she finds her balance. "Are you okay to walk?"

She nods. "Yes, but I'm a little chilled. Can we stop by my room to get a sweater?"

My hand slips around her lower back, guiding her to my closet. "I had Antonia transfer your clothes to this room. All of your sweaters are in here."

Ivy sucks in a sharp breath, and I can't tell what she's thinking when her brows pinch together. "Your room?"

"Our room," I answer stiffly.

"Is this to make sure I don't run away again?" She frowns.

"You won't run from me again," I tell her with certainty. "You wouldn't even make it past the front gate. But that's not the point. I wanted you here so I can... keep you safe."

Her face softens, and she wraps her arms around me, hugging me. It's a strange gesture of affection. One I've never understood before. But it doesn't feel unpleasant when it's from her. In fact, I think I wouldn't mind standing here all night while she does this.

"Where is Eva?" she asks.

"She's on the first floor. Antonia made up a room for her there. She mentioned something about purchasing new bedding for her. Pink, I believe."

Ivy pauses, glancing up at me. "You're buying her new bedding?"

I shrug. "I assumed you would prefer she feel comfortable here."

"Yes, but... she won't be staying that long." Sadness fills her voice.

"I suppose not," I agree. "Unless you would rather change that."

"What do you mean?"

"She'll be here until her safety is guaranteed regardless," I answer. "But I am not opposed to having her stay longer if you'd like."

She smiles again, and I think I must have said something right. "You mean like take over her guardianship? Can we do that?"

"You are a De La Rosa now." I lean down to brush my lips against her cheek. "We can do whatever we like."

She squeezes me tighter, tears clinging to the edges of her eyes. "I would like that very much, Santiago."

"Pick out a sweater," I tell her. "There is something I'd like to show you."

"What is it?" She grabs a cardigan from a hanger and wraps it around herself before rejoining me. I secure my arm around her waist and lead her into the hallway, pausing at the room right next to mine.

"This room is connected to mine," I explain as I open the door. "You can enter through the passage behind the dresser, which I'll show you later. But I thought this would be a starting point for a nursery."

She pauses inside, eyes roaming over the space. There are already a few gift bags and a rocking chair inside, gifts from Antonia. It appears she has been planning for this day as well.

"This room is beautiful," Ivy whispers. "And huge."

"I assumed you'd like to decorate the space."

"I think I'd like that very much," she agrees.

"Here." I leave her to pick up the box on top of the empty chest of drawers. "I have something for you."

When I hand it to her, Ivy looks at me as if I've had a personality transplant, and I suppose I have. But the doctor told me how important it was that she was not under any stress, and I'm trying my best to make that a reality, though I can't tell if I am.

"What is it?" she asks.

"Open it."

She rolls her eyes at my command but does as I request, removing the baby book first. When she looks up at me, I recite the information from the pregnancy book I've been reading.

"It's for keeping track of milestones. At least that's what we're supposed to do with it."

She stifles a laugh, and I don't know why. She seems to be enjoying a joke at my expense, but it doesn't bother me like it normally would.

"That's exactly what it's for."

"There's something else." I gesture to the box,

and her smile fades when she removes the necklace. I watch her closely as her fingers move over the white gold rose encrusted with diamonds. I don't think she likes it, but I can't be certain.

I shift uncomfortably. "This one is for you to wear when you want," I say. "I just assumed women like jewelry, but if you don't approve—"

"It's beautiful, Santiago." She smiles up at me with glassy eyes. "Thank you."

10
IVY

Santiago has done a one-eighty. And as happy as I am, something is still niggling at me. Maybe it's the fact he won't yet take me to see my father. Or maybe it's that he won't allow me to have a cell phone. I don't know.

I could chalk all these things up to him being overprotective. Considering all that's happened, I understand. We almost lost the baby. No. We didn't almost lose it. It was almost taken away from us. By my brother who is still out there somewhere.

That worries me too.

I'm sitting in the nursery in near darkness, the only light the carousel of animals in pinks and greens circling the soft yellow walls. I rock gently in the cushioned rocker, knees pulled up underneath me, fingers worrying the beautiful diamond-encrusted rose pendant Santiago gifted me. When I first studied it, I half expected a skull to be hidden inside the design.

I shake my head at the strange thought. I'd *expected* it. It wasn't there, of course, but I don't know. I guess that's bothering me, too. Skulls along with roses, morbid and beautiful, and our very limited past together. The ugly months. It's all too much.

I put my hand over my stomach because now there's a baby to consider. It raises the stakes.

And this is what it comes down to. This one-eighty turn. He wants an heir. He needs one. Did he suddenly fall madly in love with me once I became pregnant? Did he suddenly set aside years' worth of vengeance and hatred the moment he learned I was carrying his child?

I feel a little sick at the thought. At what it could mean for me.

What if he's acting? Given all that's happened, it's a miracle I've held on to the pregnancy. Maybe he's worried if I'm stressed or upset, I'll lose the baby. And then what? Back to square one? Will he remember his hate of me? Lock me in my room, daylight barred from my windows again?

I get up and pad barefoot over the plush new carpet to the dresser, where a few boxes sit on top. I open one, take out the little outfit. It's for a boy. Any clothes that have arrived whether from Santiago or The Society are all for a little boy. Only Antonia is buying clothes in neutral colors and even some little dresses. What if we have a girl? What will that mean?

I touch the gold bracelet on my wrist. Hazel's. I'm still wearing it. Will we receive another one with our little girl's name on it welcoming a daughter of the Society, the gesture itself almost mocking?

You didn't have a son. A boy.

I shake my head. It's not like that. IVI isn't like that. The doctor has been wonderful. Attentive and caring. Colette has had nothing but good things to say about them, all the help they've provided since little Benjamin Jackson was born.

That's another thing. I haven't been to see her either.

My mind wanders back to Hazel. Santiago has promised to take me to her, too, to meet my nephew, but he has yet to deliver. He insists he'll be the one to bring me once he has some time. Once things have quieted. Once everything is safe. And seeing as how Hazel ran away from The Society, ran off on a Sovereign Son, he hasn't said as much, but I know it won't look good for him if they find out he knows where she is but hasn't brought her back.

But then there is the guardianship of Evangeline. If she's in our care, my mother and brother can't hurt her and he's willing to do that for me. He's put everything in motion already.

I bite the inside of my lip and think about Abel and what he'd said about Eva. What he'd do once he had guardianship which he assumed, since my father lay dying in a coma, was inevitable. He'd said those things to manipulate me into cooperating. He is manipulative. But is he capable of murder like Santiago believes?

The lipstick would prove Santiago right.

"There you are."

I startle, turning to find Santiago standing in the doorway. He's still fully dressed. He must have just gotten home. I smile as he closes the door and comes up behind me. He kisses my cheek and wraps one arm around me, hand over my stomach. I look at that hand. At how big it is. How strong. How possessive.

I'm not showing yet, but I've put on a few pounds. I feel it when I put on jeans, not to mention my boobs are fuller. Santiago seems pleased by both.

"What are you doing here in the dark?" he asks, nuzzling his chin against the back of my ear.

"I'm not in the dark," I say, melting into his touch. He's so warm and big and safe.

The instant I think that last part I close my eyes to ward off the thoughts that begin their incessant circling again.

But when his hand dips lower and slides under my nightie and into the lace of my panties, all thoughts are banished. I turn my head a little, enough to feel his breath on me, enough to open my mouth and take his tongue when he kisses me.

We've always had this insane attraction, Santiago and I. This fiery passion for each other.

"Always wet for me, my sweet Ivy."

I can't help but remember when he called me Poison Ivy.

He closes his other hand over my breast, the lace rough against my hard nipple as he kneads it, the fingers of his other hand still working my clit. "So very wet."

"I'm going to come," I manage as he tickles the shell of my ear with the scruff of his jaw, and when my knees buckle, he tightens his hold on me, his cock hard against my lower back.

"That's the point," he says with a chuckle, and I arch into his hand, eyes closed, head resting against his shoulder as I pant my release.

When I turn to him, I find he's watching me, the un-inked corner of his mouth turned upward in a grin. He slides his hand out of my panties and brings it to his nose, then to my mouth. I open, lick, taste myself before he slides his fingers into his own mouth, that grin widening.

"So sweet," he says before kissing me on the mouth, one hand on my shoulder guiding me to my knees.

I look up at him, aroused again at us like this. Him standing over me, big and dominant.

"Take me out," he says.

I lick my lips and shift my gaze, undoing his belt, his zipper, pushing his pants and briefs as far as I need to before I free him. He's hard, and I listen to his deep sigh as I stroke his length and lick the tip, tasting him. He cups the back of my head, weaving fingers into my hair, grip just tight enough so as not to hurt but to control.

"Open."

I do, and I keep my eyes on his as he moves slowly at first, savoring each stroke of my tongue, pushing deeper as I relax, my hands on his thighs, my own cum leaking down the insides of my thighs as he takes my mouth because no matter how gentle he is, how careful with me, it always comes to this with us. Fucking. Wild. Feral. Like animals as he bends me backward, setting one knee to the ground and pushing in so deep that I gasp for breath between thrusts, and when he throbs in my throat, and I feel him empty, I think about how beautiful he is when he comes. How his eyes glisten, almost black, how his chest heaves with heavy breaths. How sweat beads on his forehead. And mostly how he can't drag his gaze from mine like he can't get enough.

Because this is the thing with us. I can't get enough either. And I'm banking on this new Santiago. This man who cares for me. Who takes care of me. Who treats me like I'm precious.

Because if I'm wrong, if I'm making a mistake,

the price I'll pay will be a heavy one. One I won't recover from.

He draws out, then watches me swallow, and we straighten so we're facing each other on our knees. He adjusts his pants but doesn't bother with the belt. He brings his thumbs to my eyes, wiping away the tears at the corners.

"I was too rough."

I smile, shake my head, and touch his cheek. I want so badly for this to be real. For him to be real. I kiss him gently, and he looks confused when I draw back.

"Are you all right?" he asks.

"Just tired." It's a lie but also not. He swoops me up in his arms, and within moments, I'm lying in his bed, and he's tucking me in, and it's me who's confused now.

"Aren't you coming to bed?"

He kisses my forehead, stands to look down at me, buckling his belt and tucking his shirt back in. "I have to do some work."'

"You're always working."

"Saturday night, we have a dinner at IVI. It's a smaller affair than the last time."

I climb up on my elbows, forehead furrowing. I still remember the gala. "Do I have to go?"

"It's important we're there together." He pauses, and I sense hesitation. "For my sister's sake."

"Mercedes?" He hasn't mentioned her in a long

time. "Where is she? You never said. Did something happen?"

He sighs deeply and sits on the edge of the bed. "You know I will do anything to protect my family."

I study him.

"That includes you, Ivy. But it also includes my sister. No matter what she's done."

"What did she do?"

He considers. "Well, strangely, I guess she was protecting her family."

"Protecting you."

He nods.

"From me?"

"She did something stupid, honestly. But it led to more dangerous things. She's accepted the consequences with some grace, I must say, but there have been questions about her sudden disappearance at IVI and, well, she's your family too now, and we need to protect her."

"Protect her from whom?"

Again, there's hesitation. Then finally, he speaks. And his words send a shudder down my spine. "The Tribunal."

"What did she do, Santiago?" I push. "She was just gone, and you never said."

His forehead is creased, and I swear I can see the pain in his eyes, and I hate it.

"Tell me."

"I chose you. I chose you over her, Ivy. I chose *our* family."

"What?"

"Will you go with me?"

I nod, although I'm reluctant. Because no matter what she's done to me or anyone else, I don't want to see her standing where I stood before The Tribunal.

11

IVY

My conversation with Santiago leaves me more confused than ever. Why did he have to make a choice between his sister and me? What did she do?

But a part of me is warmed by what he said, too.

He chose me.

He chose *our* family.

On Saturday morning, a box arrives from a boutique in New York City, and later that evening, I am dressed in a floor-length satin gown in a deep emerald, and if I look down, I can just see the tiniest swell of my stomach. I am sure it will be unrecognizable to anyone who doesn't know, but I see it. It's the way the fabric drapes itself over every curve, and I'm sure when I look at Santiago's face, when I see his eyes alight on exactly the same place, this is why he chose this particular dress.

He nods, his pride obvious, and wraps a hand around the back of my head to draw me in to hug me, kiss me. But when he pulls away, I see anxiety there, too, in the crease between his eyebrows.

"You look beautiful."

"Wow, you really do," Eva says. Walking out of the kitchen, she's shoving a handful of popcorn into her mouth from a giant tub under her arm. She's also barefoot and wearing bright yellow pajamas, and I realize how comfortable she feels here. How at home.

Santiago checks his watch. "Didn't you eat dinner?"

"That was an hour ago. This is called a snack." She makes a point of saying the word snack slowly for him.

"Eva," I say.

"Besides, it's movie night," she continues.

"Movie night?" I ask.

"Marco set up a TV in my room."

"He did what?" It's Santiago.

"And he gave me his Netflix log in." She shrugs a shoulder and turns away. "You guys have fun at your boring dinner."

"I'm going to need to talk to Marco. She shouldn't have a television in her bedroom."

"Why not? She's a kid."

"I'm not sure—"

I put a hand on his shoulder. "Do you know my

mom wasn't feeding her breakfast so she wouldn't put on weight?"

He looks at me like he's confused. "She what? The girl is too skinny if anything."

"I'm just saying she's had a lot of restrictions placed on her already so let her be."

"Fine. For now. But I'm still talking to Marco. Come on. We're going to be late."

"You do you," I say and let him lead me out. We take the Aston Martin again, but I follow Santiago's gaze to the rearview mirror to see two men follow us off the property.

"Additional security," Santiago says. "Nothing to worry about."

"What are you going to do to Abel if you find him?"

"*When* I find him."

"Okay. When you find him. What are you going to do?"

He glances at me quickly, then back to the road as he shifts, driving twice the speed limit. "Nothing you need to worry about."

"Do you realize that's like a standard answer for you?"

"What?"

"You don't tell me anything. Not about Mercedes. Not about my father or Hazel and now Abel. He's still my brother, Santiago."

"Half brother."

"I'm not saying he shouldn't be punished, but..." I trail off, remembering the bloody scene I glimpsed at the house where those men had kept me. "I don't want you to do anything...I don't know...illegal."

He looks at me, eyebrows high.

"Even if he's only a *half* brother, he's still that."

"Do I need to remind you of what he's done?"

I look out the window and watch the city come into view as we ride in silence for the rest of the trip. When we arrive at IVI, I can see the number of people is about half what it was the last time, but I swear all eyes turn to us as we walk onto the courtyard where refreshments are being served, and men and women are gathered in small groups talking and drinking.

Santiago must feel my hesitation and rubs a circle on my lower back. The dress is cut low and feeling his warm hand on me is reassuring. I lean a little closer to him.

"Santiago, it's been a long time," an old man I don't know says and pats Santiago's back.

"Jonathan!" Santiago smiles—an actual smile—but he checks himself quickly. "It's been long because you ran off to Europe for a year chasing after a pretty thing far too young for you." They shake hands.

"Entirely too young but well worth the effort." He winks. "And Europe was nice."

"It's good to see you. I didn't realize you'd be here tonight, actually."

"I'm not here for the dinner but when I learned your new bride would be accompanying you, I thought I'd love to meet her." He turns a broad smile to me. "This must be the beautiful Ivy. My dear, it is a pleasure to meet the woman who has managed to move this man's heart."

The words take me by surprise, and I know they do Santiago too as he clears his throat, hand stiffening at my back.

"I am Jonathan Price, your husband's godfather, believe it or not. Known him since he was oh…so big." He leans down so his hand is at knee level, then extends that same hand to me, palm up.

I slip my hand into it. "It's nice to meet you, Mr. Price."

"Jonathan, please," he says, cupping my hand between both of his.

"Jonathan," I repeat, smiling, liking the old man. "You're Santiago's godfather?"

He nods. "His father and I went way back. Shame what happened to him and Leandro." His expression darkens.

"I'm sure Ivy doesn't want to hear about all that," Santiago breaks in.

Jonathan lets go of my hand and turns to Santiago. "Of course. I saw your sister just inside on the arm of Lawson Montgomery?" he asks that last part, eyebrows high on his head.

"Inside, you say?"

"Can't miss her. Never could miss Mercedes." A man who looks familiar, but I can't quite place walks toward us, his expression serious. It's not until he's almost upon us and his eyes fall to my stomach that I realize who it is. One of The Councilors of The Tribunal. "It was nice to meet you, Ivy. Santiago, I'll see you another time," Jonathan says and turns to walk toward the man.

My heart is pounding.

"Relax," Santiago says. He must feel my anxiety as he leads me toward the open French doors of a dining room I've not been in before. It's beautiful, the walls, heavy curtains, and seating in various shades of red. Even the ceiling is draped with a silky scarlet fabric gathered at the center around a beautiful crystal chandelier.

"Wow," I say, unable to help myself. The Society has deep pockets, as do its members, and I know a bulk of that is due to my husband's skills with numbers and markets and things I don't even try to understand.

A waiter comes over with a new bottle of whiskey that he shows Santiago. Santiago looks at it, nods, and watches as it's opened and a glass poured.

"For the lady?" the waiter asks him.

I almost roll my eyes. Santiago turns to me for my answer. "Water is fine," I say.

"You heard her," Santiago tells him when he continues to stand there waiting for Santiago to reply. A few minutes later, I have a very fancy flute of water.

I've barely taken a sip when I hear Mercedes's laughter coming from the other side of the room. Santiago has already spotted her, and I see she's seen us. She doesn't miss a beat, though, as she tells a story to the half dozen people surrounding her and the man at her side. He seems familiar although I can't place him, either. It's his stance, tall and broad-shouldered, and his commanding presence.

It's when we're closer, and I hear his voice that I realize who he is.

I stop dead, and I am grateful for the music and for the laughter that erupts from the group surrounding Mercedes because I make a sort of choking sound as I feel the blood drain from my face, my body going cold.

I turn to Santiago and shake my head, my heart beating so fast I'm sure he can hear it. "Please."

As if sensing I'll bolt, he wraps a hand around the back of my neck and pulls me to him and anyone who is looking at us would think he was kissing my cheek but he's not. He's whispering to me.

"Judge is my friend. You'll need to get used to him."

"He's...I can't."

"I asked him to take you, Ivy. If anything happened to me, he knew what to do."

"What?" I ask, pulling back to look up at him. "How?"

"It is the Rite."

The Rite. God. It's like we go back in time every time I set foot in this place. The Rite is when one Head of Household, if he's the only male of age, passes on those in his charge to another in his absence or death or if he were to become somehow incapacitated.

"I trust Judge with my life. I trusted him with yours."

"When you thought I tried to kill you."

"Did he hurt you, Ivy?"

"He kept me in a cellar. He kept me—"

"Did he hurt you?" he asks again.

I shake my head.

"If he hadn't stepped in that night, you'd have spent those days in a Tribunal cell, and trust me, that would have been far worse."

"So, what? I should thank him?" I try to pull away, but he catches my arm.

"You should be respectful," he says, and I realize it's grown quieter. Santiago smiles and pulls me close again. "And you will behave." There's a pause after the *will*.

"Well, well," Mercedes says, approaching with a

wide grin on her face, drink in hand, eyes dropping instantly to my stomach before returning to mine. Her disdain or outright disgust of me is so apparent I'm sure Santiago must see it.

Judge has a hand at her elbow, eyes on me. He must know I recognize him.

"Santi," Mercedes says. "So nice to see you two out and about together, a little family in the making." She swallows what's left in her glass, sets it on a passing waiter's tray, grabs a full flute, and brings it to her lips.

"Easy," Judge tells her, but I hear it, and I wonder if he's keeping her in the cellar too because she gives him an annoyed glance but doesn't sip from her glass.

He nods. And I try to understand the dynamic. Surely Santiago wouldn't have sent her to him for whatever it is she did. Surely, Judge wouldn't be the consequences he talked about.

Just then another man comes to us. I don't know him, but he whispers something to Santiago. Santiago nods and turns to us.

"Do you ladies think you can behave yourselves for five minutes?"

I am about to say no, but Mercedes beams and comes to take my hand. Her nails dig into my palm. "Don't worry about us. We'll catch up." She turns and walks us to a private sitting area before I can get a word in. We sit on the plush velvet couches. "You're showing."

"Not really."

"Should I congratulate you?"

"What do you want, Mercedes?"

"You have no idea, do you?"

"I need to use the bathroom." I try to get up, but she puts her hand on my thigh and digs her nails into it, smiling when someone walks by to greet her.

"Don't look so smug. You haven't won the war," she says.

"What are you talking about? Any war is in your head."

"Innocent Ivy. Sweet, precious Ivy. This battle goes to you, I'm graceful enough to give you that, but I'll win in the end. You'll see."

"Seriously, Mercedes, you're fucking delusional." I shove her arm off and stand. I get about two steps away before she speaks.

"In nine months' time, I'll be back in my rightful place."

I turn to her, her choice of words stopping me. "What did you say?"

"Or eight months, I guess?" She sips from her drink.

"What are you talking about?"

She stands and walks toward me. "What did you think? That you could steal my family from me?"

"I'm not stealing anything. Your brother made a choice. He chose me."

She pauses, cocks her head to the side. Then laughs. "Oh my god! I don't believe it."

I should walk away. I know I should, but I can't.

"You're in love with him. You are seriously in love with him."

"I—"

"Well, poor, stupid Ivy," she says, leaning closer, twirling a strand of my hair around her forefinger. "He doesn't love you. He could never love you. Not after what your father did to him. To us."

My throat is so dry I can't speak. Her smile fades, and I see the circles under her eyes that I hadn't before.

"So, enjoy your little victory. For now. But remember what you are to him. What he needs you for. Once you give him his heir, it's bye-bye Ivy."

12

SANTIAGO

Ivy is quiet for the duration of the ride home, arms crossed as she stares out the window. She's barely spoken a word all night since her run-in with Mercedes. A conversation I watched from a distance, as Judge looked on too.

I hadn't planned on it happening, but it was a good test to see how far Mercedes had come. They are the two most important women in my life, and I would like them to find some common ground. But so far it appears the only thing they've found is a deeper resentment of one another. I don't know what Mercedes said to her, but it was impossible to miss the expression on Judge's face when he took her by the arm and led her away. She would be punished for whatever it was.

Security follows us through the gate to The

Manor, and Marco opens up Ivy's door for her when I park. I hand the keys off to him, and when I slip my hand onto Ivy's lower back, she pauses to look up at me. Her eyes are hard, conflicted. And I find that it is exhausting trying to figure her out.

"Let's go inside," I murmur.

She pivots forward, silently stalking through the front door and up the stairs while I trail along beside her. When we reach my room, she breaks away to grab a nightgown from the closet before she storms into the bathroom and slams the door shut behind her.

I wait for her, hands stuffed into my pockets. Five minutes pass. Then ten. And I'm losing my goddamned patience. I don't know how to deal with these emotions. The pregnancy book said mood swings are to be expected, but I've been trying to put her at ease, and so far it appears my efforts have been in vain.

When she finally returns to the room, she walks straight to the bed without looking at me and climbs in, tucking the covers around her.

"Would you care to explain why you're acting like a petulant child?" I demand.

"That's rich." She turns to glare at me. "Coming from you. Why don't you just go hole yourself up in your office, or whatever it is you do. No point sitting in here when you won't even sleep in the bed with me. I can assure you your child will be just fine without you looming over us."

"Our child," I correct her because it's the only thing I can think to say. On this point, she has been adamant, so I don't know why she seems insistent on reminding me otherwise now.

"I'm just the vessel, remember?" She bites out. "Your host."

"Fucking Christ." I drag a hand through my hair and turn away, trying to rein in my temper. "I don't know what you want from me, Ivy. I've been trying. Can you not see that?"

She doesn't reply, and I hear her sniff, but I can't look at her right now. I can't bear to see her disgust, her hatred. Every time I think we might actually be making progress, another clusterfuck presents itself.

I move toward the door without looking back, voice solemn when I speak.

"I'll be down in my office, should you need anything."

My ringing phone stirs me back to consciousness, and when I blink, I realize I must have fallen asleep in the chair at my desk. A quick glance at the clock on the wall confirms it's just past midnight. I'm usually wide-awake at this time, but since I've been keeping Ivy's hours, keeping watch over her, I've only managed a few hours of sleep at a time in the chair across from the bed. I am too fearful of losing control to sleep next to her, yet I don't want to be away from her.

Tonight, my body made the decision for me, and I am finding it difficult to rouse myself.

I reach for my phone, which has now gone silent, checking the screen. There are two missed calls from Judge, and a text message that simply tells me he found something.

I find it odd that he'd be up so late, digging through anything related to my problems. But I have a notion that Mercedes probably gave him hell once they got back to his house this evening. Perhaps he needed the distraction.

I reach for the bottle of scotch on my desk and take a long drink, soothing the dryness in my throat. When I return Judge's call, he answers on the first ring.

"Hello."

He sounds a little drunk, which is unlike him.

"My sister hasn't been giving you too much difficulty, has she?"

A long sigh is answer enough, but he replies as coolly as he always does. "Nothing I can't handle."

"It sounds like she did a fine job of making both of our nights unpleasant." I stretch my neck.

"Well, I am sorry for that," he responds. "I thought she would behave herself better. She was warned, and she has been punished for upsetting your wife."

"That isn't why you called though," I venture.

"No, I didn't call to discuss the ever-changing temperaments of women," he chuckles. "I've been digging through those files you sent and accessing some of the legal records from The Tribunal."

This information has me sitting up straighter. Judge's profession grants him access to The Tribunal's legal recordings. Something I myself do not have.

"What did you find?"

"I thought it strange that some of the names on those files you sent me are from members who have been excommunicated, so I followed those leads. As far as most of The Society is aware, they were found treasonous for one reason or another, and nobody blinked an eye when they were removed. But there was a common thread there."

"What was it?" I ask.

"Eli was the one who brought their names forward to The Tribunal in the first place. There aren't many details, but there are notes about some red flags he found in the financials linked to them. He believed there was a division taking place in that group, and it was noted that his son Abel had been helping him to investigate, a position he volunteered for."

"Of course he did," I mutter. "Any excuse to feel

important. Do you suspect those members were set up by Eli and Abel?"

"I don't know. The files I was able to access didn't have complete notes, which is common with The Tribunal. What takes place within those walls is often protected, but they will have at least some notes for reference in case it does come up again. I do find it difficult to believe the members of that group went quietly. I am curious if The Tribunal has investigated a possible link to the explosion. It would seem odd if they hadn't."

What he's telling me makes sense. Any normal person could draw that same logical conclusion, but I can't help resenting the fact that he's placing doubt in my head.

"Or it's possible that Eli and Abel set them up for reasons of their own."

"That is possible too," Judge agrees hesitantly.

"You don't sound convinced."

"I think if those members were set up, they would be trying to claw their way back in and prove their innocence. I don't know what evidence Eli could possibly have manufactured against all of them that was rock solid enough for The Tribunal to excommunicate them. Whatever he brought forward, it would have had to be very convincing, considering his position and their authority in the hierarchy."

"Well, I suppose I will have to ask him myself," I declare.

I'm already standing up to grab my jacket and seek out a guard to drive me to the hospital.

"I figured as much," Judge says. "I'll send you a secure email with the list of names."

13

SANTIAGO

Eli blinks at me, half-dazed as the nurse helps him to sit upright.

"What are you doing here in the middle of the night?" he croaks. "Has something happened to Ivy? I've been going crazy sitting here with no information, and the guards won't even tell me if you found her yet—"

"Here, take a sip of water." The nurse holds his cup up for him. "You can talk when your throat isn't so dry."

I allow that much before I glance at her. "You can go now. We need some privacy."

She doesn't argue. As a Society nurse, she knows who I am. In this hospital, the staff doesn't question the authority of a Sovereign Son.

She slips away quietly, shutting the door behind her, and I take a seat next to Eli's bed. He seems disoriented and anxious, and I suspect whatever they give him to help him sleep is partly to blame. But he'll have to wake up because I'm not about to leave.

"Is Ivy okay?" he asks again, desperation coloring his voice.

"I'm surprised you seem to care," I answer coldly.

"Of course, I care. She's my daughter."

"Yet, what exactly have you done for her?" I demand. "What have you done for any of your children? You left them in the care of a mother who worries more about her reputation than the welfare of her own flesh and blood. You allowed Ivy to suffer from a condition throughout her life instead of seeking the treatment she deserves. You permitted your wife to restrict Eva's food, a growing child, I might add. And you've facilitated Abel's power to terrorize his siblings along with God knows how many others—"

"Enough." Eli's jaw rattles, and spittle flies from his mouth as his face mottles with red. "You don't get to come in here and tell me what kind of father I am."

"That's exactly what I get to do." I glare at him. "Have you forgotten who you're speaking to?"

"I know exactly who you are," he says, his voice lowering. "And I know exactly who I am. What I meant was I don't need you to point out my shortcomings. I've had plenty of time to sit here and contemplate them myself in this prison cell of a hospital room."

His words surprise me, and when I study his face, all I see is sincerity. He isn't angry with me. He's angry with himself. Or at least, that is what he'd like me to believe. But I've fallen for that act before, haven't I?

"I didn't come here to talk about your fatherly failings." I change tack. "I came here for answers, and I won't leave here without them."

"What answers?" He searches my face as if he really doesn't know.

I'm beginning to wonder if that cardiac arrest damaged his brain beyond all reason as well. Surely, he must know why I'm here. He must not think I am such a fool I can be dissuaded so easily.

"If what you say about your own self-reflection is true, there is something you should know before we begin," I tell him. "I have Ivy's hand in marriage, which means I can do whatever I like to her. And if that is still not enough to motivate you, I think it would benefit you to know that I am also taking over guardianship of Eva. She is at my home. Under my control. I want you to think carefully about that before you consider lying to me."

"You have Eva too?" He swallows, terror streaking through his eyes. "Whatever it is you think I've done, Santiago—"

"Tell me about the sector you and Abel had a hand in excommunicating from IVI."

"The sector?" he repeats, confused. "What does that have to do with anything?"

"I'm asking the questions, Eli. I have a list of their names I can give you, should you require a reminder. There are notes in The Tribunal's files. A history. You can't deny it."

He sighs, shaking his head. "I'm not denying it. I just don't see what that has to do with anything. But if you want to know I will tell you."

"I'm waiting." I lean back and watch him closely, searching his face for any sign of dishonesty.

"They were involved in shady dealings. Something the Society was not aware of. I only stumbled upon it myself, by accident. I had access to bank accounts in their names. One of the member's wives asked me to do some bookkeeping. She wasn't aware of her husband's activities. The other accounts were those I would add the normal monthly deposits to. When I started to look through the first account, something caught my attention. There was another monthly deposit coming through from an offshore bank account that wasn't noted in his Society income. Upon further investigation, I realized he wasn't the only one receiving these payments. It was a lot to dig through, and I was only one person, so I had Abel start assisting me. After a while, we began to uncover an entire sector harboring income not affiliated with IVI. They were prominent members, their lineage within the Society had been embedded for generations. I was shocked, and still in disbelief because honestly, they really hadn't covered their tracks very well. But I knew I needed further proof."

"So, you sent Abel to investigate?"

"Yes," he admits. "He is good at that sort of thing, and he wanted to prove himself useful. I felt it was a good opportunity. And he did uncover a great deal of information on their back door dealings. We took all of the evidence to The Tribunal, and they felt the only choice was to excommunicate them."

"It couldn't have been that easy," I remark.

"Well, no," he concedes. "There was a consensus that they might try to enact revenge, but The Councilors have men keeping a close eye on them."

I'm waiting for him to tell me that they were somehow possibly involved in the explosion. Now would be the perfect time for him to plant that seed in my mind and draw attention away from himself. But Eli doesn't mention it, which I find odd.

"Have they made any attempts to harm IVI?" I ask.

"Honestly, I couldn't tell you," he says. "After the initial discussions took place with The Tribunal, I was cut out. Deemed too unimportant to be involved any further in the matter, given my position. They assured me it was handled and rewarded me generously for bringing it to their attention, and that was that."

"I see."

My jaw hardens as I consider that I've hit another dead end. While I don't necessarily believe Eli without a doubt, what he's telling me makes sense. The Tribunal would not have involved him any further in the matter than necessary.

"It sounds as if you have made some enemies within the organization," I point out. "Perhaps what you are trying to suggest, without saying as much, is that it was one of them who poisoned you?"

"Poisoned me?" His lips set into a grim line, and he shakes his head in disbelief before something seems to occur to him. "Are you telling me I was poisoned?"

"Yes. That is exactly what I'm telling you. Your bloodwork confirmed it."

I allow him a moment for this information to really settle over him, and as it does, I realize he's coming to some sort of silent conclusion as he processes it. At first, he appears angry, and then confused, and then... hurt.

"You know who it is, don't you?"

He shakes his head. "I... no, I don't know for certain."

"Spit it out, Eli. I saw the anguish in your eyes. You think it's someone close to you. Perhaps even your own son."

"No," he declares. "I don't believe that."

"It wouldn't be a stretch to consider." I examine him as I deliver the next blow. "He poisoned me as well."

"What?" His eyes snap to mine, and his anguish morphs to fear.

Eli understands what this means. I don't even have to tell him. But I will.

"He also kidnapped my wife and attempted to abort our baby. There are hundreds of Society hired men out combing the streets for him as we speak. His time on this earth is coming to an end, Eli."

"No." He looks at me pleadingly. "Please, let me talk to him. There has to be something I can do to make this right—"

"Come clean," I suggest. "And perhaps I will consider not bringing forward the evidence of his attempt on my life to The Tribunal."

"You haven't yet?" He searches my face, his love for his son foolishly overshadowing everything else I've just told him.

"No, I haven't yet. But there is still time."

"What do you want to know?" he asks. "Come clean about what?"

"Why were all those files in your ex-wife's house? Dossiers on me, other members of IVI. All the members who were killed in the explosion..."

I want to believe the confusion on his face is real.

That it can't be faked. But it also angers me because I am certain he must know.

"I... I don't know. I haven't even been to that house since Hazel..." Panic washes over his features when he realizes what he's just admitted to. He helped her escape.

"So, you are telling me that was Abel's doing then?"

"No." He clenches his hands on the bed railings, trying to drag his slumping body farther upright. "You are twisting reality to suit your own paranoia."

"Am I?" I laugh caustically. "And would I be twisting reality to remind you that you were the one who called me the night of the explosion? Too sick to go in, you said. That's how Leandro and I ended up there with our father. That's how I lost both of them. Because you set that chain of events into motion with one phone call, banking on the fact that I would help you."

My voice continues to rise as I do, looming over him as I clutch his hospital gown, lowering my face to his as I snarl the truth.

"You made me believe that you were a trusted friend and advisor. And you were the one who betrayed me."

Realization dawns on his face, and he shakes his head in denial. "No, Santiago. You have it all wrong. I was sick that night. I was vomiting uncontrollably. Believe me, if you think I haven't considered that very fact... that I sent you there, and what happened... it could have been myself and my own son. I have thought of it every day since it happened. I never stop thinking of it."

My hands fall away from his shirt, and I stumble back, angry with myself for giving him the opportunity to defend himself when he doesn't deserve it. I thought of him as a father once. Someone to look up to. Someone I admired. And now, he is a shriveled husk of a man who still has not one ounce of honor to his name.

"Your days are numbered, Eli," I inform him as I move toward the door. "And as for your son? You can consider him dead. When I find him, there won't be a soul on this earth who can save him."

14

IVY

I can't get Mercedes's words out of my head. Can't stop seeing her face, the hate in it. What she said, what she suggested, it's what I've been thinking. It's the thought that's been in the back of my mind since Santiago rescued me from the doctor who would abort our baby and brought me home. But it's not that alone that's bothering me. Before coming into this house, before having the De La Rosa siblings in my life, I never felt hated. And being hated is different than being ignored or even disliked. It's almost a palpable thing, a weighted thing.

And the fact that Mercedes hates me shouldn't bother me. I know that. And I can live with it, but it's what she said and how it just confirms what I've been worrying about. That this new Santiago, this kinder, better man, the doting husband, it's a ruse. Not real.

And she saw right through me.

I am in love with Santiago De La Rosa. I am in love with my husband which in a normal world would be a wonderful thing. But in our world, it's dangerous. It's a weakness. Does he see it too? Does he see it and is using it to manipulate me? To have an obedient wife who will accept his wishes, submit to them without an opinion of her own? A wife who carries and births his heir?

His.

"Ivy?" I blink, look up at Antonia who asks me again if I want something else to eat.

I glance down at my plate, see the eggs are still there. Cold now. My toast is untouched. I don't remember buttering it but I haven't eaten a single bite.

And Santiago is sitting at the head of the table, tired eyes locked on me.

"No, thanks. I'm just a little nauseous this morning," I lie. Although I'm sure if I keep going down this road it will be the truth. "I'll just have some tea." I pick up my now tepid tea and realize I haven't sipped that either.

"Let me get you a fresh cup," Antonia starts but Santiago puts a hand on her arm.

"No."

"It's cold—"

"Leave us."

"It'll just take a minute, sir."

But he shifts his gaze up to hers and what she must see in his eyes sends her hurrying away.

"You should be nicer to her. To all your staff. *Master*," I say.

The line of his jaw hardens.

"You don't deserve her as it—"

His fist comes down on the table so hard it rattles the silverware and dishes, making me jump. "What the hell has gotten into you?"

I put my tea cup down and set my hands on my lap. I don't want him to see they're trembling.

"You're still wearing the clothes from last night," I say.

"And?"

"You didn't come to bed at all. At least not our bed."

His eyebrows rise. "Whose bed do you think I'd have gone to if not my own?"

"I don't know, Santiago. Ever since you moved me into your room it's not like you've ever actually slept beside me. Did you think I wouldn't notice? Did you just do it to shut me up? Stop my whining, I think you'd said before."

"Of course not. What is going on with you?"

He looks taken aback. I pick up my toast and pile scrambled eggs on top but when I take a bite, the now hard toast breaks apart and the eggs slip off onto the table, my lap and floor. "Shit." I drop what's left of the toast onto my plate and begin to scoop up the mess on the table but Santiago's hand closes over mine.

"Stop."

I try to shove it away. "Let go. I don't want Antonia to have to clean it up."

"She has staff for that."

"No." I push my chair back, sliding my hand out from under his to gather the mess on the floor.

"Ivy, stop."

Mercedes's words come back to me and I hate that they have the power to hurt me. She's right. I am in love with him. And she knows her brother better than me. He can never love me.

"Ivy. Goddammit!" His chair scrapes back loudly and he's behind me, hands on my arms, lifting me out of my seat.

"You're making it worse," I say, my voice breaking a little as I step on a piece of toast.

"It doesn't matter." He turns me, shifts his hands to my face to make me look at him. "What is it? What the hell has happened between yesterday and today?"

I look up at him and all I can hear is her. I have to think about what's important now. Whether I love him or not and whether he is capable of loving me back or not can't matter.

"Are you going to take the baby away from me?" I ask outright, my throat feeling tight to say the words.

"What?"

"Are you? Just tell me. I'm not going to run away. You said yourself I wouldn't get past the front gates." I remember when he'd said it. How it had stood out. "I just need to know."

He exhales, shakes his head like he's disgusted. He pulls his hands away and wraps one around the back of his neck, shaking his head, lips in a tight line.

"I just want to know. So I'm ready." Can someone be ready for something like that?

"Is that what she told you? What's turned you against me?" When I look away from him, he cups my face again to tilt it up, brushes a strand of hair behind my ear. He sighs deeply like he's very tired. "No, Ivy. I am not going to take our baby away from you. Can we lay this to rest once and for all? Can you trust me and let this go? Because that's what it comes down to. Trust."

Before coming down to breakfast I'd walked past my old room. It's cleaned up, more of a guest room now, the dark panels still there but open. The bed made to welcome someone new. The mask in its glass case gone. The rosary he'd made me wear since our wedding night not on the nightstand where I'd last left it but gone. I'd stood outside the door and thought about how much time I'd spent in there.

How easy it would be for him to just put me back in, lock the door and forget all about me.

Trust.

He wants me to trust him.

I blink, my eyes focusing on his, something in my stomach fluttering when he smiles as if trying to draw the same from me, and I remember something else about last night. Something else she said.

That he could never love me because of what my father had done to him. To their family.

"I want to see my father," I say.

His expression changes. Darkens.

"You want me to trust you, but all I seem to do is give, and all you seem to do is take."

"That's neither right nor fair, and you know it." His voice is harder.

"Yes, you've come through on my sister. And I'm grateful for that. I'm grateful that we, you and I together, will have guardianship of her."

He doesn't say anything.

"That's right, isn't it? You and me together will have guardianship. Not just you."

"No, not just me. That's correct. Would you like to see the paperwork so you believe me?" His words are clipped.

I shake my head. "I understand about Hazel. About it being dangerous for her and maybe even for you to be keeping her location a secret from The Society. I don't understand why I can't have a cell phone or access to a phone and at least call her, though."

He doesn't say anything at that.

"And I'm willing to let that go. For now. But you have to give me something, too. In addition to Evangeline. I want to see my father. I want to see him today." I don't ask it. I don't say please. Because what I want is not extraordinary. It's not some ridiculous request. He's in a Society hospital. He'll be guarded. I will be too. No chance of Abel or anyone else getting to me. No risk to my safety. "You can take me, Santiago. I want you to take me."

He studies me for a very long moment, and I watch how his left eye narrows, see the tic in his jaw, and I'm sure he's going to say no, and then I won't know what to do. What my next move will be. But he surprises me when he nods.

"You eat something, and I'll take you to see your father."

I almost don't believe him, and he must see that because he turns me around puts a hand on the back of my chair, and gestures for me to sit back down. So, I sit, and I let him make a fresh plate of eggs and toast from the sideboard, and he sits down too and watches me eat.

"My sister is jealous," he says once I've finished and set my napkin down after wiping my mouth. "It's ugly on her. On anyone. But she'll come around."

"No, she won't, Santiago. And you'll have to keep choosing, and I'm just afraid the day will come when you choose her, and I'm back in my room or banished to wherever, and I don't think I can survive that. Especially now that there's more at stake than just me and you." My throat tightens as I say the words, but I swallow them down.

"Ivy—"

I stand. "I'm ready."

15

IVY

I realize my father was in the same building as me when I was brought here after the aspirin incident. He was just a few floors above me kept behind secured doors not accessible by anyone without a reason for being there and with an additional guard at his door.

"He was here all along?"

Santiago nods as he guides me down to the last room.

"Why didn't you tell me?"

"You didn't ask."

"Would you have?"

"I haven't lied to you, Ivy. Not once."

Is that true? I'm taken aback. Confused.

We stop a few feet from the door, and he turns to face me, backing me into the wall. "Like I told your sister, you may not like what I have to say, but I won't lie to you."

He dips his head down, so his forehead is touching mine. His eyes travel to the pendant hanging at the hollow between my collarbones, and he touches it, then takes my left hand to finger the rings there, the salt and pepper engagement ring, the wedding band. He shifts his gaze back to mine.

"I am trying, Ivy."

I reach up, I can't help it, but I stop myself before I touch his face. Instead, I smooth his shirt down—he changed before we left for the hospital, showering and putting on fresh clothes—and when I do, I realize my hand is resting over his heart, and for a moment, I keep it there and just feel it beat.

He closes his hand over mine.

"I know you are," I say and feel a little guilty because right now, I'm the one with the agenda. I'm the one lying because omission is a lie, and I am here not only to see my father, to hug him, to know he's okay but also to ask him about what Mercedes said. To find out what it is they think he did that is so terrible that Santiago would do what he's done. The thing that would leave him incapable of loving me.

He nods and takes my hand as we step in front of the door. The guard nods his greeting and opens it, and I see him. My father. And for as frail as he looks when the nurse turns his wheelchair around and as different from the tall, commanding man I remember before the coma, I am relieved.

"Daddy!"

Santiago releases me, and I run to my father, who looks surprised and then happy, so happy. He opens his arms, and I'm careful when I hug him, feeling his arms around me, having mine around him.

When I pull back, he takes both of my hands in his and looks me over, pausing at my stomach momentarily before smiling back up at me. I'm wearing a Henley and jeans, but I don't think I'm showing in this. He glances over my shoulder then, and I follow his gaze to see Santiago standing by the door, one arm folded across his chest, the hand of the other closed over his chin, watching us.

"Thank you, son," my father says, and when Santiago opens his mouth, he catches himself. "Santiago."

Santiago nods and shifts his gaze to me, then opens the door without a word. He gestures to the nurse, who leaves and then follows her out.

He is trying.

And he's right. I know Mercedes is just jealous. And I get it. I usurped her throne. It's not even about me. I'm sure she'd hate anyone who took her place in Santiago's life. It would be strange in a normal situation, but given what they've gone through, the loss of both brother and father on one terrible night, the death of their mother soon after that, then the near loss of Santiago, I can see how they'd become so central to each other. Although I don't think it's quite the same for Santiago. But then again, maybe if Mercedes found someone, maybe Judge, she would be different too.

I turn back to my father, who is studying me with a smile. "He married you."

I nod.

"What about school?"

"That's not really in the cards anymore."

"Perhaps in time. Sit down, Ivy." There's a small couch along one wall, and I take a seat there. The room isn't big, and my father rolls himself closer. "I'm sorry I don't have anything to offer you."

I smile a little awkwardly. It's been so long since I've seen him and so much has changed. "It's just really good to see you like this."

"Well, I've been better."

"You've also been worse. I'm glad you woke up from the coma."

"That's thanks to your husband."

"Santiago?"

"I was poisoned, Ivy. I read the report. What he said is true. It wasn't cardiac arrest or a sudden stroke or whatever they told you. What happened to me was brought on by poison."

I'm not sure how I feel about this. Fear, I guess. Cardiac arrest or a stroke would have been better.

Poisoned means someone tried to kill him, and my mind wanders to that lipstick I found. To Abel's silence when I questioned him.

"Is he treating you all right?" he asks.

I nod. "And Eva's at The Manor too. She's actually really happy there. I think so at least."

"I'm glad. Your mother?"

"I haven't seen her." Silence. "Dad, did you help Hazel run away?"

He is obviously surprised by my question. "Is she safe?"

"I think so. Santiago knows where she is. He said she has a little boy."

"Michael. He's a good kid."

"You know?"

"I helped her, Ivy. You were too young to know anything about it."

"You helped her run away?"

"And stay away. It's very hard for a single mom out there. I'm sure you can imagine."

"Why?"

"I wouldn't force her to marry someone she didn't love, and the fact that she was pregnant with another man's child, well, that changed things. At least she came to her senses about that one, though."

"But The Society…"

"Does not come before my family. I've made that mistake more than once."

"Abel's mom?"

He nods and tries to smile, but I see something is worrying him. "Among other things."

"I need to ask you something, Dad." I glance at the door, not sure how much time I'll have.

"Go on."

"What happened with Santiago? You were like a father to him. I remember that. I remember how much you loved him."

"I love him still even if he is misguided."

"What happened?"

"Do you know he paid me a visit last night?"

"Last night?"

My father nods. "It's good he did. Good he told me about the poisoning. But also, about what Abel tried to do to your baby." He quiets again, looking away from me momentarily, any pretense of a smile fading. "I did wrong by that boy. It's not his fault."

"Abel's a grown man."

"If I'd given him half the attention I gave Santiago, if I'd put my family first, then things would be different now."

"What do you mean?"

"I've been thinking about this all night. Trying to piece the puzzle together. I should have known better than to trust him blindly, although it's what he needed. His father's trust. But when those names came up, when ties to the Grigori mafia family were mentioned. The De La Cruz Cartel—"

"What? Mafia? Cartel?"

He looks at me, and I get the feeling he's considering how much he's already said.

"What are you talking about, Dad?"

"They're not associated with IVI. Not the Cartel and not Grigori. IVI, as it stood, would never have accepted the likes of them into the fold." He stops, shakes his head. "I should have looked into it myself first and verified things. I would have known if I had, and many lives would have been saved, including Santiago's father and brother."

"I'm sorry, you lost me."

He focuses his attention on me and tries for a smile again. "To answer your question, Ivy, Santiago thinks I, along with your brother, sent him and his family not to mention other countless Sovereign Sons, to their death."

"What?"

"The explosion, it wasn't a simple gas leak. I think it was revenge, and I set it in motion. Abel handed me the evidence of wrongdoing, and I took it to The Tribunal, unknowingly starting it all. Because those families that were excommunicated, that lost everything, they had their revenge that night or at least that is how it appeared. I need to talk to Abel. To hear it from him. Hear what he did. How many lives he was willing to forfeit."

"Dad, I don't understand."

The door opens then, and Santiago stands in the

entry. He locks eyes with my father, and I watch his throat work as he swallows.

"You heard, I'm sure," my father says calmly.

"What?" I ask, standing, looking between them.

"If you're saving your neck—"

"By hanging my own son?"

Santiago doesn't reply.

"I won't have more blood on my hands. I won't have my grandchild's blood on my hands. Not even your blood, Santiago."

"What are you talking about?" I ask.

"I think I know how Abel was funded," my dad says. "I need my computer, some files I kept, but I think I know."

"Ivy," Santiago says, not looking at me. "Marco will take you home." As if on cue, Marco appears behind Santiago.

"I'm not going anywhere until I know what's happened."

My father reaches out to take my hand. "You want to know why he hates me. Why he hates us. He thinks I set him up. He thinks I orchestrated the explosion that killed his family."

16

SANTIAGO

Ivy is waiting for me on the stairs when I walk in the front door, bundled up in my bathrobe, which seems to drown her small frame.

"What are you doing sitting here in the dark?" I ask.

"We need to talk, Santiago. I'm not going to bed without having this conversation."

I sigh, already dreading the inevitable fight as I join her at her side and help her up. "Come. Let's get you upstairs."

She doesn't protest as I lead her to our bedroom, but I know it can't be that easy. And I am proven right when I shut the door behind us and toss my jacket aside.

"I'm worried about my father," she says, emotion choking her voice.

That suffocating anguish in her tone lances

through me, and I don't like it. I find that I am compelled to fix it for her, even though I know I can't. Not without sacrificing my own promises to my dead father and brother.

"Your father is well cared for," I answer stiffly. "He has the best medical treatment money can buy. He's in a secure facility—"

"You mean a prison," she interjects. "You have him locked up in that room like a common prisoner, dictating who comes or goes."

"It's a kindness he does not deserve," I mutter, turning away to unbutton my shirt and discard that too.

"I should be helping him." Ivy sniffs. "He shouldn't be there alone, recovering without any of his family. He should be here with us where I know he's safe. Where the guards can protect him too. Now that I know someone poisoned him, I won't be able to relax thinking that it could happen again."

"It won't," I assure her, leaving out the part that his death will not be so kind.

"Please." Her voice wavers. "I want you to promise me you won't hurt him. I need that from you."

I turn back to her, rigid and frustrated. I can't give her that. Doesn't she understand? I can give her anything else in this world she might desire, but not that.

"I can't make you a promise I have no intention of keeping."

Her face falls, and she staggers back, using the bed for support as she stares at me with watery eyes.

"But he told you he would help you. He told you it was Abel or those other members. Not him."

"He told me what he thought I wanted to hear," I say. "Any man in his position would do the same."

"You'll never accept it, will you?" She swipes at the tears that are starting to spill down her cheeks. "You won't accept that you could be wrong about him because it means you would have to admit you've been wrong about me too. Then you'd have to open yourself up and learn how to love someone other than yourself, but you can't because you're so blinded by your own hatred."

"You think I'm in love with myself?" A bitter laugh escapes me. "Oh, sweet, naïve Ivy. You have no idea what I feel."

She dips her head, a flush creeping over her cheeks. "You can be so... infuriating!"

"I'm going to take a shower," I growl. "Go to sleep."

I slam the bathroom door behind me, sealing myself in as I close my eyes and drag in a deep breath. Ice runs through my veins as I play her words over, dissecting the meaning behind them.

You'd have to open yourself up and learn how to love someone other than yourself.

How could she not realize I have no love for myself? It should be evident every time she walks through these darkened halls. And who does she expect me to love, exactly? Her?

Answers to those questions are in short supply, but it doesn't stop me from playing them on repeat as I turn on the shower and step into the hot spray. I turn to face the wall, eyes shutting as the warmth flows over my face. Why would she possibly think I'd ever be capable of love?

This sick feeling in my chest isn't that. It's something else. I've already decided that because it's the only thing that makes sense. I can't love my enemy's daughter. Granted, I have made concessions. I have been too soft with her at times, and perhaps I have even lost sight of my goal, changing course entirely. But just because I've decided to keep her instead of kill her it doesn't mean anything has really changed. It's simply the sensible thing to do. She will be the mother of my children. The warmth in my bed at night. The body that brings me pleasure. Those are all practical considerations in a marriage. Feelings have nothing to do with it.

Why can't she see that?

There is truth in her prediction, and she should know it. Eli will never be able to prove his innocence to me. He can search through files and attach all the blame to his son as much as he likes. But it doesn't change the facts. He was the one who called me that night. He was the one who asked me, Leandro, and my father to go in their places. If he hadn't, they would still be alive, and I wouldn't be... *like this.*

Frustration wells inside me as I consider how much I need him gone. Ivy will never accept it. The battle lines have been drawn, and I can't win either way. Judge was right. I have to decide what's more important. Having the satisfaction of my revenge, or the warmth of my wife.

A hand on my back startles me from that unpleasant thought, and when I glance over my shoulder, Ivy is behind me, wrapping her arms around my waist and leaning her face against my skin.

"I don't want everything to be a fight," she whispers.

"Then don't make it one," I answer childishly.

She sighs, tightening her grip on me.

"I can't imagine the pain you must have felt," she says. "Losing your father and brother that way. It hurts me just thinking about it, and I'm sorry that nobody has ever apologized to you and meant it, Santiago. That isn't fair and it isn't right. My father should have addressed the situation with you right away, had an open conversation to start. But he let it fester like he always does, and now, we're here."

"What happened is between me and your father—"

"I'm not finished," she cuts me off stubbornly. "Just let me say what I want to say."

When I indulge her with silence, she continues.

"I'm sorry for the pain you've endured. I'm sorry for the incredible loss that's changed your life forever. But I am not sorry for your scars."

She turns me slowly, forcing me to face her as she cups my jaw in her hands. "These scars are a part of you, and I wouldn't change them because they prove that you are strong, a survivor. Every one of them are a testament to what you have endured and overcome. And to me, they are beautiful."

"There's no need to lie."

"It's not a lie, and you know it." She tightens her grip on me. "Stop projecting your own insecurities onto everyone else. People aren't afraid of you because of these scars, Santi. They are afraid of you because you stomp around like a fire breathing demon who will burn anyone who dares to look at him."

"It's... all I know," I confess, regretting the words as soon as they fall from my lips.

"No, it isn't." A small smile curves her lips as if she's recalling something. "I have seen your softness. You are capable of letting your guard down. Eva has seen it. Antonia too. I just think you are terrified of giving it away so freely, in case anyone gets the wrong idea about you. That you are actually good and decent inside."

"Well, that would be the wrong idea," I murmur.

"Give me an inch," she says. "I'm not asking for

leaps and bounds. All I'm asking for is that you try to trust me, like you asked me to do."

"Trust you like I did today, when you went to your father with one motivation in mind?"

"I wouldn't have to sneak around if you'd just talk to me," she retorts. "And I did want to see my father. It wasn't just to interrogate him."

"I suppose you want me to trust your word that your father wasn't involved too?" I ask. "That's what this is all about."

"Partially, yes. I know him, and I know when he's being truthful. I'm asking you to trust my intuition on this. At least until you have solid evidence to otherwise condemn him, and not just your own suspicions."

"How do you know I don't already?"

"You would have brought it to The Tribunal if you had, surely."

I have to give her that. She has a good point, but I wouldn't have brought it forward because this justice will be doled out myself.

"You are too close to the situation to be unbiased," I tell her. "What you're asking me is to give up my revenge."

"I'm asking you to give my father time to prove his innocence. Now that everything is out on the table, we can all work toward the same goal together. Let me help you. As your wife and your partner."

I stare down into her eyes and swallow. She isn't

in a position to barter for her father's life, but right now, I can't seem to tell her no.

"I will... consider it."

My voice is strained, but somehow it still manages to produce a relieved smile on Ivy's face. She presses her naked body against mine, the softness of her skin rubbing against my cock. I drag my fingers up to the base of her skull and hold her there while I lean down to kiss her.

Her hands stroke over the scars on my back as she parts her lips for me. I swallow her soft moans, pivoting her body toward the wall and walking her backward. She reaches down between us wrapping her fingers around my cock, greedy for it as our kiss deepens to something hungry and feral.

She's stroking me, driving me mad with need. I want to fuck her hard and rough, reclaim her all over again. But I don't know that it's safe.

I pin her against the wall, my fingers sliding down over her throat, her collarbone, and then stopping to pinch and grope her nipples. She arches her head back, biting her lip, and then sucks in a sharp breath when I lower myself to my knees before her.

Our eyes connect as I lift her legs and drape them over my shoulders, using the wall against her back as leverage. She tangles her fingers in my hair, arching her pelvis forward at the same time I dip my head between her thighs.

The first lash of my tongue seems to send a

shockwave through her body, thighs clenching around my face as she tightens her grip on my hair. I groan and do it again, and again, watching her come undone for me, losing herself to the pleasure. But through it all, her eyes never leave mine. She's watching me watch her. It's an intimacy I am unfamiliar with, yet, neither one of us seems willing to break it.

"Tell me what you're thinking," I demand.

She pants broken fragments of her thoughts. "So good... it's so hot. Watching you do this."

My dick jerks in anticipation, and I squeeze the bottoms of her thighs in my palms, spreading her wider for me.

"Where do you want to come, Mrs. De La Rosa?" I tease her with my nose, dragging it along the seam of her pussy, inhaling her. "On my face, or on my cock?"

"Both," she answers breathlessly.

"Someone is greedy today." I thrust my tongue back inside her and she squirms against me as I bury my face deeper. Devouring her.

Within seconds, she's rocking, tugging on my hair, crying out as her orgasm rips through her. She clenches around me, toes curling into my back, hands falling loose as her body nearly collapses in the aftermath.

I hoist her up into my arms as I stand, adjusting her body so her legs are wrapped around my waist.

She watches me, face soft and relaxed as I fumble to get my dick inside her, sliding around the wetness and pushing the head deeper and deeper until I've sank all the way in.

I release a contented sigh, rolling my hips against her, and she reaches up, pulling my face down to hers. We kiss as I fuck her and hold her, and I can't stop it.

I can admit that her hands on my body, her lips on mine, feel better than anything else ever has. Her pussy may as well have been molded for my dick. It's so warm and soft I don't ever want to leave.

I'm too drunk on this feeling to unpack the meaning behind it. So I just thrust. In and out until she's crying my name, coming for me again like she wanted. And then it's my turn as I bury myself inside her and groan out a release that seems to last for minutes. I'm still rocking in and out of her as my dick begins to soften, come dripping down between us.

She reaches up and touches my cheek, warmth in her eyes. Something happens at that moment. It feels like I'm being electrocuted, and all I want to do is get away. I'm thinking about it already, setting her upright and telling her to go to sleep while I go to my office. But Ivy seems to sense this weakness in me, and she cuts it off before it can sprout wings.

"Let me wash you. You've had a long day."

She wiggles free from my arms, and my dick falls

sad and limp against my thigh as she reaches for the soap and squirts it into her palms. While she lathers, I turn away, offering her my back as I try to catch my bearings. When I feel her hands on me though, all my fleeting thoughts fall away.

"I didn't mean it," she says quietly. "What I said about you being in love with yourself. I just... it came out all wrong."

"I've forgotten about it already," I lie.

She doesn't reply, and we settle into silence as she washes me like one might detail a car. Slowly tracing over the ink on my skin, examining every line and swooping curve. It's something I never would have allowed anyone at one time, but with her, I don't mind it. I want her to know this part of me, even though I can't understand why.

What the fuck is wrong with me?

She's halfway through the front of my body, already teasing my dick again when I reach behind her and grab the soap.

"Your turn."

She frowns like a child who's just been told playtime is over, but she gets over it quickly enough when I start by massaging her shoulders. I wash her arms and breasts and slide my soapy fingers between her legs, to which she reacts with a soft moan. A side effect of the hormones, I tell myself. But when I reach her belly, splaying my palm across the small curve taking shape there, it hits me unexpectedly.

We are making a human together. A tiny human that will have her qualities and mine. It chokes me up unexpectedly, and I hope she can't see it. This is just the natural order of things. This is what we were supposed to do as husband and wife. But right now, I feel oddly... proud. And content.

"You're thinking about how you impregnated me, aren't you?" She rolls her eyes.

"It was quite the accomplishment," I remark without reservation.

"It's biology, Santiago."

"And the De La Rosa virility," I argue.

Her smile fades as her palms come to rest on my forearms. "What will happen if this baby is a girl?"

"Then we will have a daughter," I answer, not understanding her point.

"But it won't be the same as a son." Sadness tinges her voice.

"Do you want a boy?" I furrow my brows.

"No, that's not what I'm saying," she huffs. "I'm saying you do."

"I want a boy," I agree. "We will need male heirs, certainly. But I want girls too. A mixture would be good."

Her eyes widen. "How many babies do you think we're going to have?"

"As many as I can put inside you."

She does not look amused as she shakes her head. "I'm not a baby factory."

"I know. But you have to admit it isn't a chore to make them."

"Make them, no. Carrying them around for nine months and raising them? Yes, that will be a lot of work."

"We'll have help," I assure her. "Antonia—"

"Santiago." She traces her fingers over my lips, quieting me. "Let's just get through one baby at a time, okay?"

I shrug, and she seems to let the issue go, for now. We wash off beneath the spray, and then towel off and brush our teeth at the sinks. The entire ritual is oddly domestic, and I feel a suffocating weight on my chest, like I need to leave. To escape for a while. But then Ivy ruins it all with one request.

"Will you stay with me tonight?" she asks. "For at least a little while."

"Okay."

She pauses to look at me like she doesn't believe me. "Okay?"

"Don't make a big deal of it."

She fights a smile and nods, and together we go back into the bedroom and crawl in bed, still naked. For a few minutes, we lay there, side by side, staring up at the ceiling. Not touching, neither of us speaking. And then beneath the covers, I feel Ivy's palm on my dick.

Next thing I know, I'm balls deep inside her

again, fucking her into the bed as she cries out my name, digging her nails into my ass.

Once we have both come, I collapse beside her, and she nestles her head into the space between my arm and shoulder, curling her body close to mine. My hand falls around her naturally, and I close my eyes, just for a minute. That minute turns into an entire night, and the next time I open them, I'm surprised to see it's morning.

I spent the entire night in bed with her.

17
IVY

The next month passes peacefully between Santiago and I. There's no sign of Abel. It's like he's vanished off the face of the earth. Any bank accounts in his name have been frozen, according to Santiago, who has somehow gained access to them. There's been no credit card activity on any known cards for weeks. Between Santiago's men and the soldiers, The Society has stationed throughout New Orleans and anywhere else Abel has ever had ties, I can't fathom where he'd be hiding.

Did he have more than one safe house? He had to have. He needs a place to lie low. He needs money.

Unless, of course, someone is hiding him.

Santiago hasn't said as much but I know it's on his mind. A man I've yet to be introduced to has come to see Santiago multiple times and with

Santiago's tendency to become more animated and raise his voice when it comes to my brother, I've overheard a few things. It's not that I'm eavesdropping exactly. It's just if I didn't happen by his office door during these visits, he'd never tell me anything.

He's been to see my father almost daily and when I ask my father what they talk about, what has him and Santiago so worried, he changes the subject, maneuvers me around on tiptoe. At least I'm allowed to see him, though. Although I'm still not sure Santiago's feelings for my father will ever change. If he'll ever not blame him for what happened the night his father and brother were killed along with so many others. The night he walked away a scarred, broken man.

I know Santiago doesn't want me to worry. I know he's keeping things from me in order to protect me, protect our baby. At least I believe that's his thinking process. I don't like it, but I can't seem to budge him on that. In some ways it's endearing me to him. I like seeing how careful he is with me. Different than he is with anyone else. He's gentle and thoughtful and I realize I feel safe. Safe in this house. This home we're making. Safe in his arms and in his bed.

I haven't told him my feelings for him yet. Haven't said the words I love you. But they're creeping up more and more often when we make love. When he holds me afterward. And it's getting harder to swallow them down.

He's let Eva and I video call Hazel and her son, Michael. Michael looks like a mini version of my sister, and seeing her, even over a video, was so much more emotional than I ever thought it could be. I missed my sister these years but I didn't realize how fresh that hurt was.

We keep the conversations pretty light with Michael and Eva around but it's okay. At least we've reconnected. At least I know she's safe. And the best part of it is that Michael already calls me Aunt Ivy and has begun to randomly call me when he gets home from school to tell me about his day. He most often forgets he's on the call after just a few minutes and puts the iPad he's using down to go off to play or eat a snack. It's the sweetest thing.

Eva's been back to school, too, at her own request which shows me how bored she was getting. Although Santiago has stationed two guards to remain at her side. She tells me they at least stay in the hallway when she's in a classroom. I love watching them interact especially. My little sister taking on Santiago De La Rosa, poking holes in his armor, even having him outright laughing when she's not testing every boundary.

He's a different man from the one I met just months ago.

I would feel better having my father moved into the house, but he still refuses me that.

Today, though, I am going to see Colette. It's late afternoon by the time Marco returns to take me but I don't complain. I know he's one of Santiago's most trusted men and when it can't be Santiago himself to accompany me to the few places I am permitted to go, it's always Marco and only Marco.

"How is he?" I ask Marco as I settle into the Rolls Royce. It feels strange sitting in the back seat when it's just the two of us but when I tried to slip into the front seat once, I realized quickly how uncomfortable it made him.

"Working too hard and sleeping too little," Marco says, knowing I mean Santiago. He cares about him. I wonder if Santiago realizes it. If he even sees how many people he has around him who truly care about him. It makes me sad to think he finds himself unlovable.

"And my father?"

"Same as your husband."

I want to ask more, but I don't. He won't tell me anything else.

We're silent on the drive to Colette and Jackson's Garden District house. It's a sunny day, the temperature warmer than it's been in a while. I have always loved spring in New Orleans. I'm wearing a simple cotton dress and a light sweater, and you can see my rounding belly clearly now. It's a small bump, but it's definitely there, and I put my hand over it, waiting for the day I feel the first little flutters of movement. According to the books Santiago bought me, it'll be a few weeks before that happens, though.

When we get to Colette and Jackson's house, Marco grumbles something under his breath as he turns onto the circular drive to park behind the other Rolls Royce that's already there, the driver standing outside smoking a cigarette. The man looks into the windshield at us but doesn't smile or greet us. Instead, he takes the last drag of his cigarette and flips the butt onto the manicured lawn.

"Prick," Marco says.

"Who is he?" I ask, but before he gets a chance to answer, the front door opens, and Cornelius Holton walks briskly out of the house, his face red, his step angry and hurried.

I want to shrink away and hide. I will never forget that man. Never forget how he looked at me, how his fingers felt when he opened my robe as I'd tried to cover myself that horrible morning before the wedding.

God. I feel sick. But instead of allowing myself to cower, I take a deep breath in to steel myself. I narrow my gaze and look at him straight on.

He's so wrapped up in his own thoughts that it almost appears to surprise him when he sees our car, and he stops momentarily. Through the windshield, his eyes alight on me. Not Marco but me.

And I don't look away.

"Wait in the car," Marco tells me as he opens the door and steps out, then closes it behind him. He doesn't approach Holton, but his hulking presence does drag the older man's gaze away from me and I swear for a moment, there's a flash of insecurity there. A twinge of fear or even panic. And I know Marco is making sure Holton sees him. Making sure he knows he's been seen.

Holton clears his throat. I don't hear it, but his hand moves to cover his mouth as he does. He nods once to Marco before he slips into the back seat of his own vehicle, and they're gone.

"What was that?" I ask Marco as I climb out of the car.

"Like I said, a prick." Marco closes the door and reaches for the bag I'm carrying.

"I can carry it," I say. It's a gift for the baby.

He nods, and we walk up to the house together, where even through the door, I can hear Jackson and Colette arguing, her voice higher than usual, her upset audible from here. His is lower but obviously agitated.

"What should we do?" I ask Marco, who is making no secret of listening.

He puts a finger to his lips.

"You can't listen!" I ring the bell when there doesn't seem to be any break in the conversation inside. As soon as I do, the house falls silent. Marco and I look at each other momentarily before I hear hurried steps and a baby's cry. The door opens, and I see Colette. Jackson is a few steps behind her. The men exchange a look, but I don't bother with them. I'm worried about my friend. It's obvious Colette has been crying. Her skin is blotchy, and her eyes red and puffy.

"Ivy," she says, trying to pull a smile together. I'm not sure if I should make an excuse or ask if it's a good time which would reveal that we heard them arguing and possibly make things more awkward but I'm grateful when the baby's crying grows louder. "Come in, come in. Ben must be hungry."

She takes me by the arm, and we hurry through the living room and to the stairs. I barely have time to smile a hello to Jackson whose eyes are hard when I meet them. Unreadable. But there's no mistaking the ice inside them.

Before we're even at the top of the stairs, I see the woman I'd met last time come hurrying out of what I guess is the nursery, the screaming little bundle in her arms. Colette rushes to her to take the baby who must sense his mother—or the food source—nearby and his cry changes to a gasping catching of breath as he smashes his head repeatedly against Colette's breast, his frustration growing again when he can't get to her breast fast enough.

As I follow Colette, I hear the deep rumble of Marco's voice but can't make out what he says before

Colette and I are in Ben's nursery and she's closed the door behind us.

She relaxes a little as soon as we're alone and plops down onto the big rocker to feed Ben.

"I can come back. If it's a bad time," I say, looking at her worried face.

"No, it's okay, Ivy. It's good you're here. I'm glad."

I set the bag down and sit on the chair opposite Colette. I take in the room, the walls painted a soft blue, the same mobile hanging over the cradle that Santiago had had delivered to our house.

"We have the same one," I say to fill the silence. The room overlooks the garden and it's so peaceful and quiet, so different from the mood downstairs.

"The mobile?" Colette asks.

"Santiago bought it. It's one of the first things."

She smiles. "Stand up, let me see you while I get this guy fed. Then you can meet him."

I do and turn a little so she can see the bump.

"You look beautiful, Ivy. Truly glowing."

I sit back down. "Thank you. I feel good. Not much nausea and, well, things with Santiago are better so that makes a really big difference."

"I bet," she says, her face faltering again. Ben gives a cry and reaches a small hand up to cup her chin. She smiles down at him, using the muslin to wipe milk from the corner of his mouth.

"He's beautiful, Colette."

She's teary-eyed when she looks up at me. "I love

him so much already and honestly, I thought I already loved him before he was born but it's nothing like when you first see his little face. When you first hold him." She wipes her eyes with the same muslin.

"What's going on?" I ask, worried.

She glances out the window and shakes her head and I get the feeling she's replaying a conversation in her head.

Ben falls asleep and she runs a finger over his cheek to rouse him. He starts to suck again as soon as she does.

"I don't like that man," she says to me finally as a few more tears fall. "And Jackson," she falters here, shakes her head and looks at me but I get the feeling she's miles away.

"I heard you fighting. I'm sorry. We'd just walked up to the door and I could hear."

"I'm sure the whole street heard. Everyone but Jackson, that is."

"What do you mean?"

She sighs deeply. "Can I tell you something?"

"Anything."

"This is big, Ivy. Like really big. But I think Jackson is making a mistake and there's no one I can talk to." Her voice breaks and she's openly crying now.

"Colette," I get up, take some tissues from a box

nearby and hand them to her, then crouch down to take her hand. "Whatever it is, you can trust me."

She nods, squeezes my hand.

The door opens quietly then and the same woman who'd served us last time brings in a pitcher of iced tea and a plate of small cakes. She smiles warmly but doesn't speak and just glances at the baby. I know she's trying to keep quiet for Ben.

Colette thanks her and a moment later she's gone.

"I love those cakes. I can't get enough. I'm going to be big as a house if she doesn't stop baking them." She's attempting humor and I smile but it's not quite working.

I get up, put one of the cakes on a plate and bring it and a glass of iced tea to her. She takes the cake and I set the tea on the nearby table then make myself a plate too. I don't eat it, though. I'm too worried about her to eat.

"I saw Holton leave," I say.

"He's a bastard." She falls silent, distant again and sets the barely nibbled on cake aside.

"Colette?"

She just shakes her head like she can't speak just yet.

"He was there when my...when I had the virginity test." I manage the words, feeling my face flush.

Colette's mouth tightens into a thin line. "Santiago made you—"

I shake my head. "He didn't know. It was my brother. My half brother."

"Abel."

"You know him?"

"Not personally," she says, but from her tone I know she doesn't like what she does know and I wonder if Holton's visit is somehow tied to Abel.

"Santiago wouldn't have made me do that," I say with the knowledge that it's true. Even then he wouldn't have submitted me to that humiliation. "But Holton stood as witness and I still shudder when I think of his eyes on me. His hand when he—"

"God, Ivy." Her hand is covering her mouth, her eyes wide.

I shake my head. "What did he do to you? Why do you hate him?"

"You can't tell anyone. If The Society finds out..." she trails off.

"I won't. I promise. Tell me what it is."

"Jackson's uncle, one he never even really knew, it turns out he was involved in some pretty bad things. He and Jackson's father never were on good enough terms for Jackson to even know much about him. It just makes no sense."

I wait as she gazes down at Ben, rocking him a

little as he sleeps again, his tiny mouth barely hanging on to her nipple.

"I think he's scared," she says, and looks up at me. "Jackson I mean. I think he's scared they won't believe him. That he'll be guilty by association."

"Guilty of what?"

Again, she's quiet for a very long time and when she turns back to me, she looks like she's going to be sick. "You know about the gas leak a few years ago?"

I feel the blood drain from my face and Colette's eyes fill up with tears.

"The one that killed Santiago's father and brother. The one that burnt him so badly," she continues but she doesn't have to. I know.

"I know The Tribunal has been investigating. Even though they said it was a leak. An accident. They've been investigating for years. And Jackson, as an advisor to The Councilors he's been privy to all those meetings." She breaks off altogether unable to speak for a moment. "It needs to come from Jackson, you know?" she asks, her voice strange.

"What does?"

I see how her hand is trembling when she brushes a finger gently down Ben's cheek again. "Holton is blackmailing him."

"Blackmailing?"

"Threatening him."

"For what? With what?"

"Jackson's uncle was one of the men who funded it."

"Funded it?"

"It wasn't a leak, Ivy. It was planned. It was murder." She breaks down entirely on that last word. "I told him he needs to go to them. They'll listen to him. They know him. But if Holton goes through with his threat," she stops, shakes her head. "I don't know what they'll do, who they'll believe. Jackson had nothing to do with it. He only found out about his uncle's involvement when Holton came to him with evidence." She looks at me, sniffles back her tears. "Evidence he claims your brother gave him."

18

SANTIAGO

"It's been too long," I growl. "Something should have shaken out by now."

Marco watches me quietly as I toss the stack of files onto my desk. More crap that Eli has sent over. Some of the evidence Abel gathered on the excommunicated members. I'm beginning to feel like he's sending me on a wild goose chase.

"He's only giving me this to distract me from finding his son," I mutter.

Marco scratches at his chin. "Possibly."

When I meet his gaze, I can tell he wants to say more.

"Just tell me." I gesture at him. "You won't offend my delicate sensibilities by being honest."

"I understand you are in a difficult position," he offers carefully. "Being that Eli is your father-in-law. But if you feel like he's fucking around with you—"

"Why don't I just torture it out of him?" I shake my head, disgusted with myself.

"Yes." He jerks his chin. "You could keep your wife away until he healed. She wouldn't ever have to know. Eli won't tell her if you don't let him."

But I would know.

And that's the fucking problem.

I collapse into my seat and reach for the bottle of scotch, which seems to be the only answer to my current problems.

"There are only so many sewers a rat can hide in," I say.

"In one city," Marco agrees.

He's right. Abel could be anywhere. And Eli isn't offering up any ideas. My men have searched every inch of this city and turned up nothing. He seems to have disappeared. And he isn't the only one. The Society is known for having a vast reach, but even they haven't been able to track down everyone involved in this scheme who's turned up MIA.

"Chamber's family," I murmur distractedly, spinning the bottle around in my palm.

"What about them?" Marco asks.

"They still haven't been located."

"I thought we assumed he must have killed them too."

"We did," I admit. "But what if Chamber's had the foresight to send them away? He had far more connections and money to buy them a new life."

Marco's brows pinch together. "And Abel found out where they were?"

"It's not outside the realm of possibility. He cleaned out Chamber's office. Maybe Chamber's had something there. Maybe he was planning to leave too."

"It sounds reasonable. But would they take Abel in after he murdered their husband and father?"

"I have a feeling Abel doesn't ever wait for an invitation. He just arrives as he pleases."

Marco considers the idea for a moment. "I think you had a point earlier. There are only so many sewers he could hide in. If we want to get him out, we have to flush him out."

"Hard to do when he doesn't care about anyone but himself," I note.

"He cares about his ego though. How he's perceived. It must be killing him to be invisible right now. He's thirsty for power."

I blink at Marco, surprised by his observation. It's simplistic, but so obvious I can't believe I didn't see it myself.

"Why would he need his father dead?" Marco states the obvious.

"So he can become Head of Household."

"Exactly. And I don't think he's disappeared with any notion of giving that up. He's still delusional enough to believe he can take back his power. He's just trying to figure out how."

"There is one way to speed up the process," I remark.

I don't know if it's the scotch talking, or me anymore, but when Marco nods, I know he agrees.

"If Eli were to die for real, there would be a temptation waiting there even Abel couldn't resist. The elevation of his status in the Moreno family."

It's the undeniable answer to all of my problems.

Vengeance for my family's death.

A honey pot to lure Abel back to the Society.

There's just one thing standing in my way.

My unfortunate wife.

"**K**nock, knock."

I drag my attention from the knife in my hand to the doorframe. I'm surprised to find Angelo standing there, but I suppose it shouldn't be much of a shock. I've been expecting him to come back and claim the final piece of the puzzle he asked me for.

"You look tired." He walks inside and drops his body into the chair across from me.

"I am fucking tired," I murmur unintelligibly. "Life is exhausting."

"Yet here we both are, still waking up every day," he muses.

I offer him the bottle of scotch, which he declines.

"I know, you aren't here for pleasantries." I fumble around with the keypad on the safe in my bottom drawer, opening it up to retrieve the file I need.

When I sent word to Angelo that I finally had a name for him... a record of who was funding the mysterious bank account he asked me to track, I expected him to arrive within a couple of days. It's been less than ten hours, which tells me he jumped a flight from Seattle this afternoon.

"It's all in there." I set the file onto the desk between us, my palm covering it as if it can shield him from this news.

He glances at it, arching a brow. "You're sure?"

"The proof is there. They were good, but not as good as me. I have a name, an IP address, and every location they've funneled it through, traced back to the origin point."

He reaches out to take the file. But I still can't seem to lift my palm.

"Is this the person who incriminated you?" I ask. "The one who sent you to prison?"

He gives me a stiff nod. "Yes."

Both our hands are on the file now. His inching it toward him, mine adding resistance.

"Once you see this, there's no going back," I tell him.

He freezes, searching my face for answers. And at this moment, I think his betrayal was far worse than mine. I was betrayed by someone I thought of as a father. Angelo was betrayed by his own blood. He is the rightful Sovereign Son. The firstborn heir. But someone wanted to usurp him, and I'm not sure I can be the one to deliver this news.

If I'm being honest, I know he knows already. Intuition is a powerful thing. That's why I know I could not have been wrong about Eli. I felt his betrayal, and I still do.

"Give me the file, Santiago," Angelo tells me calmly. "I can handle it."

Slowly, I release it. And then I watch him as he opens it, studies the name, blinks twice, and shuts it again.

"You are certain?" he asks again.

"I would bet my life on it."

Silence settles between us as he digests the news, his face unmoving. He stares at the closed folder, and I stare at him.

"What will you do?" I ask for my benefit as much as his.

Angelo has found himself in a predicament so similar to mine, and admittedly, I want his answer to reflect the one I feel burning within me right now.

"I will destroy him and take everything he loves." He rises to his feet, tucking the file inside of his jacket. "Including her."

I nod, and my gaze drifts back to the knife on my desk. The one engraved with the De La Rosa crest. It's the knife that's been passed down for generations to every firstborn son. It would only be fitting that it's the same knife I plunge into Eli's heart.

"And what will you do, Santiago?" Angelo asks, his eyes moving between me and the knife.

My answer is simple, a potent cocktail of my grief and too much scotch.

"I will do the same."

19

SANTIAGO

I'm stumbling down the hall when a small hand wraps around my arm from behind, determined to halt me. I sway slightly, trying to shrug it off, but the grip tightens.

"Santiago."

My wife's voice is like a sweet caress, one I have indulged in far too many times. I can't turn around. I refuse to face her. She won't poison my thoughts anymore.

This must be done tonight.

"Stop," she commands as I lurch forward again.

When I fail to obey, she wraps both her arms around my waist, as if the weight of her body could possibly slow my progress. That's what I tell myself, and if I weren't so inebriated, I would know it to be true. She is featherlight in my arms, but right now, I'm having difficulty carrying my own weight.

"Look at me," she pleads. "Turn around and look at me."

I don't. I can't. I keep forging on, dragging her along with me. The knife is still clutched in my palm, the blade heavy and sharp. Perhaps I should have grabbed the sheath. But I will not allow her to slow my progress.

"Go back to bed," I snarl.

"This isn't you." Her voice rises. "You're drunk."

I ignore her logic and put one foot in front of the other, Ivy's feet screeching against the floor as she stubbornly refuses to let go of me. We're approaching the foyer. I'm close to freedom. My escape. And somewhere in the murky depths of my mind, I'm aware when I return tonight, there won't be any warmth to be found.

I will have my relief. I will set into motion what needs to be done to draw Abel out. But the cost is too great to consider right now. Best to plunge headlong into it, worrying about the consequences later.

"Santiago," Ivy growls, finally releasing me, only to run around my front and intercept me by slamming her palms against my chest. "I know what you're doing."

"Eavesdropping again?" I stagger back slightly as I hurl the accusation at her.

She raises her chin, eyes locked onto mine. Tears hang precariously from the edges of her lids. And here I had stupidly thought I was done making her cry.

A foolish notion if ever there was one.

"Don't." I bring my thumb up to wipe the moisture away.

She grabs my forearm, her gaze moving to the knife. "You can't do this."

"I can and I will."

My voice is gravelly. The drink, probably.

Her lip wavers, and she gently directs the knifepoint to her chest, holding it there. "Then you may as well stab me first."

When I don't answer her, she draws in a ragged breath.

"You won't just kill him," she whispers. "You will destroy my heart. Can you live with that?"

"You will hate me for a time," I croak. "But you will get over it."

"No, I won't." She tightens her grip on my arm. "I will die too. Killing him is killing me. It's killing what we have together."

"No," I growl.

"Yes." She brings her other hand up to my face, and reflexively, my eyes fall shut as she strokes my jaw. "You are not this man. You won't do this to me."

I want to tell her how wrong she is, but I am failing to harness the resistance I once had to her charms. When she touches me this way, when she begs me so softly, nothing else seems to matter.

Abel is a distant memory. My hatred for Eli is eclipsed by something bigger. Something that seems to have snuck inside me like a thief in the night, replacing the darkness with a glowing ember. An ember that Ivy stokes every day.

"You are poisoning me." I toss the knife onto the floor, and it skitters away. My fingers wrap around her face, hard, and she mirrors the action with her own fingers on my jaw.

"Accept it," she bites out. "Quit fighting what you feel."

"I have no feelings."

"You're a liar."

I don't know who moves first. One second, we're ready to strangle each other, and the next, our lips are colliding. She's dragging up her nightgown as I pick her up and stumble over to the entry table with a decorative vase on top. I plant her ass on top of it, spreading her thighs open, baring her pussy to me as she fumbles with my belt and zipper.

A groan of frustration leaves my lips as I yank down the lacy material of her silk gown to expose her breasts. My mouth latches onto her nipple and tugs at the same time she finally makes entry into my trousers, pulling my dick free.

She guides me between her thighs, and I thrust into her warmth, pounding the table against the wall as I do. I fuck her like a madman, forgetting to be soft or gentle, but she makes no protest as she pulls at my hair, dragging her nails down the back of my neck and into my sweater.

She comes around me at the same time the vase shatters to the floor. We both pause long enough to look down at it, and then she grabs my ass and urges me forward.

"Come for me," she begs. "Please."

Fucking Christ.

I'll never get enough of that. My dick jerks and spasms, and I give the woman what she wants. With a long, agonizing sigh of relief, I spill inside her. I nearly collapse from exhaustion and drunkenness in the aftermath, and Ivy looks up at me with warmth in her eyes, a sign that I am forgiven. For now.

"Let's get you to bed," she says softly. "Where I can keep an eye on you."

"Lift your foot," Ivy orders.

I'm trying, but when I lift it up from the bed, it falls back down like it's weighted with lead.

She sighs and wiggles the leather Oxford free from my foot, tossing it aside as she repeats the process on the other side. Next come my socks, which she slides down, gently stroking my skin as she goes.

I close my eyes and fall into the moment completely, sighing when she massages the arches of my feet. It's a strange sort of intimacy to have someone touch you there. Nobody ever has before. I never realized it could feel so... pleasant.

When she finishes, I'm half asleep already, and she stirs me back to life, forcing me to cooperate as she tugs off my trousers and dress shirt and discards them on the chair across the room. She returns to bed and climbs in next to me, dragging the covers up over both of us. Beneath them, in the dark, my hand finds hers, and our fingers tangle together.

It all seems too easy, and I have a feeling I will hear more about what happened in the morning. Perhaps by then, I will have the solution that seems to evade me.

"Thank you," she whispers in the blackness.

I swallow the upheaval of emotions warring in my chest. I feel like I need to give her something, but I don't know what. When she pulls both of our hands to her belly, flattening my palm against the bump and covering it with hers, I think it is a silent question. An expectation perhaps, or a reminder. We are growing every day. Too slow at times, too fast at others. And I know before I can really wrap my mind around it, this tiny human will be here, bundled in her arms.

"I won't make you a promise I can't keep," I tell her.

She's quiet for a moment, her hand tightening

slightly against mine. "We can talk about my father in the morning."

"I'm not talking about your father. I'm talking about me."

"What do you mean?"

The words eject from my mouth before I can filter them. "Don't expect me to be a good father."

Silence. It fills the space between us for so long, I think she has gone to sleep.

"I think you might surprise yourself," she says finally. "Look at the way Eva has taken a liking to you. If you can win her over, you can win anyone over."

"She is different," I mutter. "There's something wrong with her."

"Because clearly there would have to be for her to like you," Ivy huffs. "That's what you mean, right?"

"I terrify children."

"You won't terrify your own. Not if you make an effort."

"I am not sure I know how," I admit.

She turns into me, stroking my arm. "Your father didn't show you?"

"My father showed me how to be cruel," I answer. "Cold and unyielding. I learned all my best qualities from him. Every lesson I learned from him came as a punishment or a beating. For many years, I thought that was how fathers expressed their... affection."

"That isn't love," Ivy says softly.

"I suppose it isn't."

"You aren't your father." She reaches up to touch my face, humanizing me in a way nobody else ever has. "You won't ever do those things to your own children."

My fingers trace over her arm. "I know I won't. I also know the limit of my capabilities. I can provide for them. I will protect them. But the softness must come from you."

"I believe you are capable of far more than you give yourself credit for." She presses her lips against my cheek. "You will see."

I don't respond because there's nothing else to say. She has expectations of me that I'll never meet. And at some point, she will be forced to accept it.

I turn into her and kiss her face. "Good night, sweet Ivy."

20
IVY

As the sun rises, I lie still beside him, listening to his even breathing. He's passed out. Exhausted probably from days, weeks even of not sleeping. Of drinking too much. Of worrying.

And I am only going to add to that worry when he wakes.

Sitting up on the bed, I pet his dark head, brushing the hair from his face.

God. What a mess this is.

He stirs but barely, and I pick up the dagger he'd been carrying last night. I went back downstairs to get it after he fell asleep when I couldn't sleep.

It's as beautiful as it is deadly. Roses and skulls always with him. I bring the tip to my finger, and it takes just the littlest bit of pressure to break the skin.

I watch a droplet of blood pool, then another. I smear it on the inside of my palm. Lay the blade flat there.

Blood on my hands. No. Not on mine. Not yet.

But on Abel's.

On my father's.

On my husband's.

"What are you doing?" comes his deep, steady voice.

Startled, I look over at him. Not asleep. Not even sleepy. Alert. Awake. Like any good predator. He's dangerous. Not to me, but to those I love. And I'm torn.

If I tell him, I betray my friend.

If I don't, I betray him.

And betrayal may be the least of my concerns. I'm sure I will have to tie him down for him to hear what Colette confided in me. If he is to remain still and listen to reason after the words are out. If not, I know my husband. This dagger will have much more blood on it than the few drops from my finger.

He's sitting up beside me, looking at the palm of my hand. At the smear of blood on his blade.

"You were going to kill my father," I say. "If I hadn't stopped you last night, you'd have done it."

He neither confirms nor denies it.

"What would you have told me this morning?"

"Ivy," he starts, reaching for the dagger.

I snatch it away and shake my head. "What would you have told me, Santiago?"

His eyes harden a little, but it's not to shut me out. I know this now. This thing, this vengeance, in a way, it's separate from me. Or at least it has become so to him. It has to be because how can he be how he is with me one moment and in the next be walking out of this house on his way to the hospital to kill a helpless old man?

Well, walking isn't quite right. He'd been staggering. Did he need to drink so much to be able to bring himself to do it?

I think about what he told me about his own father. I knew already, at least a little of it. I knew he was a cruel man. But I guess I can't imagine someone with that much power over you who is only ever cruel.

"You have to let this thing against my father go."

"That's not your concern. Give me the dagger."

"Would you have lied?" I ask instead of giving him what he wants. "Climbed into bed beside me and maybe made love to me after murdering an old man?"

"Murder?" he snorts. "An eye for an eye, Ivy. Give me my knife. Don't test my patience."

"Patience?"

"I'm not asking again."

"No."

"Be reasonable."

"Because you are?" Can I tell him what Colette told me? Would Marco help me? Would he hold him down until I made him see reason?

His expression changes, his body relaxes a little, and he smiles that one-sided smile. "You manipulated me last night."

"I stopped you from committing murder. Tell me what you would have told me this morning if you'd gone through with it."

"You want to know if I'd lie to you about killing your father? About taking my rightful revenge?"

I falter. He is painfully honest. It's just that truth has many, many sides. And believing yours too fervently is dangerous.

"I—" I start, and I'm not expecting him to move so quickly. To grab the wrist of the hand that's holding the hilt of his blade and squeeze until my fingers uncurl so he can take the dagger from me. I'm not expecting him to drag me onto my back and straddle me, the steel of the knife hard against my wrist as he holds it and me, spreading my arms to either side of the bed, face dark as he looms over me.

"You're going to stop hovering outside my study door."

"It's the only way I get any news," I say. I'm not scared of him. He won't hurt me. "And I wasn't hovering," I say as his gaze runs over me, over the nightgown that's slightly ripped where he yanked at it last night. At my partially exposed breast.

"No?" he asks, dipping his head down to flick his tongue over my nipple, the sensation sending a charge straight to my clit.

"No," I say, feeling his grip ease a little, watching as he leans over to his side of the bed, opens the nightstand drawer, and drops the dagger inside it before returning his full attention to me, eyes dark now, pupils dilated. He's aroused.

"I knew I'd have to safeguard the house for my child, but for my wife, too? That dagger is not a toy, my dear."

"I know that."

"Then you know it's not to be played with."

"I wasn't playing. And neither were you."

He leans down to graze his teeth over that same nipple, and I close my eyes as my body arches into his. "Don't get me wrong," he says, releasing my wrists to slide down between my legs. "I don't mind that sort of manipulation." He spreads my legs and pushes the nightie up. "I will never tire of fucking my wife."

He licks.

I bite back a cry and weave my fingers into his dark hair. I know it hurts him when I pull, but he only groans, dips his tongue inside me before finding my clit and sucking, and only when I'm panting, when I'm moments away from coming, does he stop. Does he climb back over my body to settle between my legs, that wicked grin on his face as he keeps his cock just out of reach.

"That's your punishment for eavesdropping," he says. "You don't get to come this morning."

"I told you I wasn't eavesdropping," I say as he straightens and gets off the bed. I see the length of his erection. I know what it's taking for him to walk away. "Come back to bed, Santiago." He turns to me. "Finish what you started." I open my legs and watch his gaze dip down.

I slip my fingers down, and he lets out a low growl.

"Finish what you started, or I will," I add.

He drags his gaze back to mine and considers, then sets one knee on the bed. "Turn over."

I look from his eyes down to his hand, which is fisting his cock. He wants there to be no doubt that he is in control. That he'll have the last word. But he can't resist. So, I turn over, get up on my knees, and keeping my head between my forearms, I offer myself to him.

"Fuck, Ivy," he says, voice thick with arousal.

I have just enough time for a victory grin he doesn't see before he's got my hips and is sinking himself into me. Within moments, we're panting, the sounds of sex filling the room as he leans over me. When I turn my cheek into the bed, he pushes the hair from my face. Sweat drops from his temple onto my forehead as my knees give out, and he's on top of me, careful to keep most of his weight on his elbows, and I watch him as I feel him push deeper inside me, feel us together, feel us so close.

"I love you," I blurt out, not even aware I'm doing it until it's too late, until I hear the words myself.

Santiago falters, losing his rhythm. He looks at me, and I stare back at him. Is that shock on his face? Is he truly shocked?

The furrow between his eyebrows deepens, and he puts a hand over my face, my eyes, and his thrusts come harder, just once, twice, the third time he comes. I feel him shudder, feel him pulse and throb inside me. Feel him empty, and when he stands, I turn to look at him, and I feel my chest tighten at the grim expression on his face.

"Guard your heart, Ivy," he says, jaw tense. "I will do what I must." He pauses, and I swear I see the battle playing out inside his head. I swear it. "I am bound, don't you see?"

I sit up, drag my knees to my chest and hold onto the blanket to cover myself. There's a weight inside my chest and something I can't quite swallow in my throat.

"You can choose." I remember my words to him about Mercedes. About it always being a choice. About how one day he may choose differently. I had no idea how much those words meant. How true they were when I said them.

I dip my head to wipe a tear on my knee.

He reaches to take my hand, and I realize it's the bloody one, although it's not bleeding anymore. His fingers trace the line of dried blood.

"No, Ivy. I can only hurt you. No matter how much I don't want to."

21

IVY

The rest of the week somehow passes. Santiago is absent from the house. I don't know where he is. Not in his office. Not home for dinner. And definitely not sleeping in our bed. Eva has noticed his absence too but is careful what she says. I get the feeling she can see I'm upset. But today is the day Santiago or Marco take me to see my father. It's always either one of them, never anyone else.

Eva is at school and I am dressed and waiting and both relieved and disappointed when Marco comes around the corner at exactly ten o'clock, keys in hand.

"Ready?" he asks.

I nod, my heart in my throat. I was hoping it would be Santiago. But this is okay, isn't it? Because after the other morning, a part of me thought he'd maybe go through with it after all. Kill my father. What does that say about how well I know my husband? I've never pretended to know him though, have I? Maybe a little. I was wrong mostly. No, that's not it. I wasn't wrong exactly.

I just fell in love with him. He's not to blame for that. And he's told me he can't love me even if it wasn't in so many words. Even if he could never bring himself to say those words.

It's not anyone's fault how I feel about him and how he doesn't feel about me. If anything, I should have kept my mouth shut. We were in a good place. Now, he's absent again.

"Mrs. De La Rosa?"

I shake my head to find Marco staring at me, eyebrows raised. "Sorry. What did you say?"

"It's a bit cooler out today, and a rainstorm is expected. You might want to grab a jacket."

"Oh. Okay. Thanks. And can you please just call me Ivy?"

He nods but I've asked him before, and I have a feeling to him it's a show of respect for Santiago.

"Is Santiago at the hospital?" I ask when we get into the car.

"No, ma'am."

I bite the inside of my lip and turn to look out the window as we drive in silence. I wonder what Marco thinks. What he knows.

When we get to the hospital, Marco takes me up

to my father's floor and stands just outside, as usual, as I walk into the small room. My father is getting stronger and stronger. Every time I visit, I see the man he once was slowly returning as he puts on weight and regains his stolen strength.

"Dad, you look good," I say, walking to where he's sitting behind a table, working on a laptop. I hug him, and he hugs me back. "This is new." The desk is sturdy and the chair a comfortable-looking office chair. Not his wheelchair, which is good to see, but I don't miss the furrow between his brows. His mind is on something else even while I visit.

"How are you, Ivy? How's Eva?"

"We're both good. Eva's annoyed about school again so that's a good sign of life going back to normal, right?"

"That is a good sign." He says the words absently.

"Do you think we'll ever get to normal, Dad?"

He blinks, then smiles at me. "Sorry, what?"

"Do you think we'll ever get to normal? Eva and I? And the baby when he or she comes." I pause. "And Santiago?" I add. Although what is his normal? Maybe this is it.

"I hope so, sweetheart."

"What are you doing with the computer? Why does he have you working when you should just be focused on getting better?"

"Ivy, your husband is a complicated man."

"Do you think I don't know that?"

"He has demons, and I know he's trying to banish them. If my work helps—"

"He's set on revenge, dad. That's how he'll banish them. By killing them." By killing you. I don't say it. He knows this better than I.

"We had a hand in what happened to him and his family."

"What do you mean we?"

He shakes his head. "Not you. I'm sorry. I didn't mean that."

"I know about Abel, but you didn't do anything wrong."

"I can't go back in time and fix what I didn't do either, so there's no sense in talking about it. He has a right, is all I'm saying."

"No, he doesn't. Not anymore. Not since he married me and since we're bringing a baby into the world. He gave up that right when he decided those things," I say, the words coming out of a place of hurt. I clear my throat and swallow back tears. "You should get some rest. Work after. When you're home."

"It's important work, Ivy. Something he needs—"

"What about what you need?"

"Something I need. I was going to say something I need as much."

The rain that had been a sprinkle on our drive now picks up hammering against the hospital window. The door opens. Marco clears his throat as another man, someone I don't know, stands just outside.

I stand. "I guess that's my cue." It's a short visit, and I wonder if it was Santiago's way of showing me he hadn't hurt my father. Yet.

Without a word, I walk out of the room and let Marco take me back home in silence. It's still late morning when I'm back, and the house is quiet except for the housekeepers doing their work. I go upstairs to change into a bathing suit and put on a robe, but rather than going straight down to the pool, I walk through the secret entrance to the nursery. I haven't been back here since the other morning, and many more boxes, presents from The Society and friends of Santiago's family, are stacked and waiting to be unwrapped. I don't have the heart for it right now, though, so I make my way to the glassed-in swimming pool attached to the house. I haven't been swimming much, mostly because he doesn't want me doing it alone, but it helps me expend some energy and clear my head. Besides, he has nothing to worry about. I am a fine swimmer, and I have never had any episodes while in the water.

I pad barefoot through the house and pass by the corridor that leads to his study, thinking about how he'd said I needed to stop hovering. I'd come to talk to him about what Colette told me when I'd overheard him speaking to Angelo, the friend who only seems to come at odd hours.

The sky is a deep, cloudy gray with rain coming down hard. It's perfect for my mood.

I close the door behind me and stand in the warm, humid room. It's pretty with plants hanging from the glass walls and the small squares of turquoise tiles making the water a gorgeous, vibrant blue. I strip off my robe and dip my toe in before walking into the warm water, extending my arms and going under. Holding my breath to swim the length of it, I love the sensation of water running through my hair, through my fingers as I glide. I swim a few slow laps before turning over onto my back, arms and legs stretched out like a star, the sound of the rain distant with my ears beneath the surface. I close my eyes and lay there, letting the water carry me, floating as I empty my mind and try to forget that morning. Forget my embarrassment at having said those words out loud. My embarrassment at his rejection.

Because that's what all this comes down to.

He rejected me.

I take a deep breath in and finally open my eyes and startle the instant I do because there, watching me, is a dark figure sitting in the shadow of a pillar at the opposite end of the pool, legs wide, elbows on knees, face dark. Not angry. Something else.

I gasp, my heart thudding.

"I don't want you swimming alone," Santiago says, his voice sounding strange.

"You haven't been here," I remind him.

"I'm here now," he says somberly. And I know something's wrong.

I swim to the edge, and he stands up, gathers my robe, and wraps it around me as I step out, eyes lingering momentarily on my rounded stomach. When he lifts his gaze up to mine, I think I know what it is I see on his face, and it twists my own heart.

It's pain. He's suffering.

"What's happened?" I ask, feeling my eyes fill up.

He tugs the robe closed, fingers warm when they touch my skin, and I miss him. I miss his touch. I miss him so much. I want him to hold me. I want to lean into him.

He cups my cheek, runs his thumb over the dot of ink, the start of something that could have gone so wrong.

"Santiago? What is it?"

"I have men picking Eva up. You'll both stay in the house for the foreseeable future."

"What?"

"No more hospital visits."

"Is it my father? What's happened?" I pull out of his grasp. "What did you do?"

"It's—"

"If you hurt him...if you...I'll never forgive you. I

swear it. I will never forgive you!" I spin to get away, but he catches me.

"Ivy." His voice is hoarse, and when I look at him, my own lip trembles with the pain I see on his face. "Your father is fine. I've increased his security, too."

"Security? What is it?"

His forehead furrows, eyes distant momentarily. "Colette and the baby—"

My stomach lurches. "Oh my god!"

"They're fine. Now. Someone took them. Someone walked into the café she'd gone to and took them."

"W...what? What do you mean someone took them?"

"She doesn't know who it was. The person said Jackson had sent him, that something had happened and he needed her back home and she went with him and...well, Jackson hadn't sent anyone. He had no idea. There was a second man in the vehicle once she got to it and she said she knew something was wrong but couldn't do anything about it then, not with the baby. They apparently drove them around then took them to the end of their street a few hours later."

"Are they okay?"

"They're unharmed. They're home and unharmed. IVI is protecting them."

"Oh, god." My hand trembles as I lay it over my

stomach. Someone took Colette and her baby? Holton had been threatening Jackson.

"And I spoke with Jackson," he says, eyes far away. "About..." he trails off, takes a deep breath in, then sets both hands at my arms and looks at me for a long, long minute before pulling me in to hold me.

I wrap my arms around his middle.

"I know you deserve better and more than I am capable of giving and I'm sorry for my failing, but I will protect you. I will keep you safe. I swear that on my own life, Ivy. I swear it."

22

SANTIAGO

I sit on the edge of the bed, studying my wife as she sleeps. The soft rising tide of her breaths is the only comfort I have found in the wake of recent events. To know that she is here, she is alive, is everything.

I understand now that there is nothing Abel won't do to save himself. There isn't a soul he wouldn't sacrifice to spare his own. Words can't describe the terror that plagues me over what transpired with Colette and her baby. What could have happened?

It could have been Ivy.

It could have been our baby.

And it also could have been Eva.

More than ever, I am confronted by the fact I'm not equipped to handle the myriad of emotions brought to the surface by this situation. The burden of responsibility is so great, and I never expected to feel... *so much.*

It isn't just Ivy, or Eva, or my sister. It's Marco, Antonia, and my entire staff too. They are embroiled in this situation merely by being in my employ, and I feel a duty to protect them all, as any honorable man should. But it goes beyond duty. It is a desperate need... the likes of which I have never felt before.

When I heard the news of Colette, I did not even think. It was second nature for me to issue my commands. To lock down The Manor, and everyone in it. But in the midst of rattling off those orders, I also found myself instructing Marco to request extra security for Eli. The man I have sworn to loathe for eternity. The man who I had intended to kill just days ago.

I can no longer deny that something inside me is changing. Call it softness, weakness, whatever the appropriate term, the ice block where my heart used to be is beginning to thaw, making room for the warmth of a spring I never anticipated. And it's all because of her.

I reach out, stroking a lock of her hair between my fingers, and my breath stalls in my lungs. She truly is the most beautiful woman I have ever beheld. A likeness which, try as I might, I cannot seem to capture in my artwork. The delicate curves and lines I draw over and over do her no justice. Nothing can imitate the reality.

I wonder why it is that every man doesn't fall to his knees when they see her enter a room. And I suppose it's because they don't see her as I do. The feelings she evokes in me are overwhelming in nature, too powerful to be defined by the prettiest superlatives. What we have together is too great to be contained by the average turn of phrase. Too rare. It is something I am only just beginning to understand. But understanding and acceptance are still two worlds apart, and I have not mastered the latter.

She possesses every quality I do not. Softness, purity, beauty... in every sense of the word. I am merely a beast of a man, yet, she professes to love me.

My darker half wants to deny it still because that is the easiest thing to do. But the lies we tell ourselves are only effective as long as we believe them. And she is still here. Aching for my company. My touch. She does not flinch at the sight of me, choosing to draw me closer in spite of everything. I would be fooling myself to insist it's a scheme of manipulation. She doesn't have that darkness in her. She couldn't fake the emotion in her voice when she confessed those haunting words.

She is in love with me... and I am helpless to it.

I don't even know what love is. What it feels like. But I know whenever she's in my presence, I can't look away from her. My blood warms, and my eyes darken, and lightning fills my veins. The organ in my chest beats harder, faster, and I count the seconds until my hands are on her. Claiming her. Owning her.

Is that love?

I don't know.

I don't know anything anymore, except for this suffocating feeling is growing every day that Abel is still out there. As long as he is alive, he is a danger to her and my family and anyone else around us.

Jackson made it very clear to me when we spoke that he believes the same. Abel will destroy anyone he can to get to me. Women and children are not excluded from that list, even if they are his own blood. We can't move forward until I know he's dead. Ivy and our child will never be safe until he's gone, and it's up to me to make it so.

Right now, that goal has to be my primary focus.

My phone vibrates in my pocket, signaling a text from Marco. The news I've been expecting. I check it quickly and then lean down to kiss my wife on the cheek, closing my eyes and inhaling her.

"Sleep soundly, sweet Ivy."

I rise slowly and head for the door, activating the motion sensors I had installed in the room and then the electronic lock. Ivy can come and go freely, but not without me receiving alerts any time the door opens.

Securing her inside, I return the phone to my pocket and head downstairs to greet my guest.

"Would you like me to stay, boss?" Marco asks.

"No. Thank you, Marco. You can go."

He nods and shuts the door to my office, leaving me alone with Eli.

The old man is waiting for me in one of the lounge chairs by the fire, a cane propped against his leg. He seems to be progressing in his recovery, but it has done nothing to alter the frailty of his appearance. Or perhaps that is just my perception of him.

I walk to my desk and eye the bottle of scotch before thinking better of it. When I turn to meet Eli's gaze, there is a resolve in his eyes that surprises me. He is solemn but resolute as he forces himself to sit up taller.

"If you are going to do this here, I ask that you do it somewhere my daughters won't hear it."

"You think I brought you here to kill you?" I reply coldly.

"I expect as much." He shrugs. "I may be old, but I'm not stupid. You want Abel. He is wreaking havoc on your life. I'm sure you have considered all the possibilities, but we both know there is only one way to draw him out."

"Yet you came willingly." I frown.

His expression softens, and for a moment, I am reminded of the man I used to know. The man who spent countless hours at my side, imparting his wisdom to the interloper who would take over his position in IVI. At the time, I had thought it strange that he seemed to hold no resentment toward me. In fact, I had only ever regarded him to have admiration for me. He spoke as if he respected me, as if he were proud of me. And I had never known that I had thirsted for such approval until I had his.

Now, everything between us has changed. I have surpassed him in knowledge and exceeded all expectations for my role. I have outperformed his legacy on every level. I have commandeered half of his family and have made known my murderous intentions for the rest. Yet, he still comes when I call for him. He still looks at me as one might imagine a father should look at their son. I cannot comprehend it.

"I came because I accept that I am partly responsible for what happened to your family," he says. "And while I cannot confess to being as devious as you would like to believe, I set the events into motion unknowingly. And therefore, I understand your position. If my departure from this life will bring you peace, then peace you shall have. I know I cannot stop you, and I won't hide from the inevitable. So long as you can guarantee that none of my daughters will ever be harmed by your hand."

I stare at him, blank, shaking my head in disgust. I can't tell if it's disgust for him or me.

"As much as I think it would please me to end your life, my wife claims she will never forgive me, and I am inclined to believe her."

Eli's hand shakes as he reaches inside his jacket, retrieving an envelope. "I have already written them both letters. I think it will be difficult for them, but in time, I hope they can move forward."

I glance at the envelope, curious at the contents, and then dismiss the thought entirely.

"I will need you to die, Eli." I prop myself against the edge of the desk and fold my arms. "But for now, it will be temporary."

His brows furrow together as his hand settles into his lap, still clinging to the letter. "You want to fake my death?"

"Thursday morning, the IVI coroner will arrive at the hospital and leave with your remains. An official statement of your death will be released by noon, and I anticipate by the end of the day, whoever is leaking information to Abel will deliver the news."

"And where will I be during this time?" he asks.

"You'll be given a sedative for transport, after which you'll be driven to a funeral home and smuggled out by my men. There's a small cottage on the property here for the groundskeeper. Marco has already secured it and outfitted the entire location with cameras. The refrigerator and pantry are well-stocked, and you will have what you need to survive during your stay there."

"How do you know this will work?" he asks.

"Because nobody but Marco and myself will know you are still alive," I answer bitterly. "Abel will have men watching, I'm certain, and it must look authentic when my wife and I attend your funeral at the end of the week. Your family's grief must be real."

"You aren't going to tell her?" he croaks.

I look away, swallowing the tension knotting my throat. "I have no choice. Ivy can't shut down her emotions. She can't keep a secret like this from her family. She wouldn't be able to watch them suffer while she knows the truth. This is the only way to ensure Abel's return. So, as far as Ivy is concerned, you will have died of natural causes."

"But she won't believe you," he protests.

I meet his gaze, narrowing mine. "That is for me to worry about."

23

SANTIAGO

I lower myself into the pew where my father once used to sit, staring up at the altar where his photo is displayed. The memorial photos of him and Leandro in the chapel have since been replaced, but something feels different about this space.

I am not the same man I was before, sitting here, mourning their deaths. I grieve for them still, but it is not the same depth of grief. When I look into my father's eyes, cold and hard, I find myself searching for his certain disappointment. And indeed, that is what I see. It is what I have always seen. If he were here now, he would tell me how weak and pathetic I am. He would rage that I have not accomplished what I set out to do.

For so long, I have carried the burden of those demands. A loyalty to a man who never spared so much as an ounce of affection for me. My guilt and shame have been heavy, weighted further by a hatred of the Moreno family. A result that felt like the natural response I should have. Somewhere to place the blame. A target for a lifetime of anger. But I am tired.

I am fucking exhausted of his expectations, even in death.

Perhaps that is what possesses me to rise and walk to the altar. When I reach up and pull down his photo, I can almost feel him rolling in his grave. He has dictated every move I have made for so long. Every emotion I never allowed myself to feel. Every failure that felt like another noose around my neck.

And when I look into his eyes, I know what Ivy said is true.

This is not love. This man who I have respected, and admired, and worshipped for so long did not love me. He controlled me. He was the master of strings, and I was the puppet. And even in his absence, he still manages to control those strings. As long as I allow him to dictate my future, he always will.

The weight of the photo pulls my arms down, and gradually, I watch it slip from my grasp, clattering onto the floor as glass shatters around my feet. For a few long moments, I stare at the remnants, and something comes over me that I can't explain. I stagger back, trying to catch my breath, my eyes burning with pain.

My breaths come shallow and then deep, turning to aching howls as I collapse back onto the pew and allow myself to feel the truth of my own emotions. My head collapses into my hands, and moisture leaks from my eyes, dripping down onto the floor.

I don't know how long it goes on for. But with every painful heaving sob, something lighter expands in my chest. I think, perhaps this is what they call relief.

A hand on my shoulder startles me, and when I snap my gaze up, I am shocked to find Antonia standing beside me. Our eyes lock, and humiliation burns my face as she slowly comes around to sit beside me, sliding across the bench like she's approaching a wounded animal.

I dip my head when I feel her studying the broken glass on the floor, the photo of my father lying in tatters.

"I always thought this place could do with some redecorating." Her fingers come to rest on my forearm, a gentility she has always offered me, even when I did not deserve it.

Slowly, I bring my focus back to hers, and I see something I never expected in the softness of her smile. I think she is proud.

"You are a good man, Santiago De La Rosa," she says. "You have always had it in you."

"I think you give me too much credit." I sit up straighter, discreetly wiping my face dry.

"I give credit where it is due. It is long past time you let go of these demons. You are beginning a new life. A life with so many possibilities. You have a beautiful wife who cares for you. A baby on the way. It's a new season. Time to clear away the old growth and make way for the new."

When she reaches down to squeeze my hand, I don't stop her. It reminds me of when I was a boy, how so often it was Antonia who looked after me. She tended to my wounds, and helped me with my homework, and taught me how to ride a bicycle and tie my shoes. She has always been there, more of a parent than my own in many ways. I have not given her adequate respect for that role. For the sacrifices she has made to work for my family for as long as she has, forgoing a family of her own. Dreams of her own.

"You are always here when I need you," I croak. "I don't suppose I have ever thanked you for it."

"You have thanked me," she answers warmly. "In the ways you knew how. You have never been just an employer to me, Santiago. I think you should know by now, I love you as a mother would love her own son."

A fresh wave of emotions chokes any response I might offer, so I simply nod, which she accepts with understanding and grace. It is twice now someone has offered their expressions of affection for me. It is a strange new world I find myself living in.

"Antonia?" I say after a few moments, when I've collected myself enough to speak.

"Yes?"

"Does love go away?"

Her eyes crinkle at the edges as she considers it. "Why would it?"

I turn my focus back to the floor, studying the shards of glass. "What if you wanted to protect someone, but to do so means to hurt them?"

She is quiet, her presence reassuring, even though I know she couldn't possibly have the answers I need. Not until she turns to look at me, determination steeling her features as I've never seen.

"If it's real, pure, and true, Santiago, love will never go away."

24

IVY

Santiago is distant. He's here, physically, and I understand the weight he is carrying. He eats meals with me. He sleeps in our bed. Or at least he lies beside me until I fall asleep because by the time I wake in the morning, his side of the bed is empty, his pillow cold.

Eva spends her days with a tutor. I spend mine with Antonia in the kitchen baking now and again or swimming when Eva can join me. Santiago finally allowed for that. I still do the exercises Dr. Hendrickson taught me, but I know the balance issues are amplified by anxiety now than anything else.

And I am anxious.

I've been able to talk to my dad and Hazel over video calls. Santiago finally relented and gave me a cell phone. He has increased security at Hazel's house as well. Seeing my nephew is still strange especially never having met him in person. But it's not just that. It's that I don't know this person. I don't know the first five years of his life and never will.

But Hazel seems all right. Not quite happy, but not unhappy either. I think once this is all said and done, she may come back home. Now that I am married to Santiago, now that we are family, I am sure he can help where IVI is concerned. In the past, I've heard of people returning. There's usually some penance to be done, some payment in skin, but surely Santiago's status will help her.

I've spoken with Colette over the phone, too. I know she's still shaken up even though she tries to put a good face on it. What happened scared her. Just the thought of it terrifies me. And the fact that Abel was somehow involved makes me feel sick.

It's the middle of the night when I knock on Santiago's office door before opening it a little to poke my head inside. I heard him get home about fifteen minutes ago.

"Ivy," he starts, not expecting me. He's just taken off his jacket and tossed it over the back of a chair, and is undoing his tie. "Is everything all right?" I see and hear the anxiety that creeps into his voice.

"It's fine. Everything is fine."

I close the door behind me and walk toward him as he nods. Rolling his shirtsleeves up, he exposes strong, tattooed forearms that send a shiver through me. When I look up at him, I find him watching me, eyes moving over me to stop on my protruding belly. It's popped straight out almost like I shoved a small basketball under my shirt.

"You're so late," I say.

"I needed to get some things sorted."

"What things?"

"Work," he says almost absently.

"This time of night?"

"I always work at night, Ivy. You know that. And now, with all that's going on, well, I don't sleep much anyway."

He wraps one arm around my waist and sets his other hand over the bump before kissing my cheek. He then pulls me in for a hug, and there's something strange about it. Something distant.

"Why are you still up?" he asks.

"I was worried about you."

"I can more than take care of myself."

"Did they find the men who took Colette and Ben?"

"What? Oh, no, not yet. I don't want you worrying about them. I'm not going to let them hurt you."

"I know. I just thought maybe you found something out."

"Not yet, but we're getting there. Why don't you go back up to bed? I'll be there soon."

"I...I wanted to ask you about something you said."

He sighs. "It can't wait?"

"No."

"All right."

"You said you talked to Jackson about something, but you never said what. The other day at the pool."

"Ah." He walks over to his desk, picks up the bottle of scotch, uncorks it, and pours himself some. He turns back to look at me. "Should we go into the kitchen? Get you something?"

"No, I'm fine. What did you talk to him about?"

He studies me, and I find myself shifting beneath his gaze. He steps closer, and I take a seat on the couch. "I wasn't going to bring it up, but since you did, I talked to him about his uncle. About his uncle's involvement in the explosion to be very straightforward."

Staring up at him, I watch him swallow another sip of his drink before setting it down.

"And I talked to him about Cornelius Holton, who is now in IVI custody. That's where I was. Interrogating him."

"He's in custody?"

Santiago nods.

"Did he...was he behind Colette and Ben's kidnapping?"

"He didn't drive the vehicle, but he was involved,

yes. He was blackmailing Jackson. But you already know that part."

I feel myself flush with heat. I'm sure he sees it too.

"Colette told him she'd spoken with you about it. I think she was hoping it would encourage Jackson to come forward on his own before Holton did."

"I—" I croak but don't know what to say.

He brushes my hair behind my ear. "It's all right. I'm not angry with you."

"I had come to tell you. The night you…the night I intercepted you on your way to the hospital with that knife. That's what I was doing when I overheard. I was going to tell you what Colette said."

"It's all right, Ivy. Truly. Things got out of hand, but Jackson's family is safe, and Holton will face The Tribunal for his role. And having Holton in custody brings us that much closer to your brother." He picks up his glass and swallows the rest of it.

"How are things with you and Jackson? And with him and IVI? Is he…in trouble?"

"There will be consequences for not coming to The Tribunal immediately with the information, but he'll be fine. Jackson is not a bad man."

"What about with you? Will he be fine with you?"

"His uncle was the guilty party, and unfortunately for me, he's already dead. I have nothing against Jackson, and I remember my debt to him for having brought the evidence forward that saved you both from The Tribunal and from me." He pauses, considers. "What a history we have, you and I."

"You're really not angry with me? That I didn't tell you sooner?"

"We all make mistakes. I hope you'll be as quick to forgive mine." He gets up, his face in shadow.

I look up at him, thinking what a strange thing to say. I'm about to ask what he means when he extends his hand, palm up.

"Come, Ivy. Let me take you to bed."

25

IVY

Something is wrong. I feel it. The next morning when I wake, I'm alone again. Although I know Santiago got a few hours of sleep, it was still dark when he slipped out of bed.

"We all make mistakes. I hope you'll be as quick to forgive mine."

His words keep playing in my head. They're strange. And they certainly don't fit Santiago. He isn't one to forgive mistakes. Or maybe it depends on who has made the mistake? Either way, he is certainly not quick to forgive. The opposite.

I've tried to call him multiple times, but my calls only go to voicemail. Just like any time I try to call my father. To say I'm worried is an understatement. At least when I finally managed to talk to a nurse, she told me my father was fine. Just sleeping.

It's not until two nights later when Eva and I are

just finishing dinner that Santiago finally returns home. And by now, I'm angry.

But when I see the look on his face, the weary, dark expression, that anger quickly morphs into something else.

Walking behind him is my obstetrician.

"What's happened?" I ask, quickly getting to my feet.

Santiago's expression doesn't change as he takes stock of me before shifting his gaze to my sister.

"Eva. Go to your room."

I glance at my sister whose forehead wrinkles with worry. "Why? What's going on?"

I turn back to Santiago in time to see him gesture to Marco, who comes to Eva. "Come on, kid," he says, his tone gentler than I've ever heard him.

Eva looks at me, and I nod, and once I do, she goes. I'm left in the room with Santiago and the doctor.

"Sit down," Santiago says as he comes closer, but I just back up a step, wrapping my arms around my middle.

"I hope you'll be as quick to forgive mine."

"Where have you been?" I ask.

"Ivy, sit down." He takes my arms, tries to maneuver me around to the front of the chair.

"What have you done?" The words come out sharper than I mean, the feeling they leave behind dark. Full of dread.

"It's not like that."

And I know what it is. What he's going to tell me. I know exactly.

"Say it," I bite out, my eyes already warm with tears as my body begins to shudder with cold. I pull out of his grasp, my hands fists at my sides now.

The doctor speaks next. "Ivy, it's not good for the baby if you get worked up."

"Say it!" I snap at Santiago.

Santiago's jaw sets, and again, I hear his words. *"I hope you'll be as quick to forgive mine."*

But I won't be. Not if he did what I think he did.

"There was a complication, something the doctor missed."

I hug my middle, my shoulders hunching as I back up another step, slipping into a chair now. I shake my head and don't look at him. I can't.

"He's gone, Ivy. I'm sorry, but your father is gone."

I close my eyes as his words echo. Gone. Gone as in I'll never see him again. Never hear his voice again. Never hug him again.

Gone as in dead.

I shake my head and make myself look at him. "I don't believe you," I say, wiping the backs of my hands over my eyes. I force my legs to carry me as I stand. "I don't."

"Ivy, you—" He reaches for me, but I slip away.

"I called the hospital. I talked to the nurse. She told me he was fine. Just sleeping. She told me!"

Santiago glances at the doctor as if they've had some private exchange, but whatever it is, Santiago raises his hand just slightly as if to tell him to wait.

"I'm truly sorry, Ivy," Santiago says, solemn gaze on me again. "He died a few hours ago. There was nothing anyone could do."

"No." I shake my head, walking a few steps away so I'm near the head of the table where Santiago's place has been empty for two days. Gone for two days. The two days before my father has a complication out of nowhere. Two days in which my father, his enemy, the enemy under guard, the weak old man under his power, dies. "No," I say again, setting my jaw. I reach for the steak knife Antonia had set for him. She didn't even know if he'd be home or not. She'd fretted about keeping his dinner warm. "Tell me the truth." I keep the knife at my side.

Santiago's gaze drops to it momentarily before returning to mine. "Put that down, and I'll tell you everything again."

"Tell me now," I say, and when he takes a step closer, I hold the knife out between us.

The doctor watches but stays where he is.

"There was a complication."

"Something the doctor missed. I heard your practiced words the first time around. Tell me how! Tell me the truth, you fucking liar!"

There's that tic in his jaw. I wonder if he's counting to ten before he speaks. He's not used to rebellion. Not used to people speaking up.

"I know you're upset. It's natural you're upset. But I'm here for you, Ivy."

At that, I laugh outright. "You're here for me? Did you just really say that?"

I walk farther away as he begins to close the space between us. Marco comes around the corner, and without taking his eyes off me, Santiago signals to Marco to stand back.

"Were you the complication the doctors didn't see coming, Santiago?"

He smiles a strange smile, but it's gone in an instant. "I can see how you'd think that," he says through clenched teeth. "But no, Ivy, I did not murder the old man."

"But it was your right. Isn't that what you told me?" I take more steps away, aware of how close Marco is. "Did you use your knife? It would be symbolic to drive the De La Rosa blade into his heart. It would make your father proud."

"That's enough." His voice is harder. "Give me the knife."

"Is this why you forgave me so easily a few days ago? You knew even then what you'd do. You thought you could use that against me? Force me to forgive you? To somehow maybe accept and forgive the fact that you murdered my father?"

He speaks, maybe asking for the knife again, but the fact of what he told me washes over me, and I can't process his words. My father is gone. He's dead.

"Tell me something. Tell me one thing," I say.

"Anything."

"Did he see it coming? Was he scared?" I feel tears stream down my face.

Something shifts in his expression, like a thing cracking, splintering. Just a little. "No. There was nothing to see coming. His heart gave out. It was all just too much for him. Now give me the knife."

I look beyond Santiago to the doctor. They're all closer. And in his hand, the doctor is holding a syringe.

They've come prepared.

"Please give me the knife," Santiago pleads, and I turn to him again. He's only a few feet away now. He's fast. I know that. He will lunge for the knife any second now. The only reason he's not is he's afraid I'll hurt myself. He's not afraid for himself. Not afraid I'll hurt him. I know that.

But he's wrong.

And before any of them can get to me, I fly at him, arm raised, my scream a proclamation of my hate for him. For this man I thought I loved. For this man who has only ever lied to me. Only ever manipulated me. Used me. And who has now taken my father from me.

It's that last thing that saves him. That final

thought. Because I know he'd stand there and take it otherwise. And when I bring the knife down, it's half-hearted because I am already defeated.

He grabs it by the sharp, serrated edge. It breaks skin, but he doesn't cry out. He barely flinches. I am not as strong as him nor am I as capable of violence. Not even against him. Not even now. And moments later, he's holding me as I sob, trapping my arms at my sides as he hugs me tight, my face pressed into the crook of his neck, the blood from his hand warm against my cheek as he cups my face, the needle barely noticeable when the doctor pricks my arm, a whispered apology on his lips as Santiago lifts me up when my knees give out, and I look up at him as my head lolls to the side.

"I hate you," I tell him, my arm not doing what my brain is telling it, my fingers not curling into claws, my hand only slapping weakly at his chest. "I hate you," I manage, my words slurring together as darkness creeps in, dulling the corners of my vision. "And I will never forgive you. Never."

26

SANTIAGO

"Boss?"

Something pokes me in the arm, stirring me. When I lift my bleary eyes, I realize I must have fallen asleep in the hall outside the bedroom door.

"What is it, Marco?" I force my aching muscles to cooperate as I rise to my feet.

"Have you been sleeping out here all night?" he asks.

I give him a stiff nod. It's not like him to ask such personal questions.

"I have some updates," he tells me. "Do you want to talk here or in your office?"

"Let's go downstairs." I pause to look at the door one more time, hesitant to leave, but aware Ivy doesn't want me anywhere near her right now either.

Marco has been aware of my struggle. The entire manor has. The past few days have been interspersed with silence and Ivy's rage whenever I try to speak with her. And I'd be lying if I said I haven't second-guessed my decision every step of the way.

I don't want to hurt her. I don't want to hurt any of Eli's daughters anymore, but right now, they are all suffering over the choice I made. And I can't even be sure it was necessary or worthwhile, since there have been no signs of Abel yet.

"You're doing the right thing." Marco reaches out, settling his hand on my shoulder. "I know it doesn't feel like it now, but this was the only way. He won't come out until he's dead sure this is real."

I wish I could be as certain as he sounds.

"Come." He jerks his chin in the direction of the stairs. "I think you will feel better when you hear what I have to say."

This news captures my interest, and without any alternative, I follow him down to my study. We step inside and close the door, and he waits until I'm settled into my chair before he removes his phone and hands it to me.

"One of my guys found someone lurking around the property. He was near the western perimeter."

I study the image of the man on Marco's screen, but he isn't someone I recognize.

"Any idea who he is?" I ask.

"From what I've been able to gather, he's a low-level criminal. There's nothing much of importance about him other than a rap sheet a mile long. Petty crimes, mostly. I already beat the shit out of him, and he gave it up pretty quickly that he was working for Abel. Said he was supposed to keep an eye on the place."

"And what exactly was he supposed to report back?" I ask.

"His orders were to look for Eli or any sightings of his daughters. There were even photos on his phone. He said Abel wanted pictures of Ivy or Eva. He wanted to see if they were distraught."

Marco is giving me the confirmation that I was right. Abel is paranoid enough to need confirmation that Ivy and Eva's grief is real. It should bring me relief, but there is none to be found. My wife is still upstairs, lost to her anguish, and I don't know how much longer I can bear it.

"He also said he was supposed to attend the funeral tomorrow," Marco continues. "He mentioned Abel had a few guys who would be in attendance, but he didn't know any of their names. They'll be reporting back to Abel, whoever they are."

I dip my head, rubbing my temples as tension clings to every muscle in my body. "I don't know if I can go through with it, Marco. I don't know if I can watch her suffer any longer—"

He lowers himself into the chair across from mine, resting his palms on my desk. "It's one more day, Santiago. Just one more day. Abel will get the confirmation that his entire family is in mourning. And then you can tell her, just as soon as we're back at The Manor."

"And what if he doesn't do what we are anticipating?" I ask. "What if he doesn't come out of hiding? His paranoia is too strong."

"He will," Marco assures me. "He hasn't waited this long for nothing. With Eli out of the picture, the temptation will be too much for him to resist. He'd rather die trying to snatch that last bit of power than be exiled to the shadows for eternity."

Instinctually, I know he's right. Abel's ego won't allow him to hide forever. But I still feel as though there could have been another way. There must have been another way that wouldn't hurt Ivy, and I just couldn't see it.

I have failed her, and nobody can convince me otherwise.

"You have less than fourteen hours," Marco reassures me. "That's it, boss. Then you can reunite them, and she will forgive you."

I nod, but it feels like a lie. Ivy told me herself she will never forgive me, and I don't think bringing Eli back from the dead will win her approval again. It's too much. This was her breaking point, I can feel it. And it all seems more hopeless than it ever has. Even acknowledging the fact that I would let him live out the rest of his natural life to keep her happy won't bring her peace. Not after a lie of this magnitude. Not after I've watched her suffer for days, her hatred of me growing with every passing moment.

"I think I know something that might make you feel better," Marco tells me.

When I meet his gaze, I know what he means before he even utters the words.

"Your prisoner is waiting for his execution, sir."

After showering in one of the guest bathrooms and washing the blood of Abel's spy from my hands, I dress in the fresh clothes Antonia brought me. I am tired after so little sleep, but I am anxious to see my wife.

I've checked the alerts on the door all morning, receiving updates from her doctor and Antonia. She has eaten a little, which is something. Other than that, there is not much to discuss. She is still in bed, resting. Alternating between crying fits and staring at the ceiling, blank.

Eva is handling it better than I anticipated. Antonia has been keeping her busy, offering her comfort and providing distractions with movies and puzzles they have taken to assembling together. On occasion, she will wander up to visit Ivy herself, but she does not stay long, insisting her sister should rest.

Their grief rests heavy on my shoulders, and even after all that Marco and I discussed, I am questioning how much harm there could be in telling them the truth now. But I know already. It isn't something I have to ask myself.

Abel is still their brother, and on some level, I'm aware that they harbor a love for him that has not yet been fully extinguished. When it comes to family, their loyalties will always be torn in that regard. But there is no question that Abel will die. They will both have to accept that, and if this is a preview of what's to come, I'm not certain Ivy and I can weather that storm. Not if she truly can't forgive me.

In the meantime, I can only cling to the belief that he can't manipulate their feelings for him if they don't know the truth. He can't guilt them into confessing the status of Eli's health if they aren't aware themselves. And judging by his past behavior, I don't doubt that he will try to get to them somehow. As much as I'd like to insist that I'm in control of everything, I can only control what I can see.

Abel has ways of gaining access to them. There are a thousand considerations to be made. He could have a rat in my own household staff for all I know. The maids, the groundskeeper, the cook... even the guards. If he has turned members of the Society against the establishment, there is no telling who he might convince to help him with his cause. It was his word, after all, his evidence, The Tribunal used to excommunicate well-established members. Abel is a manipulator of the highest order, and I can't trust anyone to be one-hundred-percent loyal. Marco and Antonia are the only ones. And the truth is, if Abel wanted to get a message to Ivy through someone, he'd find a way to do it.

It is with this tiresome awareness that I stop by my office and retrieve the small black box resting on top of my desk. As I walk up to the second landing and down the hall to my bedroom, pausing outside, I stare down to examine it, wondering if this is the right decision.

I'm aware nothing I can do will bring her comfort right now, but this foolish hope still lives within me. I unlock the door using the code and quietly step inside.

Ivy is curled up in bed, staring into nothingness. She doesn't look at me when I approach, or even when I sit on the edge beside her. Her tears have all dried up, but the pain has not. It's visceral, a living, breathing thing inside this room. I know because I feel it in my chest too. What she feels, I feel.

"Ivy?" I reach out hesitantly, stroking her arm.

She doesn't flinch or pull away, but I think I would rather that than the emptiness I see in her eyes.

I bring her hand to my lips and kiss it, and her fingers twitch in my grasp.

"I have something for you."

I slide the box onto the nightstand, and she glances at it briefly before her eyes flicker shut then open again. I don't know what to do. How to fix this for her.

"You can open it when you feel up to it," I tell her. "It's something very special to me, and I thought, perhaps it was time you saw it."

When she doesn't respond, I kick off my shoes and climb onto the middle of the bed, opening the blankets and sliding in behind her. She stiffens at first, but gradually, she melts into me, releasing a painful sigh when I wrap my arm around her waist, and she loses all resistance.

"I can't stand to be apart," I whisper, my lips grazing her ear. "I need you, Ivy. Come back to me, please."

A tear streaks down her cheek, and she shudders, slowly dragging her gaze to mine. "How could I?"

I kiss her jaw and then her cheek, tasting the salt of her tears before I close my eyes and breathe her in, hands clutching her in a silent plea.

"What if I could promise you that everything would be alright?" I choke out. "That this nightmare will all be over soon."

"How, Santiago?" she whispers. "How will this pain ever end?"

"It will end if you can find it in your heart to trust

me," I murmur against her lips. "That's all I'm asking. Trust that everything I do is to protect you."

She looks up at me, eyes hard. "I get it now."

"What do you get?"

"How it feels," she answers bitterly. "Why you wanted to kill me to avenge your father's death. I understand that now because I feel it too."

Her words ice over any warmth left between us as my hands fall away from her. Pain splinters inside me at the realization there is no fixing this. It can't be undone. Foolishly, I wanted to believe we could survive this, but now I know that we can't.

She will never forgive me. Not tomorrow. Not ever.

I can see it in her eyes.

I can hear it in her voice.

And nothing has ever felt so final when I drag myself away from her, glancing over my shoulder one last time. She doesn't look at me, and she doesn't look at the gift I left her on the nightstand.

Instead, she closes her eyes and breathes a sigh of relief as I walk out the door.

27
IVY

I don't know how much time has passed. Maybe a day or two. I'm not locked in the bedroom, but I don't leave it by choice. I don't have anywhere to go. This feeling, this ache, there's no getting away from it.

My father is dead. Murdered by my husband's hand.

Two men I love.

Two men I loved.

Why is it always past tense when they're gone? The love is still here, in the present, alongside the pain.

Santiago, though? In a way, that hurts just as much. Maybe more. His hate for my father was far greater than any affection, any feeling at all he could have had for me. Because no matter what he says, I know the truth. It's too convenient otherwise. A heart attack? Something the doctor's missed when they've been keeping such a close eye on him? I don't believe it.

I get out of bed to use the bathroom. When I'm finished, I stand at the sink and study my reflection as I wash my hands. I look a wreck. My face is gaunt, dark circles under my eyes matching those of Santiago's tattoo. I turn my head a little to look at the dot of ink. It seems so long ago, so far away. We survived that. He and I survived it. We have broken through so many obstacles set against us, some by him, some by others, but we came through together somehow.

I fell in love with him somehow.

God. I am crazy.

I switch off the water and dry my hands, looking down at my rounded stomach. There's a baby inside there. Our child. What will happen when he or she is here? I can't even begin to think about that.

I walk back into the bedroom and sit on the edge of the bed. I am tired of this room. This bed. This place. I am tired.

On the nightstand, I see the box he left and touch the pendant still lying against my chest. The diamond-encrusted rose. A gift when I became pregnant. A symbol not of love or affection but of my belonging to the De La Rosa family. My belonging to him. Like the tattoo on the back of my neck that I sometimes swear throbs to be touched. To be acknowledged. As if the ink is somehow connected to him. Like it needs to be near him.

I pick up the box and read the engraved logo. Montblanc.

Odd. But then I remember.

I lean back against the bed and bring my knees up, tucking my bare feet beneath the blankets. I lay my head against the headboard, and I remember that day. I'd been thirteen. I'd just gotten home from the new school. That awful school. I'd been teased for days, and I'd finally had enough. I hadn't seen Santiago in my father's study when I'd stormed in. Not until after my tantrum did I see him.

He didn't have his tattoo then. He was younger. Not boyish, though. I would never describe Santiago as boyish, even then.

My father had asked me to give him this box. I remember his apology that he hadn't had a chance to wrap it. I've only seen one box like it in my life. My father's. But his came in royal blue, not black.

I remember I'd felt angry at the gesture, my father giving this stranger a gift, an expensive gift I'm not sure we could afford all the while dismissing my concerns. Embarrassed even by them.

I'd slapped the box into Santiago's hand and told him off. Told him how much I hated his school. Did I tell him I hated him, too? I don't remember. I'd been a lot like Eva then.

I look down at the box now and trace the letters

embossed on the lid. I open it, and inside, cradled in a cushion of black satin, is a gold fountain pen. I lift it out and set the box aside. It's beautiful. Absolutely exquisite. I wonder if my mother knew my father had bought such an expensive gift for Santiago. Not for her. Not for any of his own children.

Turning it over in my hand, I read the inscription.

To Santiago, you make me proud, son.

Son.

My throat closes up, and tears burn my eyes.

Son.

Is Santiago taunting me now? Showing me how vile he is? How wicked? That he could murder a man to whom he'd been like a son. Because that's what he'd been to my father. He'd been more of a son to him than Abel had. More beloved than his own blood.

The realization is upsetting enough but to think that Santiago, knowing this, could murder him is beyond that.

But then I consider an alternative. Is this another manipulation of his? Something to show me he couldn't possibly have murdered a man he loved. Is this supposed to show me that somehow, after all these months of hate, these years of planning his elaborate vengeance, Santiago realized his love for my father? Is it supposed to make me believe that he couldn't kill him?

He must think me even more stupid than I realized.

I hate him.

I have to hate him.

But a part of me is breaking, too. Because no matter what I want, or what I claim, I don't. When he climbed into bed with me earlier, I didn't pull away. I curled into him. I leaned into his warmth. His strength. His blood-soaked hands. It took all I had to steel myself against him.

Because he is a master manipulator. And I cannot love him.

Determined, I get off the bed, and I hurl both pen and box across the room leaving a divot in the wall. I'm glad for it. I need to remember his violence. His duplicity. I need to remember his hate. Remember that his need for vengeance far outweighs any feeling for me.

Yes, he will keep me safe. Protect me against any enemy. But what about my heart? He won't be guardian to that. He's already told me so in exactly those words. Words I cannot confuse or misunderstand. No, he's been very clear.

I am the guardian of my own heart. I must be. And I have to steel myself now. Steel myself against him. Protect myself and Eva. Protect my unborn child from his own father. Because maybe the other thing he's been telling me, the fact he is incapable of love, of affection, maybe he's just warning me.

Because I think I understand that part of Santiago now. The damaged, broken insides of him. Too broken to ever be healed. Ever be made whole.

I think he meant it when he said he didn't want to hurt me. He doesn't. But he will. He told me that too. He warned me to guard my heart. And it's all truth. His only lie is in denying he had a hand in my father's death.

But whatever the case, I cannot allow him to do to our child what his father did to him. I will not allow him to twist our baby, to damage him irrevocably. To pass on the legacy his father passed on to him. That of a monster.

28

SANTIAGO

My wife sits beside me in the front pew at Sacred Trinity Cathedral, dabbing the tears from beneath her black-veiled hat as the priest reads scriptures from the altar. Beside us are Marco, Eva, and Antonia. Across the aisle is Mrs. Moreno, Ivy's mother, and by my count, she has yet to shed a solitary tear for her beloved husband.

The pews are occupied by many of the Society members. People Eli worked with and those he befriended during his time in the community. I'd be lying if I said I wasn't surprised by the turnout. I had no idea the old man who was of little consequence in the grand hierarchy of things had so many call him a friend.

But should it surprise me?

If I had not been spoiled by my own sour experience with him, I would have called him a great man once myself. I would have spoken kind words on his behalf, and I would not have hesitated to call him an honorable man.

Indeed, I would have grieved for him right along with all the others, and it occurs to me that in some ways, I already have.

I didn't just lose my family after the explosion. I lost Eli too.

The thought leaves a strange bitterness on my lips as I rest my hand on the wooden pew. A silent offer for my grieving wife. She does not take it. She does not look at me or speak to me, even when the funeral ends, and we follow the procession to the cemetery.

I spared no expense for the theatrics of Eli's fake death. There is even a jazz band leading the way, playing the somber traditional funeral music well-known throughout New Orleans. We walk behind the hearse into the cemetery, where the empty coffin is eventually deposited into a tomb.

Throughout the day, I catch myself looking around at the other mourners, wondering which of them are Abel's men. My own security is well disguised among them, taking notes of every face, every attendee. But Abel would know that, regardless of how well they blend in. Will he be convinced by the charade? Will any of this be worth it in the end?

When the tomb is sealed shut, the music

changes to a more upbeat tune, and then the procession relocates to the IVI compound for the reception. The day seems to be dragging on, and it's all I can do to stand at my wife's side while she ignores me, greeting mourners with tear-filled eyes.

She speaks to the guests for two hours as they tell stories about her father before she starts to fade into exhaustion, and I lean in to whisper in her ear.

"It's time to get you home now."

She shakes her head in refusal, but staggers, nearly collapsing into me before I grab her arm and hold her upright.

Unwittingly, she has done her part. She has grieved publicly for all to see. But at what cost? I have never hated myself more than I do when I pull her tired body against mine, forcing her chin up so she must look at me.

"It's time to get you home, angel. There is something you must see."

Her face softens a fraction before she shakes her head, stubbornly refusing to bend.

"The celebration of my father's life isn't over yet. You can go if you want, but I'm not leaving."

"Ivy." My voice is a warning and a plea. If I could just get her home, she would understand.

"I'm going to the bathroom." She yanks away from me. "Please just leave me alone."

29

IVY

I'm gone before he can stop me, almost knocking someone over in my rush before I finally find a bathroom where I stand at the sink and take a few deep breaths.

I dressed in black lace from head to toe. Santiago chose it. I didn't care what I wore. I was just grateful the veil was heavy enough that I could hide at least a little.

Eva sat beside me in our pew. My mother occupied the front pew across from ours dressed in a deep blue too-tight dress that accentuated her every curve. Her hat set at an angle, the veil purposely chosen to enhance, not to hide. Because she wasn't grieving.

I don't even really blame her. She was forced into this marriage. She was a gift to my father, whom she always considered beneath her.

When my fingers brushed Santiago's during the service, I was quick to pull away. If he noticed, he didn't comment. I looked at his hand then, and I looked at the casket again, and all I could think was what did he do to my father for it to be closed?

Eva went home with Marco and two soldiers after the service. I didn't want to go. I wanted to stay, to hear the stories my father's friends, many of them strangers to me, told about him. I had no idea he was so ingrained in IVI. Had no idea he had so many friends there and true friends at that. I see it in their eyes and hear it in the affectionate way they speak about him. I'm truly glad for that.

And now as I stand looking at my blotchy, tear-streaked face in the bathroom mirror, I think about that closed casket set with an enormous bouquet of lilies spilling over the lid, and for all of my father's faults, I loved him. I will miss him.

The toilet flushes, and a woman I don't know comes out of the little room to wash her hands.

"He was a good man, dear," she says to me.

"Thank you," I tell her but then am grateful when she's gone. I feel so sad. So incredibly sad. And the fact that I am alone has never been more obvious to me.

It's then I feel something. Something strange. I blink, looking down at my stomach. And there it is again. The lightest tapping. Like the tip of the tiniest finger just touching the back of my hand. It's so faint I almost miss it, but then it comes again. I put my hand over my round belly, and I smile, feel my eyes fill up at this first real contact with my baby, and all I can think is I need to tell Santiago. I need to put his hand on the bump and let him feel this almost fluttering sensation as delicate as a butterfly's wing.

But then it's gone, and my smile with it because I won't tell Santiago. Not now. I can't. He will miss this milestone, and it makes me want to cry all over again.

The door opens again then, and someone walks inside. I busy myself washing my hands. I should have slipped into one of the stalls.

The woman hesitates at the door, and I realize she's one of the waitresses. I wonder if she doesn't think she should be using this bathroom for guests.

"They're open," I say, pointing at the stalls.

"Um...are you Mrs. De La Rosa?"

I turn to look at her. I realize she's young, maybe sixteen. I nod.

"Here." She digs into her pocket and pulls out a wrinkled, unsealed envelope.

"What is it?" I ask, taking it, opening the flap to see a cell phone inside along with a sheet of paper.

She bites her lip, then looks at the door. "Someone just asked me to give it to you," she says and slips out before I can ask her another question.

I take out the phone, note the crack across the screen. I push the home button and gasp when I see a picture of Michael and Hazel laughing, Michael with a huge cone of cotton candy in his hand, his tongue blue as he licks it off his chin.

I unfold the scrap of paper. Just a torn sheet of paper. But I recognize the handwriting.

Do you see now what he's capable of? I can't get hold of you. He's got you locked up tight. Ivy, if he finds me, he will kill me, too, and you will never even hear about it. But I guess you don't care about that, do you? You're on his side now. Even after he murdered our father.
Just remember, I did this because you made me do it. I'm waiting in the parking lot of the Marriott two blocks away with Hazel and her illegitimate brat. Get here in five minutes and I'll let them go. Come alone. No Santiago. No soldiers. Or else Michael will learn how a real gun works.
Want proof I have them? I'm sure he's made me out to be a liar. Hazel's passcode is 3636. We took some family selfies.
Abel.

Hazel and Michael? I haven't talked to them since... well, it's been maybe four or five days, I realize. I tried to call a few times since Santiago told me about Dad but haven't gotten through, and I've been so depressed I didn't stop to think about it. I realize now Michael hasn't called me in several days either.

Santiago is protecting them. He told me he's protecting them.

My hands trembling, I punch in the code Abel gave me on the phone that I know is Hazel's and when I click on the camera icon, there they are. The family selfies.

I have to take hold of the counter to keep from dropping to my knees. Terror fills me as I scroll through photo after photo of Hazel and Michael sitting in the backseat of a car. Hazel's eyes are red and she's clutching Michael to her. His face is buried in her chest. It's the last one that's the worst. Abel's face looms in the foreground of this one and I almost don't recognize him for the grin on his face. He's in the front seat of the car and my sister and Michael are in the back and in the corner of the selfie I see the gun.

Before I can think a text pings on the phone. Two words.

Five minutes.

I set the phone and the note on the counter and move. I don't have time for anything else. Five minutes to get to the Marriott. I can't risk telling Santiago. Can't risk harm coming to my sister or nephew. Santiago will find the note. Someone will.

I walk out of the bathroom and hear the noise of

the crowded reception room. I swear I hear Santiago's voice but I don't see him and I hurry to the exit.

Abel is desperate. Was he desperate when he tried to abort our baby? No, this is different. He is out of friends. Out of choices.

And I know he means me harm. Even if he is blood. But I have no choice but to go. His threat is real.

A waiter almost barrels into me when he comes hurrying out of the swinging door of the kitchen. He begins to apologize, but I shake my head and tell him it's fine.

Before Santiago or any of his men see me, I slip into the kitchen, pausing only to spot the open door leading out into the street beyond. I hurry through the bustling space, thinking about this ceremony of serving a meal after a funeral. Wondering how people can eat on such an occasion.

And when I'm outside, I see two of Santiago's men standing at one end of the street as the one lights a cigarette for the other. I hurry to the other end, and a moment later, I am on a bigger, busier street. I rush down one block, two, and when I turn another corner I see a queue of taxis at the hotel. I'm about to cross the street to hurry to the lot when a car screeches to a stop beside me and I have to jump out of the way.

I see them then. The terrified faces of Michael

and Hazel in the backseat. Abel leans across the front seat and pushes the passenger side door open. I don't miss the pistol in his hand.

"Get in," he barks and I do and we're off before I've even closed the door.

30

IVY

"What are you doing? He's a child!" I half turn to the back and half to Abel who shifts into a higher gear as he speeds out of town.

He glances at me, his gaze dropping to my rounded stomach with disgust.

"Ivy," Hazel says. "I'm so sorry."

"Santiago... he said he—" my voice breaks. He was protecting them. He said he was protecting them.

"Soldiers are stupid," Abel says. "If you set your mind to it, you can achieve anything. Isn't that right, Mikey? Life lesson for you. You're fucking welcome."

Michael starts to howl.

"Slow down!" I yell as a he runs a red light and cars honk their horns at us. I take a deep breath in and fasten my seatbelt with shaking hands. "I'm here. Let them go, Abel. I'm here. You said you'd let them go!"

"Shut up."

"You said it! He's a child, Abel."

Abel glances at me and there is something in his expression that gives me a sliver of hope. But he keeps driving, the gun in one hand, his foot a lead weight on the gas pedal. We drive like this until we're out of town and after about twenty minutes he finally slows and pulls off at a run-down looking gas station. He brings the car to a screeching halt and makes sure we can all see the gun as he half-turns to Hazel.

"Get out."

Hazel looks from him to me. "Abel..." Her lip is trembling. "You can't hurt her."

"Get the fuck out!"

"Go! Hazel go!" I plead.

"Mommy!"

Tears stream down Hazel's face.

"You know what? Suit yourself. I'll take you all with me!"

"No!" I scream as Michael howls.

Hazel moves, pushing the door open and getting out, never once letting go of Michael as she hauls him out and closes the door. Abel's foot is on the gas pedal in an instant and Hazel jumps back as he takes off at an insane speed back onto the road.

"What are you doing? What do you want?"

My brother looks deranged. I don't know when he last showered or shaved. He is desperate and that scares me the most.

"Please, Abel. I can help you. Just slow down. Please."

He looks out the front window, face serious, but he does slow a little. "You're growing."

I touch my hand to my stomach but don't reply. I don't know what to say. We drive like this for ten more minutes before he pulls into the parking lot of a motel along a noisy stretch of road. It looks as run-down as the gas station.

"We're making a pit stop." He parks in front of one of the last doors and turns to me. "Don't do anything stupid, got it?"

I nod.

He climbs out then comes to my side and opens the door.

"Get out."

I do. "Have you been here all this time?"

He shakes his head. "Just got to this shithole recently. My friends seem to have abandoned me."

"Your friends?"

He takes out a key and unlocks the door. I step inside the dingy, stuffy room and he closes it again.

"So, Dad's dead."

I nod.

"It's real?"

He must see my confusion at his question.

"I wouldn't put it past your husband to fake our father's death to lure me out. Would you?"

"What? He wouldn't..." I stop, think about what Santiago had said when he'd wanted to leave the reception, but I'd refused. "No, Abel," I say, shaking my head. "Dad's dead. He wouldn't fake that." Not knowing what it would do to me, to us. "What happens now? What do you want?"

He checks his watch. "Just shut up. I need to think." He reaches for the open duffel on a chair and starts to gather up the clothes strewn about the place, tossing them into the bag haphazardly.

My legs feel weak, and I perch on the edge of the bed. I close both hands over my stomach as Abel's eyes fall once again to it.

"Did you have anything to do with the explosion that killed Santiago's family and all those other men?"

"Wow. You really think I'd do something like that?"

"You were jealous of him. Of how Dad was with him."

"I got over that. That explosion, as you call it, was a gas leak as far as I know. If anything, The Society is indebted to me for bringing to light the families breaking their laws, potentially getting IVI into serious trouble. Not that they'd ever acknowledge me. Although now that Dad's gone..." He trails off, eyes distant momentarily before focusing back on me. "But I'm sure your husband has made sure I'll never climb the rungs of their precious ladder. You know it's a pretty discriminatory system. But no, I guess you wouldn't know that, not as *Mrs. De La Rosa*. I arranged that, you know. That was me. I didn't even get so much as a thank you though, did I?"

I don't tell him his purpose was self-serving. Instead, I watch his expression darken as he seems to disappear into his thoughts. I take in his ragged appearance and see the half-empty pack of cigarettes.

"Did you have anything to do with Colette's kidnapping?" I ask.

His forehead furrows. "Who the fuck is Colette?"

"Jackson Montgomery's wife."

"Oh. That was Holton, I guess. He was getting a little desperate. I told him it was a stupid idea. You mess with a man's wife and kid, well..." he pauses, eyes narrowing infinitesimally. "There's no coming back from that, is there?"

My phone rings then. I'd almost forgotten that I had it with me.

"You have a fucking phone with you?" he asks, furious.

I reach into my pocket as the call goes to voicemail but it starts to ring again immediately. It's Santiago. I see his name on the screen.

"You do not answer that!" Abel roars, lunging for the phone.

I'm on my feet in an instant. "Let me talk to him. I can help you. I can tell him—"

He grabs the phone from my hand and throws it so hard against the far wall I see it smash.

"That takes care of that," Abel says. "You should have told me you had a damn phone with you. He's probably on his way here now. Let's go."

He takes my arm and drags me to the door.

"Abel." I pull back, but he's much stronger than I am. And he's desperate. "I'll talk to Santiago when he gets here. You're right, he's on his way," I lie. I have no idea how he'd find me. "I'll explain—" I stop when he opens the door and turns on me, the look on his face contorting it, making it into something terrifying.

"He killed Dad, you idiot. If he's willing to kill that old man even knowing he had no fucking clue what I was doing, you think he's just going to let me walk away? You're dumber than I thought if you do."

He drags me outside and toward the car. I resist. I fight with all I have and manage to kick him in the shins hard enough that he loosens his grip, and I slip out of it. I'm almost away, running toward the street, when I hear the honking of a car horn and see the shiny Aston Martin glint in the sun. I'd thought it inappropriate for a funeral, but he'd insisted on letting Marco drive Eva in it. Saying it might help cheer her up. Several cars behind the Aston Martin is a Rolls Royce.

I slow as the Aston Martin gets closer because it's not Marco behind the wheel. It's Santiago.

It takes that moment for Abel to catch up with me, recapture me, and drag me back toward the open passenger door.

"Please, Abel!"

I fight him. I fight with all I have because if I get into that car, I'm dead. I know it. He would rather drive us into an oncoming truck and kill himself along with me and my baby than let my husband win.

Because Abel has nothing to lose. He's forfeited his life, and he knows it.

And as he forces me toward the car, I give an almighty shove and somehow, someway, manage to trip him, and I run. I run faster than I've ever run in my life, and Santiago's almost here. He's turning into the lot. I can make it. He's so close, I can make it.

I can see his face now. Santiago is so near I can see his face.

And it's that that has me stop.

His expression of horror. His open mouth. I think he's screaming. I think it's a scream I see. But he's too far away, and Abel... oh my God, Abel... But before I can finish that thought, there's a sound like I've never heard before, and I feel a pain that I've never felt before. Intense and abrupt and propelling me at an impossible speed.

I don't register the screech of tires. I don't hear the screaming of horns. And when I open my eyes, I see my hat. It's down the road caught under the tire of a car. The veil is torn, blowing in a breeze.

And I realize all the noise has stopped. No one is screaming. Not Abel. Not Santiago. Not even me.

31

SANTIAGO

Time does not slow for tragedy. It's something I know intimately, how quickly a life can be extinguished. A blink of an eye. A single breath. A split second. There one moment and gone the next.

I'm helpless to stop it as I watch Abel's car collide with Ivy's body from behind. The impact is a blur, a fraction of a moment when she is propelled into the air and then onto the pavement, rolling to a stop with such finality, it feels like I'm dying too.

Nothing can prepare you for such an event. No amount of adrenaline in the world can force your body to cooperate as the shock of what you're witnessing threatens to freeze you.

My car comes to a stop. I struggle to release my seat belt, howling in frustration as my eyes connect with Abel's for one split second. He doesn't look at his sister as he directs the car forward without slowing. He only has eyes for me. A sneer on his face, as if to say he won.

I force myself to follow a series of simple commands, even as every muscle in my body goes rigid. One is to take a deep breath. Two is to pull the brake. Finally, I manage to untangle my seat belt, flinging open the door just as Abel veers around me and speeds off toward the exit.

I glance at his taillights and then back at Ivy. As soon as I saw Ivy's phone location on the GPS, I didn't think. I just took off, Marco and the rest of the guards scrambling to catch up with me. They were following me as I wove through traffic, but they are still a few seconds behind. It's just me, standing between my past and my future. My chance to kill Abel or save my wife. It's not even a choice.

I tear my gaze away from the squealing tires as Abel turns the corner and disappears from sight. I'm running. Lungs burning. Heart pounding. Fists clenching. When I reach her, the sight drops me to my knees.

Her head is lolled to the side, blood-streaked across her face.

"Ivy." My voice is barely a whisper when I reach out to touch her, hesitant. "Wake up, angel. Please wake up."

I'm not supposed to move her, but it's the only thing I want to do. I want to cradle her in my arms and tell her it's going to be okay. I will find a way to save her. Instead, I reach for her hand, only to realize her arm and several of her fingers have been broken. They are already starting to swell, bruises forming along the skin. Her dress is torn down the side, scrapes and gashes marring her legs and her arms. She's bleeding from her lip and possibly somewhere else. I can't tell.

I'm trying to drag my phone from my pocket when I hear Marco's voice, his hand coming to rest on my shoulder. "I already called, boss. They're on their way."

I look up at him, a desperation I've never known altering my voice beyond all comprehension. "What do we do?"

He swallows, eyes glassy. "I... think you need to check her pulse."

My chest heaves, emotion threatening to break free as I stroke my wife's face. Marco watches on as I move my trembling fingers to her throat, trying to feel for a pulse. It's the most terrifying moment of my life, and I'm shaking too badly to feel anything. I dig deeper, pressing my fingers into her skin, begging for something. Anything.

"Help me," I plead. "Marco..."

An ambulance turns the corner. Marco did right. He called for the Society's medical team. Ivy will have a fighting chance. I have to believe that.

"Excuse us, Mr. De La Rosa." Someone taps me

on the shoulder as paramedics begin attending to her, rattling off information as they try to move her onto a stretcher.

I can't seem to let go of her arm. The edges of my eyes are darkening, my vision narrowing to a pinpoint as my breathing becomes too shallow to draw air.

"Santiago." Marco pries my hand from her, and instinctively, I take a swing at him as I stagger to my feet.

He grabs me by the shoulders, shaking me, and when I try to fight him off, he backhands me across the face, shocking me back to reality.

"Pull yourself together, Santiago," he growls. "Do it for your wife."

My nostrils flare as a long, painful sound leaves my lungs. He's right. I know he's right. But I don't know how to pull myself together when the only thing that matters is falling apart. I watch them load her into the back of the ambulance, and Marco ushers me forward.

"You can ride with her, sir."

I glance back at him before the doors shut, and he gives me one last encouraging nod. "I'll meet you there."

The next ten hours are a blur as I'm left to hold my breath in the hospital waiting room. I alternate between pacing the floor and collapsing into a chair to hang my head in my hands, swinging between violent despair and brief glimpses of hope.

Doctors and nurses come and go, providing updates with little information. They did imaging tests on Ivy as soon as she arrived, confirming the baby is okay, but from what they can tell so far, she has three broken ribs, a fractured arm, a ruptured tendon in her leg, and numerous scrapes and bruises. The impact was to her face and the side of her head, but they told me she was responsive to stimuli before they took her back to surgery for the ruptured tendon. I wanted to see her, but the surgery had to be performed immediately to prevent further damage.

Marco told me that was a good sign, and the nurses have continued to assure me they are doing everything they can. But hours have come and gone, and something doesn't feel right. I know it, deep in my gut.

"I have to go back there," I tell Marco.

"You can't." He stands up and forces me back into the chair.

I'm too exhausted to fight him off, and I know it isn't logical. They told me as soon as she was in recovery, they would come for me. But I can't deny this desperate sinking inside me. It's an instinct that only intensifies with time, and after another hour passes, I can no longer deny it.

"It's been hours," I croak. "They said she'd be out of surgery by now."

"It takes time for the anesthesia to wear off," he answers. "Look at the screen, boss."

He points at the monitor in the waiting room with Ivy's number on it. The one that tells me she's still in surgery. It hasn't been updated for six hours, I realize, and I know that can't be accurate.

When I stagger to my feet again, Marco sighs, and this time he seems to understand he's not stopping me. I head for the desk, where a terrified nurse blinks up at me as soon as she sees me.

"Mr. De La Rosa," she squeaks.

"I want to speak to a doctor. Now."

She swallows, nods, and scurries off. Five minutes pass, and then ten before a weary-looking doctor appears. It's the same man I spoke to earlier. One of the best surgeons IVI has on staff. He was called in specifically for my wife's case today. I was assured she was in good hands with Dr. Singh. But one glance at his face tells me I was wrong.

"What happened?" I force the words between gritted teeth. "I want to see my wife. Now. Where is she? Where the hell is she?"

"Mr. De La Rosa." His eyes bounce between

Marco and me. "I'm afraid there's been a complication."

"Complication?" The word falls from my lips in an unrecognizable voice.

"Your wife seems to be experiencing a prolonged delay of consciousness following surgery."

"She's not waking up?" My eyes move down the hall behind him to the closed doors they wheeled Ivy through. "But... she's okay? You said she was responsive earlier. You told me—"

"This can be a rare complication of anesthesia," he tells me. "There are cases when this happens without much of an explanation…"

His voice begins to fade as he rattles off rehearsed lines about post-op recovery times, organic and metabolic causes of delayed consciousness, non-traumatic causes for comatose patients. The words all start to blend, and I can't follow any of them. It's too much to process, and there's only one thing I know for certain.

"Take me to her," I order. "I need to see her. I'm going now, with or without you."

He hesitates and then offers a solemn nod.

32

SANTIAGO

The steady beeping of the monitors in Ivy's room are the only solace I have in the darkness. Those rhythms mean, in some capacity, she's still here. She's still inside her body, even if she's not awake.

It's been three days since the surgery, and she's been transferred to the ICU, where they continue to run tests. Every doctor who arrives inevitably leaves without any answers, offering the name of another colleague who might be able to help. I send for all of them. A constant parade of elite medical professionals come and go without results. There are no concrete answers, only estimations.

Some tell me it's a complication of the anesthesia. Others insist it must be metabolic in nature. One recklessly began to suggest that it was psychogenic, a state of distress so rare the body shuts itself down. They run countless blood tests and imaging scans, interrogating me about any pre-existing conditions or medications she may have taken that day. They are all looking for something, but it's become clear they don't know what it is.

Her brain scans have revealed no permanent damage. No swelling. Her spinal cord is intact. But with every passing hour, I'm beginning to lose hope that anyone can help her.

Between the influx of specialists and nurses, I take to my phone to search for potential causes myself. I read case studies about prolonged comas with unknown causes, deep-diving into the bizarre and unusual. It becomes clear the more that I read, and the longer Ivy takes to wake up on her own, the dimmer her chances are.

In the hall outside the door, the staff has lined up chairs for the other visitors. Antonia, Marco, Eva, Hazel, Michael, and Eli are all keeping vigil there, awaiting their turn to visit. We work in rotations, something that was not my idea, but one I agreed to nonetheless. I thought maybe if she felt their presence, someone she still loved, it might encourage her to come back. But so far, that has proven fruitless too.

Admittedly, when Marco brought Eli here, I was angry. But the moment I saw his face, something hit me. The unshakeable truth that he knew exactly how I felt. The pain in his eyes was a reflection of mine. And once I saw it, I could not send him away.

Marco's men are combing the city for Abel, and any plan we may have had to lure him out is in tatters now. None of it matters. The only thing that matters is that Ivy comes back, and only then will I leave her bedside to murder her brother.

Many times, I have considered moving her back home. But the hospital staff tells me it would be ill advised. It doesn't matter if I hire an army of staff and purchase enough medical equipment to outfit an entire hospital. If something goes wrong, this is the safest place for her. It's a fact I'm still having difficulty wrapping my head around. A defeat I don't want to accept. She shouldn't be lying on this bed in this cold, sterile room. Everything about it feels wrong.

"Have you tried talking to her?"

I blink up at the nurse who came to check Ivy's vitals. "What?"

"Sometimes it helps." She offers me a smile.

I glance at Ivy, her face empty. Eyes closed. "Can she hear me?"

"You never know," the nurse answers. "There have been patients who can hear everything happening around them. Either way, I don't think it can hurt to let her know you're here."

I'm still considering her words long after she leaves when I take my wife's hand in mine. Her fingers are cold, and it doesn't feel right. It feels like she's already gone, and I don't know how to bear it.

"I'm here, angel," I rasp. "I've been here the whole time."

I don't know what I'm expecting. A twitch. A change in her heartbeat. Some sign of life. But there's nothing.

"I don't really know what to say to you," I confess, dipping my head and closing my eyes. "I know this is my fault. I put you through so much... and you are tired. So, I get that you want to rest. And I'll still be here when you wake because you have to wake up, Ivy. You can't leave me. Not now. Not ever."

A single tear streaks down my cheek, splashing onto her arm. "I can't survive without you. And if you come back to me, I'll give you everything. Anything your heart desires, so long as you stay."

The machines continue to drone on, the stillness of her body untethering me in a way nothing else ever has.

"I can't do this without you." I move my fingers to her belly, where our unborn child still grows against all odds. "You have to stay with us. Because I don't want to be here if you aren't. I... I care about you, Ivy. I care about you more than I could ever put into words, and I never knew how to tell you. How to admit it. I didn't even realize until I nearly lost you... and I can't... you just can't leave me."

A knock on the door jars me from my rambling

confession, and when I look up, Eli is standing there. Our eyes lock, and he dips his head.

"You really do love her, don't you?"

He sounds both shocked and relieved by the idea. And I won't deny it any longer.

I turn back to Ivy, nodding solemnly. I want her to hear the words from my own lips. I want her to see how true they are.

"Excuse us." A ruckus in the hallway catches my attention, and Eli turns just as two IVI guards shove past him, entering the room.

"What are you doing?" I growl at them.

"You've been summoned by The Tribunal, Mr. De La Rosa," the man on the right answers. "We're going to need you to come with us. Right away."

33

SANTIAGO

"What is the meaning of this?" I shrug the guards off me with a snarl as they usher me into The Tribunal, Marco trailing us. "How dare you summon me away from my wife at a time like this—"

"There has been a serious accusation brought against you," Councilor Hildebrand interrupts my tirade. "And it is the duty of this Tribunal to investigate accordingly."

"What accusation?" I glower at the three Councilors as they peer down on me in judgment.

"We have been presented with evidence that you have altered or falsified your statements against Abel Moreno in an effort to disgrace his reputation and remove him from The Society."

An invisible shockwave moves through me as I glance around the darkened edges of the vast room.

"Abel fucking Moreno?" I clip out. "The man who just tried to murder my wife?"

"I think it was the other way around." He steps out of the shadows, a serpent who just won't fucking die.

Instinct has me lunging for him, and I manage to land one solid blow to his face before the guards yank me back again.

"You see?" Abel hisses. "He wants me dead by any means possible."

"This is a fucking joke." I turn to The Councilors, chest heaving. "You know what he's done. The poisoning, the attempted abortion, kidnapping my wife, Colette Van der Smit—"

"For every offense you have laid against him, he has provided an alternate version of events," Hildebrand tells me. "It is our duty to investigate these alleged crimes."

"Fuck your investigation!" I shrug one guard off me successfully, but the other still clings to me.

Marco steps up to his side, narrowing his eyes. "If you aren't ready to face your death, I suggest you let him go. Now."

He does as Marco suggests after a moment of hesitation, and I thank him by turning and slamming my fist into the side of the guard's skull, dropping the man onto the floor in a fit of pain.

"You will behave yourself," Hildebrand warns. "Or we will be forced to restrain you."

"I'm a goddamned De La Rosa," I remind him. "My father was your mentor. And you have the nerve to sit up there and question me like a common criminal?"

"We are simply doing our job," he replies coolly. "You are aware how this process works. Every member of IVI who brings forth a claim has a right to be heard. Even the accused."

"He doesn't deserve to bear the mark of this Society." I glare at Abel. "And if you seek to make a mockery of the serious offenses he has committed by challenging me—"

"Enough!" A voice echoes from behind me as the door slams shut.

I turn as Marco does, and the guards launch themselves toward the intruder as Hildebrand bellows in irritation. "Who interrupts our proceedings now?"

"It's Eli," the silhouette answers just before he comes into view. "Eli Moreno."

There's an audible sound of shock from Abel, but my gaze is pinned on Eli as a sickening realization occurs to me. He's part of this. He came here to set me up. Just like before.

"Eli Moreno?" Hildebrand repeats, his voice alarmed. "Back from the dead?"

"I can assure you I am as healthy as can be for my age, considering the events of the last year." His gaze moves to his son, and something pinches his features. A look of discomfort, perhaps. I can't quite place it.

"Dad..." Abel chokes out. "I thought... you were dead."

"No thanks to you, I am very much alive," he answers.

I watch the exchange between the two men, trying to decipher every micro expression. Every hitch in their tones and shift in their posture.

"Well, congratulations on not being dead," Hildebrand tells him dryly. "But I'm still unsure what your purpose is here."

"I came here to put a stop to this." He looks at The Councilors and then back to Abel. "Once and for all. It's enough, son. There has been too much damage. Too much destruction. I can't allow it to go on any longer."

Abel's face flushes with red as his fists clench at his sides. "You would choose to defend him over me? Your own fucking son?"

"I don't know where I went so wrong." Eli dips his head in shame. "And I'm sorry that I've let you down, Abel. I'm sorry for hurting you and not being there as much as I should have perhaps... but this has become too large. Too many lives have been destroyed, and I can't in good conscience allow anyone else to suffer over your anger with me."

He walks up to the dais where the three Councilors are seated, handing Hildebrand what appears to be a flash drive.

"It's all on there," Eli tells them solemnly. "The truth about the excommunicated members. The explosion that killed Santiago's family and the other Sovereign Sons. The attempt on my life. Everything is right there."

I watch on in disbelief as Marco clears his throat beside me. He seems to be as uncertain as I am. But when Eli turns around and meets my eyes, he nods to me, a sign of respect and so much more.

I think this is his way of trying to make amends.

"It can't be you, Santiago," he tells me. "He will pay for his sins now, but it can't be you. Not if you truly want to move forward with Ivy."

34

EVANGELINE

I'm trying to stay upbeat for my sister. For my father and for Santiago. I'm really trying. But it's getting harder and harder the more time goes by.

For four weeks, she has lain like this. Unmoving except when the nurses move her. Her expression unchanging. Her belly still somehow growing. I don't even know if she can hear me, and I'm sure I sound pretty stupid to anyone passing by, but I want her to know I'm here. That we're all here and waiting.

So, I drag the chair over and sit down, and I take my sister's hand.

"You'd think they'd have one comfortable chair in this place. I swear my butt feels like wood every time I leave here."

I turn her wedding band around and around.

Santiago took the engagement ring home, but he wouldn't let them take the wedding band off.

"Did you hear your crazy husband lose his shit when they tried to take this off you?" I ask out loud. "It was sort of funny. It will be anyway when you wake up, and we can relive the moment. They almost had to call security." I wipe my eye. I don't want her to hear that I'm crying. I cry every time I come in here. I hate this. Hate seeing her like this. Hate knowing it was Abel who did it to her.

I set her hand back down and put mine to her belly when it moves. "Can you feel that?" I ask. I'm not sure if I'm asking my sister if she feels the baby or the baby if she feels my hand. "It's the freakiest thing," I tell Ivy. "I've been making videos so you can see when you wake up. I know that sounds creepy, but I thought you'd want it."

My niece or nephew—Santiago won't find out the sex of the baby without Ivy—presses a hand or foot against my sister's belly. I say hand or foot, but for all I know, it could be her butt.

"I think it's going to be a girl. And I'm making a list of names so you'll have plenty to pick from. Dad's doing better, by the way. He'll come to visit you later, too." She must know by now that he's not dead. That Santiago had devised that plan to lure Abel out. It just went so horribly wrong. But I'm not going to think about Abel now.

"Antonia and I have unpacked most of the baby

gifts, but they just keep coming. There's so much, Ivy! Everyone is excited about this baby, even Santiago's weird sister," I say, leaning in close to whisper the next part. "She wants to come home, but Santiago won't let her." I keep an eye on the door. "I overheard him tell her the house will be ready for you. That he's going to bring you home any day now." I leave out the part about not wanting any additional stress for Ivy when she gets home.

I straighten again and tuck the blankets closer around my sister. I look at her face. Then at the monitors. Nothing.

I can't help a sob when I look down at her again and try to suck it all back in.

"Sorry," I say, wiping my tear off her face. "I'm trying really hard to keep it together because someone has to, but it's getting tougher. You need to wake up, okay? You just need to push through whatever is happening inside you and wake up. There's no reason you're not awake. The doctors say so." I take a deep breath in and pull myself together. "I've never seen Santiago like he is. If he's not in here, he's in his office in the dark. He just sits there like a ghost or a vampire or something. Never comes out when anyone is around. I think he doesn't know how to be without you. We all just really need you back home."

The door opens, and I turn my face away to swipe at my eyes.

"Hey." Hazel's greeting is soft, warm, and

concerned. She's my sister, I know, and I've gotten to know her over the past few months, but it's still weird. I barely remember her being home, but she left when I was six or seven, so I guess that's normal.

"Hey," I say.

She reaches into her bag and takes out a candy bar for me. "Michael says it's your favorite."

I take the candy. "Yes! He came through. Here." I reach into my pocket and pull out a mini bag of gummy bears. "These are for him."

"You guys have a junk food swap going?"

I shrug a shoulder. "I'm his aunt. I'm allowed to spoil him."

"You're thirteen," she says, dropping the bag of gummies into her bag. She looks at Ivy and sighs deeply. "Anything?"

I shake my head. "How's Michael?" I still can't believe Abel kidnapped him and Hazel. I just don't get it.

"He'll be okay," she says but I know she's not telling me everything.

"You?" I ask.

"I'm fine," she says with a warm smile as she squeezes my hand. "Thanks for asking."

"The baby's awake," I say as we both look at the blanket move over Ivy's belly. "Let me get my phone." I dig it out of my back pocket and start to record it.

"You know that's kind of creepy right?"

"I don't care. She shouldn't miss this. I'll show her when she wakes up." When the baby settles down, I put the phone away and find Hazel watching me with that pitying look I'm getting to know. "She will wake up. You don't know her like I do, Hazel."

"Okay, Eva."

"Not *okay, Eva*. She will."

"I know she will." She squeezes my hand, and we just sit there for a while. Hazel chatters on about Michael, telling Ivy what he's up to. The nurses said it was good to do. To keep talking to her. Let her know we're here, and we miss her.

Santiago arranged things with IVI with Hazel and Michael. I don't really know what he did or what the problem was exactly, but she's living back at home now. Dad's back home, too, but Mom's moved out. It's like musical houses with us. I could have gone back too, but I chose to stay with Santiago. He needs me more than they do.

Hazel stays an hour and then gets up to go as the sun is starting to set. "I need to be home for dinner with Michael. And I'm sure Dad wants to come see you, too." She's talking to Ivy. "I'll be back tomorrow, okay?" She adjusts her blanket. "You want a ride home?" she asks me.

I shake my head. "I'll just stay until Santiago gets here. Marco will drive me home after."

"All right." She hugs me, then leans over to kiss Ivy's forehead. "See you guys tomorrow."

I watch the parking lot from Ivy's window, and like clockwork, Santiago's car pulls in as soon as the sun's gone.

"I swear he's a vampire," I whisper as I watch him walk, head bowed, to the entrance. "Most people can't have visitors overnight, but they've made an exception for him," I tell Ivy as I sit back down. "Compulsion probably. I heard vampires can do that."

"Or charm," Santiago says from the door.

"See, how'd you get up here so fast?"

He smiles, waggles his eyebrows, and hangs his hat on the hook by the door. When he looks at Ivy lying there, his expression darkens. His face gets so sad it's almost hard to look at him.

"You should stop with the hat, you know," I say, shifting my gaze away from him.

"What do you mean?"

"You don't have to hide your face."

I feel his eyes on me, but he doesn't answer. "You should get ready to go. Marco will be here soon and Antonia's getting dinner ready."

"Is he bringing the Aston Martin?"

"Of course."

"Good." I sigh. I don't really care about the car. That's just me trying to keep it light. Marco was the one who told me about my dad on the way home from the fake funeral. If Ivy had come home with me, then she'd know too, and she wouldn't be in this mess. "The baby's really active today," I say before I can cry in front of him. I should have made her come home with me. I should have forced her.

"Did you film it?"

"Of course."

"Good. She'll want to see that."

I look over at him. "I'll help you, you know."

"Help me?"

"If the baby comes and she's still sleeping."

His jaw tightens, and his eyes are red, but they're always red these days. "She'll wake up." He turns to her. "She has to."

There's a knock on the door, and Marco peers into the room. He glances at Ivy, then at Santiago. They have a wordless exchange. I know he's asking if there's any change, and Santiago is telling him no. Then Marco turns to me.

"You ready, kid? You've got school tomorrow."

"Yeah, yeah." I get up and lean in to hug Ivy. "Please wake up," I tell her, holding on to her just a moment longer until I'm sure I won't look like I'm about to lose it before I straighten up.

Santiago is watching me when I do, and I know he knows. But he doesn't say anything. Instead, he pulls me in for a hug, which is weird because he's not a hugger. He barely lets anyone touch him, but here he is, hugging me, smashing my face into his belly, and I'm going to lose it again if he doesn't let me go soon. He's going to squeeze the tears out, and no one needs that right now.

"Give me room to breathe already. Geez." I pull away, quickly wipe the back of my hand across my face and turn to grab my backpack and the candy Michael sent my way. I'm about to slip out the door, but Santiago grabs my arm and bends a little so he's at eye level with me.

"Your sister is strong. And she's stubborn. She's going to wake up. Understand?"

Biting my quivering lip, I nod, but I can't really hold back the tears anymore. He pulls me into his arms again, and by the time he lets me go, his shirt is soaked where my face was, and I just keep my head down as I walk out with Marco.

35

SANTIAGO

Time passes. Seconds, minutes, hours. Somehow, we fall into a familiar routine. We rotate visits, and Ivy is never alone. I go home to shower and perform the duties that are expected of me, and then I come back here to this lifeless, sterile room where my wife is trapped in a perpetual sleep.

The days blur together, inevitably turning into months. Three months, to be exact. Her external injuries have healed, but the invisible wounds have not. There are still no answers to her condition, but with every passing day, the bleakness of the situation can't be evaded.

We've tried everything. Hypnotherapists. Experimental sleep medications. Natural doctors. Doctors from the largest academic medical clinics in the nation. Even a few specialists from Europe and the

UK. Psychologists. Integrative specialists. Neuropsychiatrists.

I've spoken to physicians around the world and consulted with neuroscientists. I've even had conversations with other patients who woke from comas of unknown origin. Cases where patients who had recently experienced trauma could not be roused after minor surgeries. But one thing differentiates those cases from Ivy's. Hers is what they call persistent.

It's been too long, and they are pushing me to move her to a long-term facility after the baby is born. They are already speaking as if it's inevitable that she won't be awake when that day comes. But she has to. *She has to.*

For the first time in over two decades, I fell to my knees and prayed this morning. To whatever God or deity actually exists. Whatever metaphysical force that seems to be controlling the puppet strings from a place I can't touch.

I think, perhaps, this is my punishment. For losing my way. For falling away from the virtues the nuns tried so hard to instill in me. I allowed my rage to fester until it was a malignant disease, metastasizing to every cell, blackening my soul.

I prayed for forgiveness. I promised to be a better man. To do right by her, if I could only have the chance. Just one more chance. Because I know now that nothing else matters. Not if she isn't here. I tell her so every day, and still, she will not come back to me.

Admittedly, my mood swings on a pendulum from profound sorrow and grief to hurt and anger. How could she leave me here alone? Why won't she stop punishing me?

"Please." I bow my head, kissing the back of her hand as I cling to it. "Please forgive me, Ivy."

The monitor beside the bed changes rhythm, beating faster. I snap my eyes up, glancing at her heart rate and then back to her face.

"Ivy?"

Her arm goes rigid in my grasp, and a nurse enters the room, her brows furrowed as she glances at the monitor.

"What's going on?" I ask her.

She ignores me and starts checking Ivy's vitals. Her temperature, blood pressure, and continually increasing heart rate.

"Tell me what's happening," I demand.

"She could be going into labor, Mr. De La Rosa. I need you to step outside—"

The on-call doctor appears, followed by several additional nurses. Within seconds, they have Ivy's bed surrounded, and a hospital guard enters, trying to usher me out of the room.

"It's too early," I protest. "It hasn't been nine months."

"Sir, I need you to step outside."

I shrug off the guard, glancing back at Ivy, and I could almost swear I see her face pinch in pain. But she doesn't move.

"What's going to happen to her?" I plead.

I watch on helplessly as the doctor lifts the bedding and examines between Ivy's legs. He rattles off some information I don't understand and then turns to me.

"Mr. De La Rosa, she's in good hands. We'll need to give her some medication to increase contractions. If they are strong enough, we won't need to take her to surgery. But right now, you can't be in here. It's not safe for her or the baby. Do you understand?"

"Santiago?" Marco's voice comes from behind me, his hand settling over my shoulder. "Come outside with me. Let them take care of Ivy."

I don't want to leave her because I'm fucking terrified I might not get her back. The helpless uncertainty hanging over me makes me desperate.

"Please take care of her." I reach out and grab the nurse by the arms. "Please don't let anything happen to her."

She swallows, sadness reflected in her eyes. "I will treat her as if she were my own sister, Mr. De La Rosa. We'll do everything we can."

With that last assurance and a fleeting glance at my wife, I'm dragged out of the room by Marco and directed by the hospital guard to go to the waiting room. With nothing else to do, I hang my head and silently plead for a miracle.

"Mr. De La Rosa?" I whip my hazy eyes up to the nurse standing at the entrance of the waiting room.

She's smiling reassuringly as she draws closer. "Are you ready to meet your daughter?"

"Daughter?" I stagger to my feet, eyes darting behind her, searching for any sign of the baby. "Where is she?"

"We have her in the NICU right now as a precautionary measure, but you can see her now," she tells me. "Follow me, and I'll show you."

"What about Ivy?" I ask. "Why aren't they together? Is she okay?"

"I know this is very difficult." The nurse settles her hand on my arm in a gesture of comfort. "But your wife's vitals are stable. The doctor is finishing up with her now. We'll continue to observe her, but the delivery went very well. Right now, I think the best thing you can do for your family is be there for your daughter. She's doing very well, considering the circumstances, and we just want to monitor her to ensure she remains healthy and stable. She is the daughter of a Sovereign Son, after all, and we want to ensure she has the best possible care."

I glance at Marco, and he nods in silent agreement. "I'll stay right here, boss. I'll keep an eye on your wife when they let me back in."

"Thank you, Marco."

Hesitantly, I follow the nurse down the hall and into the elevator and through another maze before we reach the NICU. She uses a badge to enter the doors and then walks to the room where the nameplate outside reads "baby De La Rosa."

A choking sensation lingers in my throat as we enter the room, and I see the tiny baby for the first time. She's tucked inside a clear plastic encasement with holes on the side.

"Why is she in there?" I ask. "Is something wrong?"

"It's an incubator," she tells me. "Baby is doing okay, but she's early, so we want to monitor her closely. Keep her temperature stabilized, her oxygen, heart rate. This is how we keep premature babies safe."

"But she's okay?" I ask again, my eyes moving to the small human I'm too nervous to approach.

"Her vitals are good," the nurse explains. "The doctor has given her a full exam to test her reflexes and muscle tone, and everything is as expected. She'll need to spend time in the incubator, but for now, would you like to hold her for a few minutes?"

"Hold her?" I repeat. "Is that... safe?"

"It's okay." The nurse smiles. "She's stable right

now, and skin-to-skin contact is very important for preemies. It encourages bonding, and it can even help regulate her breathing, heart rate, and blood sugar. If we can do skin-to-skin contact every day, we aim for that because it usually means the babies will get to go home sooner."

"So, what am I supposed to do?" I ask helplessly.

She glances at my shirt as if it should be obvious. "Usually, skin-to-skin is during breastfeeding, but in this case, you'll be bottle feeding, so—"

"I need to take off my shirt?"

An image of me holding my daughter for the first time nestled against the scars on my chest makes me ill. She will hate me from the start.

"It's okay to be nervous," the nurse assures me. "But just think of it as a way to help your baby. You'll give her all those feel-good chemicals, help her sleep better, and give her the best possible start."

Not seeing an alternative, I reach for the hem of my shirt and peek up at the nurse. "You may not want to look at this."

"Trust me," she says. "I've seen it all. But you just get comfortable in that seat, and I'll get baby out for you."

I do as she says, awkwardly folding up my shirt and setting it onto the table beside me when I sit down. My hands feel hot, and my chest is tight when she removes my daughter from the case, adjusting the wires on her body and removing her hat before she brings her to me.

Extending her arms, the nurse leans down toward me and waits for me to take her.

Terror claws at me as my eyes move over the tiny face in disbelief. *I have a daughter.* And I'm alone, and I have no fucking idea what to do with her.

"Here." Sensing my shock, the nurse settles the baby next to my chest, helping me cradle her in my arms before she covers us with a small blanket.

She's warm, and soft, and I'm expecting the screaming to start right away, but it doesn't. One second passes, then two, and I draw in a quiet breath, settling into the position as the cloudy blue eyes open briefly and then shut again.

And finally, I get a good look at her. The small swirl of dark hair on her head. Pink cheeks. The tiniest nose I've ever seen and even smaller fingers. She's the most beautiful baby in the world. I'm certain of it.

Emotion wells up in my chest, and there's nowhere for it to go. Already, I'm horrified that I might fail this tiny human who depends on me. There's nobody else to do this for me. I have to do it on my own, without Ivy, until she wakes up. Until she comes back to us.

And I've never been so scared in my life.

36

SANTIAGO

"Have you thought of a name for her yet?" Katie asks.

I look up at the nurse watching me from the doorway. She's been here every step of the way, keeping me updated on Ivy and helping me process each milestone of my daughter's transition from the womb to the incubator to the real world.

My daughter's tiny fingers curl inside mine as I cradle her against my bare chest. Something I've admittedly come to look forward to every day. They tell me she's doing well, and every day seems to be a new learning curve. So far, I've accomplished feeding her and changing her diapers, though I still feel as if I'm fumbling through the process every time.

She hasn't been allowed to meet any of the other family just yet, but they've been able to see her through the window of a special visiting room, offering smiles and waves with tears in their eyes.

Ivy is still in the ICU, still asleep. Unchanging, even as my world is changing every second. She should be here for this. She should be holding our baby's hand too. Stroking her hair and laughing at how terribly I fail when I try to bottle-feed her, or as I'm trying to ascertain which part of the diaper is back and which is front.

It's all so overwhelming and painful. And it's all I can do to focus on each moment rather than the large picture in front of me. The one where the dark reality is, I might not ever get to see Ivy with our baby.

"I don't want to pick a name until her mother wakes up," I confess quietly.

Katie offers me a sad smile, leaning against the doorframe. "I get it. But at some point, that little beauty will need a name. Maybe you can think of something you would both like. Her mother's middle name, perhaps."

"Perhaps." I shrug noncommittally.

Agreeing means admitting that Ivy won't ever be able to help me choose, and I don't think I can ever accept that.

Katie slips away quietly, leaving me alone with my daughter. Her eyes are less cloudy now, and when she looks up at me, there is a fascination in her features as her gaze moves over my face. I was so convinced she would be terrified, but all I see is wonder. I understand that because I feel it, too, whenever I look at her.

So small. So fragile. The tiniest fingers and toes. Skin softer than I even knew was possible. It seems like everything is a threat to her, and I am already dreading how I will manage to protect her from the overwhelming dangers of this world.

"You are beautiful," I whisper to her. "Just like your mother. I think you will meet her one day soon. Let us hope."

Her eyes grow sleepy, and she scrunches up her face, a tiny smile forming as she starts to drift off. Katie told me newborns do that sometimes when they have gas or when they are cozy. I suppose right now, she must be cozy.

It is the smallest sign of relief in this landscape of uncertainty.

"We're going to miss you, little beauty." Katie strokes the baby's cheek, and I nod at her.

I appreciate everything the staff has done for us. If I'm being honest, I would not have survived these last few weeks without them guiding me every step of the way. But now we are being discharged, and I am free to take my daughter home.

A new, alarming journey.

"Thank you, Katie."

She hands me the diaper bag and holds the door open, where Marco is already waiting for me in the hall.

"Everyone is waiting to meet her," he informs me. "The staff cordoned off a section of the waiting room on the fifth floor for the occasion."

I grimace, and Marco shrugs. At times like these, being at a Society hospital is not necessarily a good thing. They can be too accommodating when they think it will please their patients.

I follow Marco down the hall, and we step into the elevator together. He glances down at the baby and then back at me. "You look like a natural."

"None of this came naturally," I answer dryly.

My brow is sweating, and I'm clammy, already considering a hundred different things that could go wrong. The elevator getting stuck. The cables snapping, plummeting us to the ground floor. Trapping us in here without formula for the baby. A gas bubble getting caught in her belly that I can't dislodge. Vomit. Poop. Pee. Those are only just the beginning.

There will be colds and shots at the doctor's office. And boys. Oh God, she's going to date someone eventually. And I'll have to murder him, and then she's going to hate me too.

I glance at Marco with panic in my eyes. "I don't know if I can do this."

"You can." He reaches out, squeezing my arm. "You will just take it one day at a time. Don't think about anything else. Just this minute. Then the next. Don't even think about tomorrow yet. We'll worry about that when it comes."

I release a shaky breath and nod. Just this minute. I can do that.

The elevator opens, and I step out, concentrating on putting one foot in front of the other. A group of smiling, eager faces is waiting for us when we turn the corner into the waiting room. Eva is the first to approach, so excited she can barely contain herself.

"Oh my god," she whispers, eyes huge. "She's so beautiful."

"I know." I nod approvingly.

Antonia squeezes in beside her, followed by Eli, Hazel, and Colette, and Jackson too. They all make complimentary observations, gushing over my daughter while she watches them curiously.

"Can I hold my granddaughter?" Eli asks.

I meet his gaze, and something softens in me. When I consider it, he seems surprised, and I think I am too. I'm surprised how relieved I am to have him here at this moment.

I move to hand the baby over, and panic ensues again as I withdraw her.

"Wait." I glance up at all of them. "Maybe... I should just hold her for now. There are germs, and the nurses said she can get sick easily."

Marco chuckles under his breath, and they all join in with him. I'm not ready to let her go just yet, but they all seem to understand, settling on observing from nearby for now.

The festivities continue for the next thirty minutes while they offer gifts and congratulations, but as happy as they all are, they can't hide the worry in their eyes too. There's a dark cloud hanging over the occasion, and the truth is, there's only one place I want to be.

When I finally make my escape, Marco takes all the gifts down to the car while I head back down the familiar hall, stopping outside my wife's room.

I stroke my daughter's face, heaviness settling into my soul. "Let's go see your mother, baby girl."

Ivy's room has remained unchanged during the course of my brief visits these past few weeks. The only difference is that beneath the hospital bedding, the protruding belly has retreated. Her small frame takes up little space, and I never realized how fragile she was until I saw her this way.

I remember my time in the hospital, between surgeries and rehabilitation and recovery. My feet would touch the end of the bed, even with my head at the top of the mattress. Ivy's feet don't even come close to the edge.

She is delicate in a way I've never noticed before. The human fragility I fully intended to exploit when I married her now frightens me more than anything.

I love her.

I love her so fucking much I can't stand to see her like this any longer. And as I linger at her bedside, holding our daughter, I consider the darkest possibilities. The truth I can no longer deny.

I want to bring her home, but it's not even an option. Not with the level of care and monitoring she needs. Too many things could go wrong. But leaving her here feels unnatural. She doesn't belong in this place. She should be with our daughter and me, wherever we are.

They keep mentioning the long-term care facility. A place where she will undoubtedly have everything she needs, should something go wrong. But how could I ever allow her to be in a place like that?

It isn't fair for her to be trapped in this state. I know that, but what alternative is there? It's not as simple as making a decision of life or death. She can still breathe on her own. They feed her, and sustain her, and monitor her. Her brain is alive. Her organs function. But there is some invisible barrier we can't seem to breach, no matter what we try.

Every day, I live with the fear that she will slip away from me. But I also dread the long-term consequences if she doesn't. What will become of her? Will she lay like this for the rest of our lives? Will she still be trapped in this bed when I take my last breath?

And what about our daughter? All the milestones Ivy will miss. Her first words. Her first steps. Her school years, and then, inevitably, her wedding.

I close my eyes and mourn all over again until the baby starts to fuss. Quietly, I rock her in my arms until she calms, marveling over the fact that she does this for me. That I have the ability to calm anyone.

"There's someone here I'd like you to meet," I whisper to Ivy as I lean down and lower our daughter to her chest, holding her there.

She squirms against her mother, her tiny body settling in as her eyes grow heavy. After a few moments, she falls asleep that way, and I continue to hold her there, long after my arms have gone numb and my back begins to cramp.

I can't say exactly why, but this moment feels important. Like I need it to go on for as long as it possibly can.

"That's our daughter," I tell her in a hushed voice. "Can you feel her, Ivy? Can you come back for us now?"

My eyes move over her face, my voice breaking as I go on, each declaration more desperate than the last.

"I'll do it all. I'll feed her. Change her diapers. Get up with her in the middle of the night. You won't have to do a thing if you don't want to. You can keep resting, just as long as you're here with us."

"Mr. De La Rosa." A soft knock on the door interrupts us, and I look up to see one of the nursing assistants standing there.

"I'm so sorry," she says, gesturing to the familiar cart in front of her. "It's bath time."

"Right." I offer her a tight nod and gently remove my daughter from Ivy's chest, cradling her in my tired arms.

"I know you usually offer," the nursing assistant says as she wheels in the cart with the plastic basin. "But you've got your hands full now."

I frown as I acknowledge her observation. Since Ivy has been here, I felt like it was my job to take care of her in this way. The only way I still could. But now, I can't.

"It's okay," the assistant assures me. "I'm sure she's just happy to have your company."

I blink up at her, replying without giving it enough thought. "Do you believe she's still in there?"

She freezes, her features morphing to panic before she carefully resumes her clinical smile.

"Well, I don't think any of us really knows for certain." She glances over her shoulder, eyeing the door, and then lowers her voice to a whisper. "But between you and me, how is she still doing all of this? Breathing, functioning, delivering a baby? How could she perform all these miracles if she wasn't in there?"

Her words bring me a long-overdue sense of relief from an unlikely ally. Everyone else has been very careful with their words, cautious about giving me too much hope while trying to draw me closer to accepting what they see as reality. But this woman just confirmed it's not as crazy as it might seem to think otherwise.

"Thank you." I glance at her name tag, which I never bothered to check until now. "Madison."

She smiles and gets to work, lifting the blankets and slowly washing my wife's legs and towel drying them before moving onto her upper extremities. She hums while she works, massaging Ivy's muscles a little, and I think about how much I owe these staff members. It's something that can't be quantified. A debt of goodwill. And at that moment, I make a silent promise to myself. I will find out who Madison, Katie, and all the other nurses are and what they need. Student loans paid. Houses. Cars. Whatever it may be, I will provide that for them because they deserve nothing less for the dedication they have shown my wife.

"Hey, look at that." Madison smiles, pointing at Ivy's arm. "She has goose bumps."

"She does?" I perk up, leaning over to see it.

Madison nods, reaching to lift Ivy's wrist, and then her eyes widen in shock. "Oh my God."

"What?" I move around to that side of the bed. "What is it?"

"She twitched. I swear... I felt her wrist move."

A flicker of hope alights in me as we stand there side by side, staring down at Ivy's arm. It feels like a dream. And the longer we watch with no activity, the more I'm questioning if Madison is insane like me. Seeing things that aren't there.

"You try." She releases Ivy's arm and gestures for me.

Shifting the baby slightly, I free my right arm and reach for Ivy's hand. But it doesn't twitch. It does something else entirely. Her fingers curl so slightly, I'm certain I must be imagining it.

"Is that just a reflex?" I whip my gaze back to Madison.

She looks nervous but giddy at the same time. "I think we better get the doctor in here."

37

IVY

I'm cold. My fingers close around something soft, but it's gone a moment later. A baby cries out then it's quiet again. Dark again. I don't know for how long until I feel something pinch at my arm.

"What the hell are you doing?" a voice booms as I pull my arm away as much as I am able.

It's too loud all of a sudden. Too bright when I manage to partially open one eye, so I close it, and I'm drifting off when I hear him again. Hear the baby cry again.

"Ivy?"

I want to sleep, but something inside me responds to that voice. Whatever it is wants to wake up. Is fighting to.

"Ivy, can you hear me?" It's another man's voice

this time. It's quieter and calmer than the first one. "Can you open your eyes for me?"

I try. I manage to open one, but again, it's too bright.

"Turn out the overhead light," the first man commands, and it's gone, the light softer now. Natural so I can rest.

"Sir, we need you to step out of the room."

"Like hell I will!"

I hear a scuffle and then the baby again. "I'll take her outside," a woman says. "I'll just be right out here."

"Ivy. Can you hear me?" It's the other man, the calmer one, and this time, he doesn't ask me to open my eyes but pulls one lid up and shines a bright light into my pupil. When I try to pull away, someone laughs. It's the loud man. And it's a strange laugh. Relieved. Happy and sad at the same time.

"Ivy, angel. Ivy. I'm here."

"Sir, please."

A warm hand takes mine. I squeeze it. I try to at least because I don't want him to let go.

"There. She did it again. I felt it. I swear I felt it!"

"Mr. De La Rosa, if you can come with me, we can give the doctors room to do their work."

Mr. De La Rosa.

Santiago.

"Your wife is really in the best possible hands.

But you need to give them some space to do their work."

Someone pinches me again, and when I make a sound of protest, they laugh. Why are they laughing?

"There she is. Ivy, my name is Dr. Singh. Do you think you can open your eyes for me?"

I want to. Where is Santiago? I don't hear him anymore.

"You're upsetting her! Whatever you're doing is fucking upsetting her!"

There he is, and he has my hand again.

"Ivy, it's me, angel. Santiago. Your Santi."

Santi.

He didn't let me call him that. Not at first anyway.

I remember Mercedes then. That's her nickname for him. And I remember how mean she is, at least toward me.

The beeping of machines becomes more hurried, and Santiago speaks. "It's all right, Ivy. No need to get upset. If you can't open your eyes right now, it's okay. Shh. Just relax. You can open them later."

I hear a chair scrape across the floor, and I want to squeeze his hand. Tell him not to let go. And I remember he came for me. He was racing to get to me.

But where was I?

Warm fingers brush my forehead. He's pushing my hair back. I like when he does that. And then he's close, and I can feel him, feel his warmth. Smell his scent. Familiar. I breathe it in.

I make a sound, but it's hard to move. Everything feels heavy, but I hear a choked sound come from him as he lays his cheek against mine. I want to hug him. I want to hold on to him.

And when he pulls back, I try harder to open my eyes. I force all my energy into just opening my eyes, and I see him. I see his face close to mine, inches from mine. I see his hazel eyes. I see tears inside them, and then his hand is on my face cupping my cheek, and he's so beautiful. Even sad like this, I love him so much. It's all I can think about. All I can feel.

But then I hear the baby's cry again. It's coming from farther away, and I see Santiago's mouth move into a smile when he hears it, and he shifts his gaze in the direction of the sound. I follow it too, and I see figures in white coats, maybe six of them standing around me, looking down at me, their faces blurring as I struggle to keep my eyes open. I look down the length of my bed to the door but stop, confused, and I close my eyes and force all of my energy to move my hand over my belly.

It's flat.

They all go into a panic when the beeping becomes frantic, and Santiago's hand is gone. He's gone. And my baby's gone. And all I feel is the trickle of a tear slide down along my temple before I sleep again.

38

IVY

This is a different kind of sleep than it's been. Not so heavy. And I hear voices as I start to wake up, wondering again where I am when my eyes open, and a stranger comes into blurry focus.

"Good morning, Ivy," he says. "It's me, Dr. Singh. It's good to see you again."

I turn my head when I see movement in my periphery. It's not as heavy as it was a little while ago. Santiago comes into view, and he looks like he hasn't slept in days. His hair is standing at all angles, and his eyes look so red and tired.

But then he smiles, and the thing he's holding moves and makes a sound.

My hand creeps toward my stomach.

"This is our baby, Ivy. Can you see her?" Santiago says.

I can't, though. All I see is a bundle of blankets. Our baby. *Her.*

"Here. Here she is."

And there she is. Her little weight on me as Santiago holds her against my chest, her tiny cheek against me. Her breath warm and her lips soft when she nuzzles against my neck her mouth searching for something to latch onto.

I want to move. I want to hold her. Bring her to my breast. But it's too hard, and he must sense it because he takes my arm and sets my hand over my baby's bundled form. I feel the tears come as I turn to look at her little face, at her eyes that open just for a moment, that barely focus on me before they close again. She is having as hard a time as I am keeping them open.

"It's okay. Go to sleep. We'll both be here when you wake up. You just keep waking up. Do you understand me? You just keep waking up."

39

IVY

It's easier to open my eyes the next time. It's dark in the room but for a night-light plugged into the wall and the ghostly green of the machines. This time, it's just Santiago and me. No doctors. And he's asleep.

I watch him. He must have drifted off because he's seated in a chair with his head resting on a pillow lodged between the chair and the wall. It can't be comfortable. Beyond him, I see a cot. It's empty. He must have brought the pillow over to keep an eye on me.

I manage to lift my arm and reach toward him. I look at my hand as I bring my fingers to his cheek. My fingernails are cut short and the wedding band looks like it's too big on me. My engagement ring is gone. I want to brush his hair back, but it's harder than it looks to be precise so I let my hand fall onto his thigh, and he startles awake.

After a moment of confusion and worry, his eyes focus on mine, and his expression changes to a warm smile spreading across his face.

"Ivy."

"Baby," I croak, my voice sounding broken and foreign.

"Our little girl is right there," he says, pointing at a small bassinette I can just make out the outline of in the dark corner. "She's okay. Healthy and beautiful and perfect."

I try to nod but only manage a small one. I wonder if he sees it.

"How long?"

As I ask the question, I start to remember. We were at my father's funeral. But that's not possible. I heard him. I swear I heard him. Was I dreaming?

"A few months."

Months?

"Three, to be exact," he says as if he hears my confusion.

Three months? I've lost three months?

I see the nervous girl who handed me Abel's letter. I see his words again, his threats. See Hazel and Michael's terrified faces in the back of that car. And then out in the parking lot. Abel trying to get me into the car. Santiago speeding toward us. And Abel driving toward me...

"Shh." Santiago coaxes when the beeping sound picks up as my anxiety does. "You're safe. Our baby is safe. Your father and Eva are safe. Hazel and Michael and everyone you care about are safe."

He touches my cheek, and I put my hand over his as he wipes a tear away with his thumb and then gets up, moves the blankets, and very carefully nudges me over a little, just enough that he can lie on the bed beside me. This is better, I think. Much better. Now we're face-to-face on the same pillow, and he's warm and solid. His arm is around me, and I can feel his heartbeat under my hand before I move it to touch his face, to trace the lines of his mouth, the ink of his tattoo.

"I am sorry," he says after a very long time. He brings his mouth to my forehead and kisses it, one big hand never leaving my cheek. "I am sorry for everything that's happened to you because of me."

"No." It's another croak. My throat almost hurts with the effort.

"Shh. Just rest."

Again, I try to nod. Again, I'm not sure I succeed.

"I love you, Ivy. I know that now. I've known it on some level for a while, I think. Or at least I've felt it even if I couldn't or wouldn't put words to it. I love you."

I smile, open my mouth to tell him I love him, too, but he puts a finger to my lips when I try but struggle to form the words.

"I know, angel. Shh. You deserve so much better than me, but you're stuck with me because I can't be without you again. I can't live without you, Ivy. I won't." His voice breaks. He kisses my mouth, and I close my eyes. It's a chaste kiss. Lips touching lips. And my heart flutters at the sensation. At this thing I have missed. Santiago kissing me. Santiago holding me. I missed it. Even as I have lain here these months—*months*—in this strange sleep, I have missed him.

"And I will do right by you. I will make you happy. I will be worthy of you. Of your love. I swear it. I swear it on my life, my angel."

40

IVY

Several weeks pass before I am released from the hospital, and Santiago helps settle me in the wheelchair I must be rolled out in before setting our little bundle in my arms.

Elena De La Rosa. I chose it because it means bright, shining light. That's what she is for me. For us.

Santiago has yet to decide on her middle name, but she's gone without a first name for the first weeks of her life, so this is a start. He apparently refused to choose a name without me.

He closes one hand over my shoulder and squeezes as he leans close to kiss my cheek. "Are you sure she's not too heavy?"

"I'm sure," I tell him. "She barely weighs nine pounds."

"All right. If she gets too heavy—"

"I know. I'll tell you."

He nods, runs a knuckle over Elena's cheek as she smiles up at us before closing her eyes and nuzzling into her blanket.

I've been in a coma for three months. Elena somehow survived the accident. No. Not accident. It makes me sick to think of it. Of Abel, my own brother, willing to run me down to wound Santiago.

I wipe my eye, and Santiago squeezes my shoulder again.

In those months, Elena grew strong inside me for as long as she could or as long as my body could manage it. She was early but not so early that she couldn't survive.

Eva showed me all the videos she'd made of Elena moving in my belly while I lay still. It's eerie to see it, see myself like that, see my stomach move with this human being inside it. And I have decided in the weeks that I've been back that Eva's a lot like my husband. Obsessive and a little crazy in the best way.

She was upset I didn't choose her first choice of name, which was—surprise—Evangeline. But she'd done some research choosing names with care and swore she knew it would be a girl all along.

My father is home now. He's healthy and more fit than I've seen him in a long time, actually. He's still working with his physical therapist and will for a while and has modified his diet even though we know his unhealthy habits weren't what put him in a hospital. But it's better that he takes care of himself. I feel that Hazel moving back into the house with Michael is the reason for a lot of this. She's pretty strict when it comes to Michael, and she won't let my dad eat anything she wouldn't let her son eat. My dad complained about it, but I could see he was happy to have her home. Happy to have them both home.

My mother is gone, and a divorce is in the works. I hope she'll find happiness, too. I know she didn't visit me in the hospital. Not once. Eva told me that, but I don't think she meant to. I would have known anyway because my memories have returned, and I recall hearing Eva in my room talking to me or the others who kept watch over me. I recall many of their visits even though they feel like wisps of dreams. Not once did I hear my mother's voice.

The doctors never did solidify what they think happened to me. Why I remained unconscious and unresponsive for so long. There is a theory that it was my body's reaction to the physical impact of the accident after such stressful months. A sort of PTSD. It scares me sometimes to think of it. To think it could happen again even though the rational part of me knows I'm safe. I haven't told Santiago this. He already keeps vigil over me 24/7, and I don't need him worrying any more than he already is.

I look down at Elena's face as she stirs in her

sleep when we get outside. It's a chilly day, so I tuck her blankets closer.

I am sad about having missed her final months in my belly. Sad that she may have felt alone with me so unresponsive to her movements. At least I got to feel her once before everything.

I'm also sad I can't breastfeed her. My milk never did come in. But Santiago reassures me that I will breastfeed all of our other children and that Elena will be fine. She is healthy and strong.

Looking at the photos the nurses managed to snap of him feeding her those first few days makes me giggle. He looks so uncomfortable, shoulders high with stress as he cradles this tiny thing against his bare chest while feeding her.

I reach up and squeeze his hand at the memory of those pictures.

When we get to the car, Marco is waiting with the door open. I try to get up on my own, but Santiago is beside me in an instant. Marco takes Elena as Santiago guides me into the car before taking Elena and strapping her into her car seat between us in the back seat.

Eva is here too. She's already seated in the passenger seat typing out a text to someone. She's going to stay with us even though we've stopped the legal process of taking over guardianship of her. There's no need for it now that my father is alive and well, and Abel is out of the picture.

Abel. I won't think about him yet. Not today.

Marco closes the door, and a moment later, Santiago settles on the other side of the car seat, and we're driving back to The Manor. For the first time since I married Santiago, I am happy to go home. In fact, I can't wait to get home and start our new life with our family.

41

SANTIAGO

Over the next two weeks, Ivy and I settle into a comfortable rhythm. The specialists come to the house to work with her on rehabilitation every day, and every day, we see improvements. She's walking on her own now. Eating on her own. Taking care of Elena when she can, stubbornly proving to herself and everyone else that she's capable.

I never doubted for a second that she wasn't.

I'm proud of her. I feel it every time I look at her, and I understand that's what it is because I feel the same way watching our daughter grow and change every single day. We've all come leaps and bounds from where we used to be. But there are still a few lingering points of tension that haven't been brought up.

Abel, for starters.

At first, I didn't know what to think of Eli's intervention at The Tribunal. But now that I'm a father myself, I can see it for what it is. He did it for me, and he did it for Abel. He doesn't want me to ruin what I have with Ivy. And he feels responsible for the man Abel has become. At some point, he must have realized there was no stopping him. Seeing it from a different perspective, as a father myself, I can't imagine how difficult that decision must have been for him.

He's trying. Every day, he's making efforts to be a better father. To be there for all his children, including Eva, who it looks like we'll have around for quite some time to come. But there is still the dark cloud of Abel's trial hanging over all of us. The Tribunal delayed it until their investigation was complete and pending witness availability, given the recent circumstances. But now that Ivy is out of the hospital, they are ready to proceed this week. Tomorrow, we will come to know Abel's fate.

I thought it would be the hardest thing I'd ever have to do. Giving up the satisfaction of destroying him myself. Avenging my family. But glimpsing what life was like without Ivy, I know now it is the easiest choice I will ever make. If I don't have her, I don't have anything. She and Elena are my future, and Abel's destruction is in the past. It will be difficult, but I will accept Abel's punishment handed down by The Tribunal with the knowledge that it spares my family any further turmoil. And I hope that it will resolve any lingering doubts I have about Eli, giving me the answers that I need.

The door to the nursery creaks open, and I glance up at Eva as she sneaks inside.

"What are you still doing up?" I ask her. "And what is on your face?"

She tiptoes closer, smiling down at Elena in my arms as I'm rocking her back to sleep.

"I heard the baby crying, and I couldn't sleep. I was playing around with some ideas for a Halloween costume."

"A skull face?" I arch a brow at her curiously. "Halloween is still a long way off."

"I wanted to be like you," she answers softly.

Something pulls in my chest, and I feel another piece of my ice shield shattering. She really is a little psychopath, but I think I love her. In fact, I know I do.

"Santiago?" She digs her toes into the carpet, shifting around nervously. "Are you going to send me away soon?"

"Send you away?" I frown. "Why would I do that?"

"I don't know." She shrugs a shoulder. "You have the baby now, and I just keep thinking at some point you'll probably get tired of having me around. Especially if another baby comes..."

I stop rocking, staring up at her as I try to determine the right words. This feels like a test. Something I might face many times as a father in the coming years. And I think about what my own father would have said. There would be no words of comfort. No assurances. His word was law, and there was no defying it.

I am not my father. And I want Eva to know that. I want Elena to know it. I want them to feel something I never did.

Love.

But I'm still fuzzy on the rules. How to express it. How to receive it. In many ways, I'm like a toddler, fumbling through this new existence without a guidebook. But I try, and I think that is all I can do.

"I think I can safely say for your sister and myself, we don't ever want you to leave, Eva."

She offers a small smile. "Really?"

"But someday you will."

Her smile falls, and I rush to get the words out.

"Someday, you will probably go to college and then get married," I tell her. "But only to someone I approve of. If he's an asshole, it's not happening."

She giggles at the expression on my face, which I can only imagine is murderous, and then nods with tears in her eyes.

"You'll always have a home with us," I add quietly. "Always."

She leans in and hugs me carefully, and then kisses Elena on the cheek.

"Now you better get to bed," I say. "Or your sister's going to move your bedtime up."

"Alright, I know." She rolls her eyes and then heads for the door, pausing to look over her shoulder. "Good night, Santiago. Love you."

She leaves before I can say anything, but my quiet words follow her down the hall.

"Love you too."

"Is Elena okay?" Ivy murmurs sleepily as I ease myself back into bed.

"Yes, she's asleep now," I assure her. "I'm sorry. I didn't mean to wake you."

"It's okay." She blinks up at me with soft eyes, illuminated by the bedside lamp.

Upon our return, I had Marco assist Antonia in installing lights in most of the rooms again. The lighting is softer, and there are still parts of The Manor kept dark—for the moments I feel I need to escape again—but I think I am learning to live in the light now.

"Thank you for taking care of her." Ivy reaches up to stroke my stubbled jaw as I pull her against me. "I don't mean to sleep through the night, but sometimes, I'm so tired I don't even hear the monitor."

"Don't apologize." I kiss her forehead. "Your body is still recovering. You've been through so much with the car accident, the coma, and giving birth to our daughter. I still can't believe it sometimes. You created her inside you."

"I had some help." She laughs. "I think I remember vividly how determined you were."

My face pinches, and I close my eyes, and Ivy's softness does not falter as she brushes her fingers over my scars.

"Hey, don't," she whispers. "Don't go back there."

"I'm trying not to."

"Our past is what made us strong. With everything we've overcome, we can conquer anything now."

She sounds so certain, and when I open my eyes to meet hers, I can see she means it.

"I hope you'll still feel that way tomorrow."

She nods in understanding, and then her other hand moves beneath the covers, stroking the bulge in my briefs. "You know what I think would help?"

I frown and shake my head. "It's too soon. You're still recovering—"

"It's been too long," she argues, her frustration evident.

We've had this same argument for many nights now. The doctors told us four to six weeks, and I've been determined to wait the full term out even though I've been close to giving in. The truth is, I'm terrified anything too rigorous could send her back to a sleep she won't wake from.

"Santi," she pleads. "I need this from you. I need to feel you again."

Tears cling to the edges of her eyes, and it pierces me. How can I deny her when she isn't playing fair?

For a long moment, I consider all the potential risks. The consequences. And then... the benefits. My mind is torn, but my hands are not. I'm already groping her breast, unconsciously aware of it until she releases a soft sigh of approval.

"Please," she urges, legs falling apart as my other palm slides down her hip between her thighs.

My lips fall to hers, and she cradles the back of my head in her palm as she begins to devour me. I'm trying to be gentle, but every time she moans, my fingers start to move faster, harder. And then she's sliding her fingers into my briefs, wrapping them around my cock, and I can't think straight anymore.

It seems to be intentional, this distraction, and to my annoyance, it works.

She comes around my fingers with a sharp cry that I promptly swallow, and then I'm fumbling to get my briefs off, burning with the need for my release. I'm planning to finish off myself so she can rest, but Ivy has other plans.

She pulls herself free, moving down the bed, and takes my dick back from me as she peeks up at me with heavy-lidded eyes.

"Ivy—" My protest is cut short when she sucks me into her mouth, and it's all over from there.

I watch her take me, my cock gliding over her tongue and deep into her warmth. My hand comes to rest on her head as I try in vain to harness my restraint.

"It's okay," she murmurs around me. "I know how you like it. Don't hold back."

God, she's going to fucking kill me.

There's a protest on my lips, but she glares up at me. "Do it, Santiago. I'm not made of china, and I want you to stop treating me as if I am. I miss this. I need it. So just give it to me, please."

Well, when she puts it like that...

I cup her head and slide my dick between her lips, deeper and deeper until she digs her nails into my thighs. My eyes shutter closed, and my hips move, rolling and thrusting as I fall into a familiar rhythm. Ivy moans around me, and my balls draw tight, and every muscle goes rigid as I slide in and out of her mouth, skating the knife's edge of my release and trying to draw it out. Nothing has ever felt so fucking good.

A choked growl gets caught in my throat as I start to come, trying to pull back, but she holds me there, swallowing my release as it spills into her mouth.

When I drag my softening cock from her lips, part of me feels ashamed, and the other depraved part of me couldn't be happier.

She smiles up at me, quite proud of herself for getting my resolve to break.

"You better be ready for the end of week six, Mr. De La Rosa," she tells me. "I won't let you out of this bed."

42

SANTIAGO

"Santi." Mercedes squeezes me tight in her grasp, and I return the gesture, patting her back awkwardly.

She glances up at me, half laughing, half crying over my attempt at a hug.

"I've missed you so much," she blurts.

"I know," I tell her. "I've missed you too."

She holds me at arm's length, examining me. "You look... different."

I shift, dragging a hand through my hair and shrugging. "A lot has changed."

She nods stiffly. An acknowledgment, I think. I had hoped in time, she would come around to the idea of Ivy being a permanent fixture in my life, but I suspect it will take a while until she no longer sees her as a threat.

"When can I meet my niece?" she asks, eyes darting over my shoulder to where Ivy is waiting in a chair with Elena.

"I'm not sure if that's such a good idea," I answer hesitantly.

My sister's face falls, and guilt eats at me. Judge steps forward, settling his hand at her lower back. I don't miss the action, and when he notices my eyes on him, he clears his throat and removes it.

"Mercedes will behave," he assures me. "And she would very much like to meet her niece, if you'll let her."

I glance back at my wife, remembering the fallout from their last encounter. We already have enough to contend with today, and I'm not sure I want to add more stress or tension. But when Ivy meets my eyes, she smiles as if she's aware of my predicament. It's uncanny how she has come to know me so well. How she can read me like nobody else.

She rises from the chair slowly, rocking our daughter in her arms as she approaches. I meet her halfway, my palm settling against her hip as I lean down to whisper in her ear.

"We don't have to do this if you aren't ready. Not today."

"She's her aunt," Ivy answers. "And I wouldn't deny her this meeting, but if she's rude—"

"She won't be," I assure her. "I will make certain of that."

She nods, and we walk toward Mercedes, who seems to be frozen in place. Her face is a mixture of emotions as she watches the three of us together. There is sadness in her eyes, but I think it is for what she feels she has lost.

"Ivy." She forces a smile as she nods at my wife. "I'm... happy to see you are recovering well."

Ivy arches a brow. "Is that so?"

"Yes." Mercedes dips her head, a moment of softness I rarely see in her. "I know I can be a spoiled, jealous bitch sometimes, okay? I can admit, I've done some things I'm not proud of, and for that, I am sorry. But you obviously make my brother very happy, and I see that you're here to stay, so I would like to try to get to know you. If you'll let me."

Ivy seems surprised by her admission, but I'm not. Mercedes swings on a pendulum from sweet and innocent to an angry little beast. She always has. And while I can no longer excuse her episodes, I do understand them. She lashes out because she's hurting inside, and I can only hope that one day, she will not hurt anymore.

"I think that would be beneficial for all of us," Ivy tells her, shifting Elena in her arms so Mercedes can see her. "This is your niece. Elena Frances De La Rosa."

"She's... beautiful." Mercedes brings a trembling hand to her lips, tears filling her eyes. "Can I... might I hold her for a minute?"

Ivy looks at me, and I squeeze her hip lightly. "That's up to you."

She considers it for a moment, and being the woman she is, she inevitably helps Mercedes take our daughter into her arms. We all watch her as she rocks Elena back and forth, quietly gushing over her beauty. Judge seems to stiffen at the sight before him, and I narrow my eyes at him, wondering at the meaning behind his discomfort. He's looking at Mercedes like the image of her with a child is a shock to his system. For a man who never intends to marry or have his own family, it leaves me to wonder why the idea should surprise him.

"One day, you will have your own," I tell my sister, but my eyes are on Judge.

"Maybe I'll have a whole brood of them," she remarks dryly. "Ten little monsters just like me."

As I suspected, this casual remark makes Judge so tense, he can't hide his irritation. I'm beginning to wonder if there really is something there.

"What do you think of that idea, Judge?" I cock my head to the side, studying him carefully.

"Hmm?" He shifts, stuffing his hands into his pockets.

"Mercedes having ten little monsters," I answer. "Will you be their godfather?"

At this, Mercedes looks up at him, a strange undercurrent of tension in her own features. "Yes, Judge. What do you think of that?"

"She can do what she likes," he answers tightly. "Once she's proven herself capable."

Mercedes appears to be hurt by his remark, and I realize I probably shouldn't have goaded him when Ivy nudges me in the side.

"A conversation for another time," I tell him, narrowing my eyes.

He nods in understanding, and Mercedes hands the baby back to Ivy. "Thank you for letting me meet her. I suppose we should probably get going now."

"Yes," I agree. "We'll meet you outside once we've said goodbye to Elena."

Mercedes and Judge walk out the front door, and Antonia meets us in the foyer, offering us her most reassuring smile as Ivy and I glance at each other and back at our daughter. It's our first time having to leave her, and neither one of us wants to do it. But The Tribunal is no place for a baby, and especially not today.

"I will take care of her as if she were my own," Antonia promises. "She will be in good hands."

"And I'll be here to help," Eva calls out, appearing from the corridor and walking to Antonia's side to join her. "We'll be the babysitting dream team. Don't you worry."

Ivy and I both laugh and then reluctantly place Elena into Antonia's arms.

"Thank you both, in that case."

We say our goodbyes, Ivy teary-eyed, and then walk out the door.

43

IVY

I am so anxious I'm shivering with it. Santiago takes off his jacket and puts it over my shoulders. He leans in, squeezing my hand, his expression closed off, body tense. He's anxious too.

"It will be okay."

It won't. Not really. But it will be what it has to be. This part of the trial is only a formality. Abel's fate has already been decided. Today, we will learn if his death will be a peaceful one or not. And for all he's done, for all the hurt he's caused, for all he's stolen, for the lives he's had a hand in ending and the damage to our families and countless others, I don't want this for him. I don't.

The trio of Councilors are seated in their place above all of us, dark robes on, hoods up, faces in shadow. Three grim reapers. Jackson is across the courtroom in formal attire.

Santiago told me for his part, for not having come forward sooner with his knowledge of Holton and my brother's involvement and the names of the others, he paid a fine. The way he said it makes me wonder in what currency. I have a feeling it was flesh. But he has been reinstated to his post as advisor to The Tribunal.

Mercedes is sitting beside Judge in the row below ours.

My father is seated on the other side of me. He is older now. It's expected after all that's happened. The physical and emotional attacks have taken their toll. But I think it's this last piece, sending his son to the gallows because that is what he's done, which has turned his hair white.

I squeeze his hand, and he looks over at me, his eyes shiny. I want to tell him it will be okay, but it won't, so I don't. I'm saved by having to say anything when a door opens, and two men enter. Masked guards in formal dress. Between them stands my brother, and I have to put my hand over my mouth to stifle my gasp when I see him.

Santiago tenses beside me, his grip on my hand tightening just a little.

It's been months since I've seen Abel. Almost half a year. He's spent part of that time on the run, and part of it in a Tribunal cell. I wonder if Judge's accommodation for me was a luxury compared to where my brother has stayed.

The guards walk him toward the dais where he has to take the steps up one at a time. His ankles are shackled together by heavy, ancient-looking chains. They clang as he sets his hands on the bannister, the links dangling from the cuffs on his wrists connected to those at his ankles.

He is wearing a sheath similar to the one I wore when I stood in his place accused of his crime. The thought should harden me, but it doesn't. He's still my brother. And even if he weren't, he is a man facing his end. And a part of me cannot make sense of it, cannot accept it.

Santiago and I have spoken about Abel's sentence at length. He will be put to death. There is no way around it. And for Santiago, he has made a concession in allowing The Tribunal to mete out the punishment and the execution. After all, he is the man responsible for the deaths of his father and brother. For the injury to him and the subsequent emotional injury to Mercedes. Abel is the one who literally lit the flame that caused the explosion. And even as that is enough, there is what he did to Hazel and Michael and to me.

But I tell Santiago, at least on that last part, he could have done more. He could have run me over, ensuring my death and the death of our baby, but he did not. He stopped, and he drove away. I don't think I'll ever know if that was a conscious decision. I haven't been allowed to talk to him. And when I bring this up to Santiago, he counters with Abel's last-ditch effort to save himself when, while I lay in a coma, my husband was escorted to The Tribunal's halls and accused of being the mastermind behind it all. Abel had somehow fabricated evidence to prove his statements. My father had saved Santiago. He had given up his own son to save another, a man who was always a better son to him than his own blood. And I wonder if that blow was harder than any other to my brother. Or maybe he was too far past that and had reached the point of no return. Because my father once again chose Santiago over him.

That is the thing that started this, and that will be the thing to end it.

Abel looks around the room, and I see a stubbornness in the set of his jaw. An arrogance. But when his eyes meet mine, I see fear. Not repentance. Not remorse. Fear.

He, too, has grown older in these months. His hair has grayed although it's not gone completely white like our father's. He's thinner too as though his muscles have wasted away. Or maybe that is the sheath he's been made to wear.

I look at Santiago. His eyes are locked on Abel. They're hard.

Mercedes turns to put a hand on Santiago's. She's barely able to drag her gaze from my brother, but at that moment, I see how her eyes are bright, how her mouth is set in a tight line, and I see how her knuckles go white around Santiago's hand. She has asked to be present at his execution. I am not sure what the decision was, though. I'm not sure Santiago will allow it, and even if he does, will The Tribunal?

The gavel comes down, and we all turn our attention to The Councilors who draw their hoods back from their heads. The act makes me shudder.

"Abel Moreno, you have been found guilty of the murders of..." They begin to read off names. I recognize three. Santiago's father and brother and Dr. Chambers. But as the list grows, my mouth falls open, and I see quiet tears stream down my father's face.

I lose track of the count and hug Santiago's jacket closer around my shoulders. He keeps one hand on me at all times whether on my thigh or fingers intertwining with mine. I'm not sure whose are colder, mine or his.

They don't ask Abel's plea. That's been and done. He pled not guilty, but the evidence stands to prove otherwise.

But this next part of the trial is the important part. The sentencing. Because there is more than one way for a man to die.

"Have you any final words before sentencing, Abel Moreno?"

All eyes turn to my brother. I see how his hand trembles, and the chain rattles when he brings the glass of water beside him to his lips and drinks a sip before setting it back down. He clears his throat as he turns his eyes up to the trio.

Santiago explained what comes next. What choice my brother has yet to make.

Tell the full story. Name the names. Die a peaceful death.

Don't and we shall have the full story and the names and a long-drawn-out death the likes of which I am certain I don't want to know the details of.

Abel begins to speak. His voice is hoarse as if he hasn't spoken in a long time. He begins by naming names. And a part of me is relieved, audibly so in the form of a sigh.

Santiago squeezes my hand.

A peaceful death. That's better than the alternative.

And after the names, he tells his story.

He tells how he fabricated the evidence that had many good families excommunicated from The Society after the bad ones were dealt with. He tells of the ousted men who were behind it, who backed the work with more money than I can comprehend. He talks of why. Things that send my head spinning. Drugs. Sex. Human trafficking. A contract with a Mexican cartel and an Italian mafia family and illegal, inhumane activity that some members of IVI participated in that eventually led to the moment of

Abel's personal revenge. The explosion that would kill so many of the Sovereign Sons who had a hand in ousting the members would be the culmination of Abel's singular focus. His hate of Santiago De La Rosa. His hate of the man who would take his place as his father's son. His hate of the man who, in his warped mind, stood in the way of him and greatness. Whose very life impeded Abel's ability to climb within the ranks.

Santiago sits like a pillar of stone beside me as he listens. Takes it all in. Understands the mind of a monster whose hate and jealousy led to so much destruction.

By the time Abel is finished, I am exhausted.

The Councilors sit looking down on my brother with contempt. I can't blame them. They lost family and friends, too.

Councilor Hildebrand clears his throat.

"For your role in the plotting and murders of so many of our fold, you are sentenced to death by hanging."

I clasp my hand over my mouth, and there's an audible gasp. It's my father.

Hanging. I knew it, didn't I? It would be something terrible. But what execution isn't?

"The sentence will be carried out swiftly and with a compassion you do not deserve. May the Lord have mercy on your soul." He slams his gavel down and stands, and somehow, we all get to our feet as the three walk out of the room, and I turn to watch as my brother, in a moment of panic as the guards take hold of his arms, turns his face up to us. To our father or to me, I can't tell.

He opens his mouth to say something, and I realize he must have been looking at my father because when my father bows his head, a tear drops from Abel's eye, and he bows his, too. And, without a word and without protest, he is led out of the courtroom through the same door he had been brought into it.

I turn to my father and take his hand.

He looks at it, then up at me, and I see the agony on his face.

He pats my hand. "It's right, Ivy. It's what has to be."

I hug him and hold him as he tries to stop the sobs. It's a long few minutes before he shuffles past me and leaves The Tribunal building alone. I do not know if he will witness Abel's execution.

Santiago walks me down and out of the courtroom where Marco is patiently waiting, his face, too, grave.

"Marco will take you home," Santiago says, and I know he will stay to witness. I don't blame him, and I don't ask him to come with me. I had before. I had asked him not to watch, but I realize it wasn't my place to do that. My brother stole so much from him. And Santiago needs closure.

I nod. But there's one thing. I want to say goodbye. I want to tell Abel goodbye. But I know I won't be allowed to see him, so I reach into my purse and take out a folded note. I hand it to Santiago.

He looks from the note to me.

"I want him to know I forgive him," I say. Santiago must give me this. This is my closure even though I know he doesn't believe Abel deserves forgiveness.

Santiago studies me for a long minute before he squeezes his eyes shut and closes his hand over mine. "You are too good for this world," he says, and slips the paper from my fingers to his.

I reach up to cup his face. "I love you. And I understand what you need to do," I tell him before leaning up on tiptoe to kiss him. I feel his deep, shuddering inhale of breath.

It's over.

He will witness Abel's execution, and it will be finished. And I don't know if he expected to feel joy at this. I can't say what he does feel, not really, but it's not joy. He's too human to feel joy even when his enemy is about to be executed.

I come back down to flat feet and look up at him. His forehead is furrowed, eyes heavy with emotion. He nods once and turns to walk away.

44

SANTIAGO

The compound is on lockdown, the normally soft lighting in the courtyard even more dim than usual. It's late now. The traffic outside dwindling to a silence that only seems to preface the ominous occasions on a night such as this one.

The guards are at the gates. The Sovereign Sons and their respective families are all dressed in robes, the few women in attendance donning veiled hats. The men, including myself, are in masks.

Mercedes is beside me, Judge flanking her other side while we take our place in the crowd. Time passes slowly as each family walks the stairs to the gallows erected only for events such as these.

All the Society members who have been wronged by Abel have an opportunity to speak their final piece. Every family who lost someone in the explosion is in attendance, as well as some of the excommunicated members who were wronged by his false evidence.

One by one, they approach him while he stands on the wooden platform, hands tied behind his back. Some are too grief-stricken to speak. Others too quiet to hear. The slaps from mothers who have buried their sons can be heard echoing throughout the courtyard, and Abel bears them all through gritted teeth and a hardened jaw.

He was promised a peaceful execution, and for him, this is as peaceful as it will get. He will die by a broken neck or strangulation, but even that is too much for a coward like him. Someone who has inflicted so much pain cannot even consider the notion of receiving it himself. I have no doubt he was hoping for a large dose of barbiturates, a mercy only sanctioned for the particularly weak or vulnerable.

Since his fate was announced, I have swung between two extremes. One part of me knows it isn't enough, while the other logical part of me understands why it must be this way. He would have never given up the names of the others who participated in the crimes unless there was something in it for him. Now, all of the families can be at peace. Because we are tired. It is a fact I can no longer deny.

When I look upon my sister, at the grief she has shouldered since the loss of our family, I know this is what we need. Not just for Ivy's sake, but for ours too. It is time to put these dark memories behind us, and tonight, when I go to sleep, it will be with a clean conscience.

Abel Moreno will be dead, and I will never allow him to taint my thoughts again.

"It's our turn," Mercedes whispers.

I nod at her, steadying her as we step forward together. Judge releases her reluctantly, their eyes connecting briefly before I escort her up the platform to stand before the devil himself.

Mercedes trembles in my grasp, and it is all I can do to hold her up as she meets his gaze. He won't look her in the eye. He won't look either of us in the eye.

As part of his plea, he did not hesitate to tarnish any other name in an effort to save his own. He told The Tribunal that Mercedes had hired the woman who poisoned me to lure me into adultery. He also tried to pass off the poisoning as her plan in a last-ditch effort, but the evidence against him could not be ignored. As one last parting shot, he cast a shadow over my sister's name. And there will certainly be a punishment from The Tribunal for her involvement in the scheme with the courtesan, no matter how small. Even I cannot save her from facing the consequences of her actions, but I can and will plead on her behalf. I suspect it will be a light sentence, hours of service to the Society. Time spent assisting the nuns. Whatever it may be, even Abel knows it will not come close to matching his own. Yet I believe that was his intention.

He would have my sister die for his actions. He would run down his own sister in cold blood and sacrifice his own family for his pursuit of power. How many lives has he destroyed? How many families?

The others involved in the schemes have been punished accordingly. Holton has been excommunicated for his role. Chamber's surviving family members too, who were found hiding out in the South of France. They were guilty by association with Chambers himself, his shame too great to bear. But it is Abel who was the true snake amongst us.

When I look at his face, I understand what it means to have no soul. There is nothing in him to save. Nothing that will carry from this life to the next. And I believe, for him, that is the worst punishment of all.

"I want you to know something," I begin, my voice quiet and low.

He lifts his chin slightly, his eyes meeting mine for the first time. There is the hint of a smirk playing across his lips. He wants me to know I haven't won. That he will never possess any true regret for his actions. A fact that could only wound me if I hadn't realized it long ago myself.

"From this day forward, you will cease to exist," I tell him. "You will not be remembered. You will not be mourned. Nobody in this Society will ever utter your name again."

The smirk slips from his face, and in its place, a shimmer of rage appears.

"Our lives will go on. We will raise our children and prosper in your absence. Your family will be my family. Your sister, my wife. Your father, my father. The dark days you created will be long behind us. And when we gather for every holiday, there will not be an empty seat at the table. It will be as if you never existed at all. Your memory will be wiped away, forgotten. And I think, perhaps, that is the greatest gift you have given us. An apathy so pure, we can no longer harbor hatred for you. Nor sadness, nor loss. There is nothing, and there will always be nothing as far as you're concerned."

"You aren't their family," he snarls under his breath. "You never will be. And they will remember me. They will never forget—"

I unfold the note from Ivy, holding it up for him to see, and he goes rigid.

"You should know better than anyone, Abel, what it means when someone forgives. It means they have made peace with who you are. They have accepted the truth, and they have let you go. The cord is severed. It is the very reason your own father provided the evidence against you. There is nothing worth saving in you, and he understands that, perhaps better than any of us."

"No," he growls. "You are wrong. He will grieve for me. You'll see. You will all see. Nobody can ever replace me. Least of all you."

A dark smile flickers across my face as I offer one last sentiment to carry him to his final breath.

"I already have."

We turn to go, and Mercedes halts me, glaring back at Abel, steeling her strength as she stands taller. When she pulls away from me, I am not certain of her intentions, but I do not intervene as she approaches Abel. She pauses only when the tips of her heels bump against his bare feet, and for a moment, she stares at him with such unwavering strength, it reminds me of who she is at her core. She is determined to let Abel know it too. That she will rise from the ashes of her destruction. That his actions will not ruin her.

Without warning, she whips her head back and hurls spit in his face and then slowly curls her lips into a poisonous smile.

"I will do the same to your grave. Enjoy your death, you miserable bastard. You've earned it."

When she returns to me, taking note of the surprise on my face, she offers the slightest of nods, and I escort her back down the stairs, returning her to Judge who's waiting at the bottom. He seems to be hypervigilant this evening, his eyes scanning her face through the mask. Looking for signs of distress. Weakness. Something I can't quite identify.

We move through the parting crowd together, rejoining the other families at the back. A gong sounds, and the guards take their positions at the gallows. The women all turn their backs, including Mercedes, while the men watch on.

I squeeze my sister's hand as the guard at the top of the platform makes his preparations, adjusting the noose on Abel's neck and checking the ropes on his ankles and wrists. He is not offered a bag for his head. Tonight, we will all witness the gruesome sight of his writhing face until nothing is left but his bulging eyes and gaping mouth.

His transgressions are read against him one final time, the names of the dead called out before the guard steps to the side and silence settles over the crowd. There is a restlessness in these final moments as I watch him, and strangely enough, it is my face he seeks in the crowd. His eyes fall on me, face tight, with my final words undoubtedly lingering in his thoughts.

He knows them to be true.

It is the last peaceful thought I have before the guard pulls the lever, and the floor beneath Abel drops out, his body falling through, swinging wildly as he gurgles for a few brief moments. Fleeting panic is the last earthly expression he wears on the mask he called a face. And then slowly, it fades to nothing.

A blank slate.

A man who never was.

"Is it done?" Mercedes whispers over the sound of the creaking rope.

"It is done," I answer solemnly.

"Eli?" My voice is gruff, barely audible behind him.

He turns slowly from his pew in the chapel, and I'm not certain how long he's been here, alone in the darkness. Waiting for the news of his son's death. The confirmation since he was unable to bear it himself.

Again, it hits me how difficult this must have been for him, and the respect I once had for him shines brighter than it ever did.

"Santiago," he murmurs, dragging a tremulous hand over his white hair as he rises. "I suppose you have come to deliver the news."

"No." I lift my jaw, struggling to get the words out. "I came to tell you… thank you."

There's a long moment when we study each other, his eyes shining with tears, and mine with… well, I suppose much of the same.

"I was blinded by my grief," I confess. "I couldn't let it go. And I believed the worst in you. For that, I am sorry."

"You believed what any man would have in your

position," he answers solemnly. "For that, I cannot fault you."

I dip my head in acknowledgment, and silence settles between us. I'm not certain who takes the first step, but I suspect it is Eli. Slowly, we close the distance between each other, and I extend my hand, an offer of peace. Eli glances at it and shakes his head, pulling me in for a hug instead.

"We are family now," he says softly. "And I am proud to call you my son, Santiago. You are becoming the man I always knew you would."

My shoulders relax under his praise, and I swallow, choking back the emotion his words provoke in me.

"Thank you, Eli," I answer quietly. "Thank you for seeing me even when I couldn't."

45

SANTIAGO

When I walk into the nursery, I'm surprised to find Ivy there, rocking a sleeping Elena in her arms. She looks exhausted, and I regret not being here to help her with the feedings tonight.

"What are you still doing up?" I whisper.

She glances up at me, eyes soft and calm. It brings me a relief I didn't know I needed until now. I was not quite certain how she would react when I saw her again. Knowing that I was there to witness her brother's death and that, on some level, it satisfied me beyond measure and gave me the closure I needed. I also hope she understands I know how difficult this is for her, regardless of all he has done.

Our love is a love unlike any other to bear the trials we have. It is the only explanation for what we have overcome.

"I couldn't go to sleep without you." She shifts Elena in her arms, rising to her feet. "Not tonight."

I step closer, my fingers brushing over her cheek. "Thank you."

She watches me as I lean down to kiss Elena's forehead, and then she settles her into her crib. For a moment, we stand there together, both of us watching our sleeping daughter in awe. Our fingers tangle together, and when Ivy looks up at me again, she has tears in her eyes.

"She's the most beautiful baby in the world."

"I know." I grin. "We made her."

My hand comes around her waist, and I lead her from the nursery back to our room. Ivy shuts the door behind us softly, glancing at the monitor, and then brings her palms to my chest. She starts to unbutton my shirt with a gentleness only she could possess.

When her hands slide over my skin, pulling the fabric away from my body, I close my eyes, reveling in this feeling.

"Ivy," I choke out.

"I know," she whispers.

Her hands move to my trousers, unzipping the fly as she backs me into the chair in the corner. She guides me down into it and climbs onto my lap, lifting the hem of her nightgown as she does. When the silky fabric settles around her waist, she slips her hands into my briefs, pulling my hardening cock free.

I paw at her breasts through the silk and lace, and she arches into my touch, sliding against my cock. Teasing me as my lips find her nipple, shoving the straps of her nightgown down, trapping her arms at her sides.

She struggles against it in frustration until, inevitably, I drag the entire gown up over her head and toss it aside, leaving her naked in my lap.

"I'm still soft," she murmurs, her hand gliding over her belly nervously.

"I like you soft." I kiss her throat, pulling her closer, my cock trapped between us, anxious to plunge deep into her warmth. "I like you any way I can get you."

"It's been so long." She cups the back of my head, moaning as I dip lower to lick her nipples. "Please, Santi. Now. I need you now."

Reaching between us, I fumble around for my cock, teasing the head against her entrance, still trying to be gentle. Ivy takes over, grabbing my shaft and tilting her hips as she sinks down over me with an agonized sigh.

"Does it hurt?" I ask.

"No." She falls against me, her fingers digging into my shoulders. "It feels like exactly what I need. What we both need."

She rocks against me, and I tangle her hair in my

fist, dragging her face down to mine while my other palm settles against her hip. She rolls her body against me, swallowing my groans as we fall back into our natural rhythm. We kiss until we can't breathe, hands groping everywhere we can reach. Teeth clashing and tongues dancing.

I suck her throat and worship every inch of her skin I can taste, and she cradles my head in her palms, whispering the only words that will ever matter.

"I love you, Santiago. I love you so much."

"I love you too," I confess, agony making my throat hoarse. "Fuck, Ivy—"

She smiles down at me as my grip on her tightens, fingers contracting around her as my orgasm steals any rational thought. My cock spasms and empties inside her, and she keeps going, using those last few moments to steal her own pleasure, wringing it from her body with a cry before she falls against my chest.

My arms come around her, and our skin sticks together, and there in the dim light, we catch our breaths and stroke each other and forget about everything else. The darkness of the day is gone, and I know it is not unintentional.

She knew I needed this, just as I know she does. I had wondered if we might talk about it. I had dreaded that she might ask for details, but I can see now she doesn't want them. And I could not be more grateful for her allowing me this. We each have our own endings with Abel, and now, we start again. A new chapter, just as I told him.

Ivy climbs off me slowly and kneels on the floor, removing my shoes, and pulling the unzipped trousers free. I arch an eyebrow at her as she takes my hand, pulling me up from the chair.

"Come on," she whispers. "Let's go wash this day off us."

I reach down, stroking her face and lifting her into my arms, wrapping her legs around my waist. "As you wish, Mrs. De La Rosa."

EPILOGUE
IVY

3 Months Later

It is a bright winter day. I button Elena's jacket and lift her out of the car. Santiago mutters a curse behind me, and I turn to find him fumbling with the stroller as he unfolds it.

"These things. I don't understand why we need all the gadgets. I mean, a cup holder, for Christ's sake." He gives it a shake, then runs his hands over the flat bed, tucking the blankets in around the still empty mattress with the little stuffed bear she sleeps with peeking out over the top.

He's so careful with Elena, so caring. He's a better father than I even imagined, and I had imagined him doting on her. He never gave himself enough credit.

He pushes the stroller toward us, eyes on Elena. She is reaching out for him with a big smile on her lips and her mouth open. She's all gums. Her cheeks are a healthy pink, her eyes the same shade as his. I know that can still change, but I hope not.

"You want your daddy, don't you?" he asks, smiling a bright smile. He releases the stroller and takes her from me. "I hope all those people won't expect to hold her," he says to me with a glance through the windows of the French doors leading to the room where the party will be held after her baptism. It's a baptism and a belated baby shower in one. The latter was Colette's idea.

"Of course they'll want to hold her," I tell him. "She's the reason they're here. And you will smile and let them."

"I will not."

"Mm-hmm." I push the stroller as we walk toward the small chapel at IVI. I remember our first night there. The night of the marking. It's been more than a year since that day, and any feeling I used to associate with it or with this place is gone. That's partly a choice and partly time healing old wounds. And during these past three months, Santiago and I have healed. We've started a new life together. A new life with our new family.

A pianist plays soft music, and I can smell incense burning beyond the chapel door. We park the stroller as soon as we're inside and carry Elena in. I smile to find the small gathering already at the back of the church around the baptismal font. My father is standing beside Eva. He's holding Michael's hand, and Hazel is beside Michael. Jackson and Colette are here too, the two of them seemingly even closer than before. Colette is holding Ben. Antonia is talking to Marco's wife and their two children as Marco stands nervously by.

Mercedes is accompanied by Judge. I'm more and more curious as to their relationship. They stand a little removed from the gathering. She will only stay for the baptism. I know she wanted to be godmother, but Santiago told her no. We haven't discussed it yet, but we will, I'm sure, as time passes.

Jonathan Price stands as the representative of IVI, and I'm surprised but happily so. I remember meeting him. He'd been warm and kind, and Santiago is at ease around him. We smile in greeting.

The priest who married us is wearing his ceremonial robes. He clears his throat and smiles, gesturing for us to take our places.

Santiago and I take Elena's coat off, and I leave it in the front pew so she's dressed only in the long white christening gown that Antonia made her. I had no idea she could sew, but it's beautiful and a shame it will only be worn once. Although that's not entirely true. Each of our children will wear the gown at his or her baptism.

Marco straightens his tie as we approach, and Eva steps beside him. She's beaming. He stiffens even more. It's funny to see him nervous. Eva will be Elena's godmother, and Marco will be her godfather. He actually got emotional when Santiago asked him.

"Are we ready?" the priest asks as Elena excitedly extends her arms to Eva, leaning all her weight toward her.

Eva makes a face at her that has her giggling, and her giggle is infectious. Ben starts to wriggle in Colette's arms, and Michael starts to make faces at Elena to get her attention.

The priest clears his throat, and so does Eva in a mock effort to be serious. Santiago hands Elena over to her and whispers in her ear for her to behave, but I see the wink he gives her.

Elena should have been baptized months ago, but with all that was going on, well, we didn't even think about it.

Santiago takes my hand, winding his fingers with mine, and we watch as the priest performs the ceremony in perfect Latin. Elena only fusses when he dribbles water over her forehead, her chubby little arms wriggling, hands fisted, cheeks getting bright red as she prepares to let out a howl of indignation. It makes me smile. She's so much like her father, and

I have to squeeze his hand to stop him from going forward and stopping the priest.

The ceremony is over quickly, and soon, we're wrapping her up in a blanket.

Mercedes comes to congratulate us and hands Santiago a small gift. Judge then escorts her out. I know she wants to stay and some part of me wants to tell her she can. But today is about Elena. Not Mercedes. As everyone begins to make their way to the reception room, Santiago and I hold back along with the priest as Jonathan approaches, taking something out of the breast pocket of his jacket.

"It is lovely to see you, my dear," he says to me, taking my elbow and leaning in to kiss my cheek.

"I didn't realize you'd be here," I answer. "It's very nice to see you, too."

"It is a happy surprise, old man," Santiago says as they shake hands. "I hope you'll come to the house for dinner one of these nights."

"When I heard about the christening, I volunteered to represent The Society, and as far as dinner, I would be honored." Jonathan runs the back of his finger over Elena's cheek. "She is a beauty," he says. "Like her mother."

"Thank you," I say.

"I had a little to do with it," Santiago adds. "But I am glad she only seems to have inherited the color of my eyes."

"Well, there is her temper," I add.

Santiago gives me a look.

"Then you have your hands full," Jonathan says. He holds the box out toward us and opens it.

I'd almost forgotten this part. The bracelet for all little girls born within IVI.

"Thank you," Santiago says.

Jonathan nods, and he and the priest take their leave.

Santiago clasps the chain around Elena's pudgy wrist.

I try to process what I feel about this, and in a way, it's strange. I feel nothing. At least not right now. Maybe later I will. There's one thing I've realized in the last year. The Society is a sort of extended family. And if you are on good terms with them, then they're a powerful support system.

But if you're not, if, like my brother, you turn against them, their wrath is just as powerful, their justice swift and final. But there is also compassion. Hazel and Michael were welcomed back. I don't know what my father or she or even I had expected would happen if they found her. I always imagined them hunting for her. Hunting for anyone who'd left the fold. But it's not like that. They will hunt you. Absolutely. If you've caused harm to members of The Society or The Society itself, they will hold you accountable. But walking away is not a punishable offense. At least it hasn't been in the case of Hazel. My father's fear had been in her running off, shunning a Sovereign Son. But that's not how IVI saw it. I'm not sure how much Santiago had to do with that, but I am happy for the end result.

This doesn't mean that I plan on enmeshing myself more than I would any other group or organization, but it makes me see things a little differently, and that's a good thing because I know how important IVI is to Santiago. His ancestors are among the founding families, after all. It's in his blood.

Someone clears their throat. We turn to the door to find Colette and Eva standing there.

"Are you guys coming?" Eva asks anxiously.

"The guests are getting restless," Colette adds.

"I mean, really, if you want to hang out here," Eva continues, rolling her eyes and walking toward us. "My niece is the main event so..." She trails off, shrugging a shoulder.

"We're coming," Santiago says.

"Actually," I contradict, handing Elena over to her favorite aunt. "We'll be there in a minute."

Eva's gaze shifts from Santiago to me and back to him. "Just remember it's a church," she tells him and turns to walk away.

"How old is she again?" Santiago asks as the door closes behind them, and we're alone. He turns to me, eyebrows raised. "We should go in. The sooner we do, the sooner we can go home."

"You're such a homebody."

"And you're a socialite?"

"You have a point." I take his hand and lead him to a pew. We sit down beside each other and he studies me, his expression more serious.

"Ivy?"

I see the furrow between his eyes deepen and reach out to smooth it out. "It's nothing bad. I just wanted to have a minute alone with you. We're so rarely alone now."

He smiles but waits. He knows me too well now.

"I wanted to wait until I was sure," I start, glancing up at the altar as my eyes warm with tears. Happy ones. When I turn back to him, his are nearly the same as he waits expectantly.

I touch his collar to straighten it.

He takes my hands and dips his head to draw my attention back to his face. "Ivy?"

"We shouldn't pack the christening gown away just yet."

He cocks his head, draws a deep breath in as understanding begins to dawn. "Are you—?"

"We're having another baby."

He hesitates.

"I'm pregnant," I say, just to be clear. He lets out a laugh and hugs me so tight, it hurts. But to hear him laugh and to feel him hold me like this, and to feel his happiness, it makes that same feeling of joy almost burst inside me, and tears are streaming down my face by the time he draws back. He's using his thumbs to wipe them away as he kisses me, telling me how happy he is, how proud he is of me. And when my tears stop, we rest our foreheads against one another's, and I touch his cheek.

"I love you so much," I whisper.

"I love you even more." We stay like that for a long moment before we pull apart. "Let's keep this secret to ourselves for a little while."

"Yes."

"We'd better go in," he says, pulling me to my feet.

I nod, and he places one hand at my back as we walk to the door. He opens it, and I step out.

"I'm not surprised, you know," he says as we walk through the courtyard to the reception room.

"No? Because you seemed surprised."

"Well, the De La Rosa virility is a legendary thing," he says as he opens the French door and gives me a wicked grin. "I'll show you again tonight."

I put my hands on his shoulders, lean up on tiptoe and give him a one-sided grin. "I only hope your stamina is as legendary."

WHAT TO READ NEXT

A sample from *Mine*
by Natasha Knight and A. Zavarelli

Unlocking the door, I push it open to go inside, and goose bumps rise every hair on my body.

He's been here. Inside our house. I feel it now. Feel him. Smell him?

No, that's my imagination.

I quietly close the door and lean my back against it, feeling the pocketknife in my hand. I decide to switch it out for a real one and set it on the counter. My hand is trembling as I pick up another knife, a sharper one, and I don't allow myself to think about Lev. To wonder if I'll be able to do it. To kill him.

Kill him?

I grip the lip of the sink as a wave of nausea overwhelms me.

I've done it before. I know what it feels like to plunge your knife into someone's gut. I know how warm blood is when it pours over your hand. And I know how much blood there is.

But Lev?

I wipe my eyes and steel my spine. I need to get packed. I need to get our things and go.

But just then, I hear it.

Footsteps.

Fuck.

My inhale is an audible tremble matching the slow steps. He's not trying to sneak up on me.

The footsteps stop, and the hair on the back of my neck rises, the air in the room shifting, becoming heavier, making it harder to breathe.

There's a crunching sound.

"Hope you don't mind I helped myself," he says, and his voice makes my spine go rigid, makes me grip the knife so hard my knuckles go white. "And I took a shower. Fixed the leak, too."

The leaky shower drips for an hour after every shower. It drives me nuts.

"Turn around, *Katie*. Let me see you."

I'm going to be sick. I shake my head and make some strange, involuntary sound from inside my throat.

Footsteps warn me he's coming closer, then he's

right behind me. I feel him, feel the warmth of his big body when he stops so close that another inch and we'd be touching, and I remember the last time he touched me.

But it's on purpose that he doesn't touch me. I know it when he brings his arms around me and brushes the crumbs off his hands in the sink and all I can do is look down at them, so big. They've been gentle, and they've been rough, but I haven't seen them be violent. Not yet. Not to me.

He leans his head close, and I close my eyes when the familiar scruff on his jaw scratches my cheek, when his fingers push my hair away from my ear, and I feel his breath tickle my neck when he speaks.

"Cat got your tongue, *Kat*."

One big hand closes around my knife hand while the other relieves me of it. I stand there, mute, and watch it clang into the sink.

"Now what were you going to do with that?"

The taunt animates me, and I thrust my elbow backward into his ribs. I don't know what I expect, but I hit a wall of solid muscle.

"Ouch," he says, and I hear the grin on his face.

I whirl, bringing both hands to his face, nails digging into his cheeks as I let out a violent scream and fight. I fight like this is the fight of my life because it is. He's going to kill me like he killed Nina.

Like he killed her family and who knows how many others.

I fight even though I know I'm no match for him. He's too strong, too big, and too well trained.

I got lucky once against a predator, but Lev, he's different. Smarter. Faster.

Within a moment, he has me pressed against his chest, hand crushing my mouth to smother my scream and lifting me off my feet to carry me backward.

I kick and twist and fight every step of the way as I try to pry his arm off me, but he seems unaffected as he easily carries me through the kitchen and into the living room, then through to my bedroom where he throws me on the bed so hard I bounce twice from the force of it.

I look up at him, see the rage in his black eyes, his fisted hands, the muscles of his arms, his wide shoulders. I see the new tattoo snaking along his forearm, disappearing under the T-shirt.

His hair is still wet, and I remember he said he'd taken a shower. He's not in a hurry. He's relaxed, even. Not afraid of getting caught or of me escaping him now. Because I can't. I know it. We both know it.

He sets a knee on the bed, and I roll away.

"Get away from me!" I scream when he catches me, rolls me back, and straddles me, keeping most of his weight on his knees as he takes my arms and drags them over my head to cuff me to my own headboard.

Fuck.

He brought handcuffs?

"Let me go!"

He gets off the bed and goes to the mirror over the dresser. I watch him wipe a speck of blood off his lip. At least I managed to hurt him. But when he turns back to me, I find myself backing up away from him as much as I can, which isn't much.

"Please, Lev. Let me go. Please. I don't know anything. I didn't see anything. God, please!"

He looks down at me, and I realize how dark the room is. He's closed the curtains. Not that anyone would walk by here. There's no one for at least a mile in any direction. They won't even hear me when I scream.

He sets his knee on the edge of the bed, and I cringe backward as he looms over me. Was he always so big?

He reaches a hand out, and I flinch, thinking he's going to hit me. But he only takes a lock of hair and lets it fall through his fingers.

"Told you your hair's prettier like this," he says.

I start to cry then. I start to sob. This is it. This is how it ends. And Josh will be alone. Who's going to bring him home? God, they can't bring him home. What if he's the one to walk in here and find what Lev leaves behind?

"Shh, Katerina." He wipes away my tears with the rough pads of his thumbs. "I don't like seeing you cry. Don't you know that?"

"Please don't hurt me. Please. I haven't told anyone anything. I haven't."

"What would you tell them? You just said you didn't see anything. That you don't know anything."

He's using my own words against me. He sits down, cocks his head to the side, and studies me. His gaze roams down over me, and I follow it, see how my blouse has come out of my jeans and my belly's exposed, see how one of my boots is gone, probably lost as I was kicking at him.

He touches my belly then, a soft touch, just his knuckles featherlight on me as he pushes the blouse a little higher. He pops the button on my jeans, and when I gasp, he spares me a glance, just a glance before returning his attention to slowly and purposely unzip my jeans.

I whimper, blubbering words that make no sense as he opens them, then pushes my panties down just a little, just enough to see the scar from my cesarean.

He traces it, and I quiet. He's gentle, just following the line back and forth and back and forth.

"Did it hurt?" he asks, never taking his eyes from it, and I realize what he's doing. He's letting me know he knows about Josh. About *our* baby.

And I start to cry again, sobs wracking my shoulders.

Lev returns his attention to my face, leaving the scar and watching me, eyes hard and angry.

"Katerina, Katerina, Katerina. What am I going to do with you?"

One-Click Mine here!

ALSO BY A. ZAVARELLI

Boston Underworld Series

CROW: Boston Underworld #1

REAPER: Boston Underworld #2

GHOST: Boston Underworld #3

SAINT: Boston Underworld #4

THIEF: Boston Underworld #5

CONOR: Boston Underworld #6

Sin City Salvation Series

Confess

Convict

Bleeding Hearts Series

Echo: A Bleeding Hearts Novel Volume One

Stutter: A Bleeding Hearts Novel Volume Two

Twisted Ever After Series

BEAST: Twisted Ever After #1

Standalones

Tap Left

Hate Crush

For a complete list of books and audios, visit http://www.azavarelli.com/books

ALSO BY NATASHA KNIGHT

To Have and To Hold Duet
With This Ring
I Thee Take

The Society Trilogy
Requiem of the Soul
Reparation of Sin
Resurrection of the Heart

Dark Legacy Trilogy
Taken (Dark Legacy, Book 1)
Torn (Dark Legacy, Book 2)
Twisted (Dark Legacy, Book 3)

Unholy Union Duet

Unholy Union
Unholy Intent

Collateral Damage Duet

Collateral: an Arranged Marriage Mafia Romance
Damage: an Arranged Marriage Mafia Romance

Ties that Bind Duet

Mine

His

MacLeod Brothers

Devil's Bargain

Benedetti Mafia World

Salvatore: a Dark Mafia Romance

Dominic: a Dark Mafia Romance

Sergio: a Dark Mafia Romance

The Benedetti Brothers Box Set (Contains Salvatore, Dominic and Sergio)

Killian: a Dark Mafia Romance

Giovanni: a Dark Mafia Romance

The Amado Brothers

Dishonorable

Disgraced

Unhinged

Standalone Dark Romance

Descent

Deviant

Beautiful Liar

Retribution

Theirs To Take

Captive, Mine

Alpha

Given to the Savage

Taken by the Beast

Claimed by the Beast

Captive's Desire

Protective Custody

Amy's Strict Doctor

Taming Emma

Taming Megan

Taming Naia

Reclaiming Sophie

The Firefighter's Girl

Dangerous Defiance

Her Rogue Knight

Taught To Kneel

Tamed: the Roark Brothers Trilogy

THANK YOU!

Thanks for reading *Resurrection of the Heart*. We hope you loved the conclusion of Santiago and Ivy's journey.

Reviews help new readers find books and would make me ever grateful. Please consider leaving a review at the store where you purchased the book.

ABOUT A. ZAVARELLI

A. Zavarelli is a USA Today and Amazon bestselling author of dark and contemporary romance.

When she's not putting her characters through hell, she can usually be found watching bizarre and twisted documentaries in the name of research.

She currently lives in the Northwest with her lumberjack and an entire brood of fur babies.

Want to stay up to date on Ashleigh and Natasha's releases? Sign up for our newsletters here: https://landing.mailerlite.com/webforms/landing/x3s0k6

ABOUT NATASHA KNIGHT

Natasha Knight is the *USA Today* Bestselling author of Romantic Suspense and Dark Romance Novels. She has sold over half a million books and is translated into six languages. She currently lives in The Netherlands with her husband and two daughters and when she's not writing, she's walking in the woods listening to a book, sitting in a corner reading or off exploring the world as often as she can get away.

Write Natasha here: natasha@natasha-knight.com

Click here to sign up for my newsletter to receive new release news and updates!

NATASHA KNIGHT

www.natasha-knight.com
natasha-knight@outlook.com

Printed in Great Britain
by Amazon